P9-DIZ-265

Hesitantly, Deanna Troi opened her empathic sense to the artifacts sitting in the containment field.

POWER!

It hit hard, like a blow to the skull, as a torrential flood of sensory input invaded her mind. Her head snapped back as if she had been physically struck, causing her instinctively to hold up her hands to ward off the attack.

"What's happening to her?" she heard Picard demand, worry etched in his voice, but she could not respond to him. She could only fight for her own sanity.

Something was grasping her arms: Crusher, Picard, followed by Beverly shouting, but Deanna could no longer understand the words, could no longer do anything except fall into a maelstrom of emotion, hatred, rage. Dimly, she was aware of Picard lifting her in his arms and running out of the room, as if he could outrace disaster and impending doom. . . .

Look for STAR TREK Fiction from Pocket Books

Star Trek: The Original Series

The Ashes of Eden
Federation
Sarek
Best Destiny
Shadows on the Sun
Probe
Prime Directive
The Lost Years
Star Trek VI: The Undiscovered Country
Star Trek V: The Final Frontier
Star Trek IV: The Voyage Home
Spock's World
Enterprise
Strangers from the Sky
Final Frontier

#1 Star Trek: The Motion Picture
#2 The Entropy Effect
#3 The Klingon Gambit
#4 The Covenant of the Crown
#5 The Prometheus Design
#6 The Abode of Life
#7 Star Trek II: The Wrath of Khan
#8 Black Fire
#9 Triangle
#10 Web of the Romulans
#11 Yesterday's Son
#12 Mutiny on the Enterprise
#13 The Wounded Sky
#14 The Trellisane Confrontation
#15 Corona
#16 The Final Reflection
#17 The Search for Spock
#18 My Enemy, My Ally
#19 The Tears of the Singers
#20 The Vulcan Academy Murders
#21 Uhura's Song
#22 Shadow Lord
#23 Ishmael
#24 Killing Time
#25 Dwellers in the Crucible
#26 Pawns and Symbols
#27 Mindshadow
#28 Crisis on Centaurus
#29 Dreadnought!
#30 Demons
#31 Battlestations!
#32 Chain of Attack
#33 Deep Domain
#34 Dreams of the Raven
#35 The Romulan Way
#36 How Much for Just the Planet?
#37 Bloodthirst
#38 The IDIC Epidemic
#39 Time for Yesterday
#40 Timetrap
#41 The Three-Minute Universe
#42 Memory Prime
#43 The Final Nexus
#44 Vulcan's Glory
#45 Double, Double
#46 The Cry of the Onlies
#47 The Kobayashi Maru
#48 Rules of Engagement
#49 The Pandora Principle
#50 Doctor's Orders
#51 Enemy Unseen
#52 Home Is the Hunter
#53 Ghost Walker
#54 A Flag Full of Stars
#55 Renegade
#56 Legacy
#57 The Rift
#58 Face of Fire
#59 The Disinherited
#60 Ice Trap
#61 Sanctuary
#62 Death Count
#63 Shell Game
#64 The Starship Trap
#65 Windows on a Lost World
#66 From the Depths
#67 The Great Starship Race
#68 Firestorm
#69 The Patrian Transgression
#70 Traitor Winds
#71 Crossroad
#72 The Better Man
#73 Recovery
#74 The Fearful Summons
#75 First Frontier
#76 The Captain's Daughter
#77 Twilight's End
#78 The Rings of Tautee

Star Trek: The Next Generation

Star Trek Generations
All Good Things
Q-Squared
Dark Mirror
Descent
The Devil's Heart
Imzadi
Relics
Reunion
Unification
Metamorphosis
Vendetta
Encounter at Farpoint

#1 Ghost Ship
#2 The Peacekeepers
#3 The Children of Hamlin
#4 Survivors
#5 Strike Zone
#6 Power Hungry
#7 Masks
#8 The Captains' Honor
#9 A Call to Darkness
#10 A Rock and a Hard Place
#11 Gulliver's Fugitives
#12 Doomsday World
#13 The Eyes of the Beholders
#14 Exiles
#15 Fortune's Light
#16 Contamination
#17 Boogeymen
#18 Q-in-Law
#19 Perchance to Dream
#20 Spartacus
#21 Chains of Command
#22 Imbalance
#23 War Drums
#24 Nightshade
#25 Grounded
#26 The Romulan Prize
#27 Guises of the Mind
#28 Here There Be Dragons
#29 Sins of Commission
#30 Debtors' Planet
#31 Foreign Foes
#32 Requiem
#33 Balance of Power
#34 Blaze of Glory
#35 Romulan Stratagem
#36 Into the Nebula
#37 The Last Stand
#38 Dragon's Honor
#39 Rogue Saucer
#40 Possession

Star Trek: Deep Space Nine

Warped
The Search

#1 Emissary
#2 The Siege
#3 Bloodletter
#4 The Big Game
#5 Fallen Heroes
#6 Betrayal
#7 Warchild
#8 Antimatter
#9 Proud Helios
#10 Valhalla
#11 Devil in the Sky
#12 The Laertian Gamble
#13 Station Rage
#14 The Long Night

Star Trek: Voyager

#1 Caretaker
#2 The Escape
#3 Ragnarok
#4 Violations
#5 Incident at Arbuk
#6 The Murdered Sun
#7 Ghost of a Chance

For orders other than by individual consumers, Pocket Books grants a discount on the purchase of **10 or more** copies of single titles for special markets or premium use. For further details, please write to the Vice-President of Special Markets, Pocket Books, 1633 Broadway, New York, NY 10019-6785, 8th Floor.

For information on how individual consumers can place orders, please write to Mail Order Department, Simon & Schuster Inc., 200 Old Tappan Road, Old Tappan, NJ 07675.

POSSESSION

J. M. DILLARD
and
KATHLEEN O'MALLEY

POCKET BOOKS
New York London Toronto Sydney Tokyo Singapore

The sale of this book without its cover is unauthorized. If you purchased this book without a cover, you should be aware that it was reported to the publisher as "unsold and destroyed." Neither the author nor the publisher has received payment for the sale of this "stripped book."

This book is a work of fiction. Names, characters, places and incidents are products of the author's imagination or are used fictitiously. Any resemblance to actual events or locales or persons, living or dead, is entirely coincidental.

An *Original* Publication of POCKET BOOKS

POCKET BOOKS, a division of Simon & Schuster Inc.
1230 Avenue of the Americas, New York, NY 10020

Copyright © 1996 by Paramount Pictures. All Rights Reserved.

STAR TREK is a Registered Trademark of Paramount Pictures.

This book is published by Pocket Books, a division of Simon & Schuster Inc., under exclusive license from Paramount Pictures.

All rights reserved, including the right to reproduce this book or portions thereof in any form whatsoever. For information address Pocket Books, 1230 Avenue of the Americas, New York, NY 10020

ISBN: 0-671-86485-8

First Pocket Books printing May 1996

10 9 8 7 6 5 4 3 2 1

POCKET and colophon are registered trademarks of Simon & Schuster Inc.

Printed in the U.S.A.

Prologue

Young Skel woke with a start, opening his eyes to the moonless black of Vulcan night. A noise had roused him—a soft, subtle sound that had merged into his already-fading dream, a sound that had been meant to warn him.

Just in time . . .

In the cool darkness—thin arms propping him into a sitting position, palms pressed hard against his warm cot—Skel struggled to suppress a gasp. The desperate thought had not been his own.

In time for what? *he asked its source silently.*

In time to save your life.

A telepathic message? He furrowed his brow, concentrating, but the sense of it was gone, and as he mindfully controlled his breathing, the panic slowly eased.

Look about you, Skel, *he urged himself.* Here you sit in your home, in the town of Rh'Iahr, peaceful as all Vulcan towns are peaceful. You are in your own comfortable bed, surrounded by your own things, and but two doors down the hall, your parents lie sleeping. . . . *He was only ten years old, but a good student, interested in the quantum sciences. His teachers said his emotional control was advanced for someone his age, and he knew that brought honor to his parents.*

Then why are you sitting up in your bed in terror? *He was calmer, yes—but the unease persisted. Perhaps he had had a nightmare; he had read of such possibilities. Vulcans rarely dreamed, and nightmares, even among children, were uncommon.*

No. He retrieved a few fragmented scenes from his dream. It had been a distinctly unstartling review of activities at school. . . . Then why the fear?

Because I heard something. Or sensed something. Something—I cannot recognize. Something alien. Something—evil.

His intense self-honesty demanded that he correct his own thought: Not sensed. Sense. Even now . . .

Silently, he drew back the lightweight blanket that covered him and slipped from his bed, bare feet padding across the cool floor. At the doorway, he paused, swiftly manipulating the door's control mechanism before the simple sensor detected him and opened it. Instead, the door slid open a few centimeters, its well-cared-for mechanism making no sound at all. Skel peered through the crack: beyond lay the expected wall, with its holographic display of his own childish artwork, created at school, draped in the dark of night.

Yet the illogical feeling of terror—that despite the normal appearance of his surroundings, something terribly abnormal hovered nearby—persisted. Skel pushed back a fringe of brown-black hair away from one long pointed ear, which he pressed to the opening to listen.

There would be nothing, of course, except the soft

sound of his parents sleeping; thus reassured, he would return to sleep. Yes, this was a logical way to handle a most illogical feeling.

A heartbeat of silence, and then—a sound, low and quiet, soft as a breath. Yet not a breath, for it held an undercurrent of pain. It was a moan—a low, quiet moan.

One of his parents was sick—his mother, he decided, when the soft complaint came again. Skel's slanted brows furrowed with concern. Once, when the family was camping, his mother, T'Reth, had fallen from a cliff; Skel had never forgotten the sight of her shattered forearm, pierced by ivory bone, spattered with emerald blood. His father had splinted the fracture on-site, but no sound ever escaped her ashen lips, though hours passed before they reached a healer.

If his mother had uttered this gentle murmur of pain, she must be gravely ill; no doubt his father would be tending her. Skel could provide some service. He was not an infant, after all. He was ten, and advanced in his emotional control. He would help his mother.

He moved to press the door controls, then pulled quickly away, prevented from touching them by an internal force—an emotion, a sensation of such fear and revulsion that it shamed and perplexed him. He was reacting like an infant, and yet—the emotion was so compelling that he yielded to it and dropped his hand.

Soft, familiar footfalls emanated from the corridor, moving toward his parents' bedroom; he listened with a mixture of wild, unreasoning fear and a sense of relief. This would be his father, who no doubt had been moving about the house to summon the healers and tend to his mother's illness. Skel pressed a night-adapted eye to the crack. Perhaps the reassuring, normal sight of his father would help Skel collect himself and shed these childish fears.

He watched until a figure emerged from the shad-

ows: his father, just as he had known. Skel dampened the surge of intense, irrational relief he felt as he watched the older Vulcan turn the corner of the hallway as if coming from the meditation room. His hands appeared first: they grasped a large heavy object of gleaming metal that took Skel some seconds to recognize as a lirpa, *an ancient ceremonial weapon that had belonged to his mother's ancestors.*

The sight made no sense to the bewildered boy's eyes; of all things, his father should have carried a medikit to tend to his suffering wife. But as his father passed near Skel's door and turned to reenter the room he shared with his wife, his face became clearly visible—providing Skel with an even more disturbing sight. For the elder Vulcan—a gentle, serene man devoted to the study of logic—was . . .

Smiling?

Smiling? His father?

No, not smiling. *Skel recoiled from the sight, scarcely daring to breathe. He had seen humans and Andorians smile, and this was not a smile—but a leer. A grimace. An expression, he knew from his studies of other cultures, of pure sadistic evil.*

As he stepped back from the door, he closed his eyes; yet the horrifying image of his father's face remained. It was an image, Skel knew, that would remain forever imprinted on his memory.

In that instant, such terror consumed him that Skel grew convinced he was still dreaming—trapped in a nightmare, and all his logic, all his training could do nothing to dam the flood of fear and anguish that engulfed him.

Another sound: his mother's soft low moan from the bedroom. But this time, it rose shrilly into a scream—a scream which made him want to clap his hands over his sensitive ears.

"Run! Skel, run!"

He froze, too horrified to believe such a warning,

until it pierced not only his ears, but also his mind, as his mother T'Reth cried out to him with her dying thoughts. The sound of her mental screams throbbed in his head, drowning out the terrible, real sound of her strangled shrieks.

RUN! RUN, MY CHILD, RUN! DO NOT RETURN. RUN AND HIDE! NOW! RUN FOR YOUR LIFE! AND NEVER, EVER LOOK INTO ANY VULCAN'S EYES!

The terrible voices would not stop—not the one in his head, not the one in his ears.

RUN! RUN! RUN!

All his carefully honed Vulcan discipline fled as Skel became what his ancient ancestors had been before the Reformation. Like a wild animal, he bolted for his window, opening it wide to the cool night air of the desert, and leapt from the low-built dwelling in sheer, animalistic panic.

He obeyed the voice, and ran and ran and ran, over the soft, cold sand toward the distant black mountains. His short legs pumped frantically with all his youthful energy, until, more than a kilometer away from his own house—his house where logic and rational thought had once reigned—he slammed into an immovable object, and looked up to see . . .

His father's leering face.

The elder Vulcan's eyes were wide, demented, and blazing with bizarre emotions as he clamped powerful hands around his son's head, forcing Skel to stare up, open-eyed, at that terrible visage. The voice inside the child shrilled louder, DO NOT LOOK INTO HIS EYES. NEVER INTO HIS EYES!

As Skel's father roughly pulled the boy's small face toward his, the child fought with all his strength to look away, to escape those imprisoning hands. But the crazed countenance of his father loomed closer, closer, until there was nothing left for Skel to do but disobey the terrifying, commanding voice in his mind. The boy blinked, and against his will, he stared up into those once familiar golden-brown eyes, eyes once serene that now burned with murderous rage . . .

And found the face he confronted was his own.

The Vulcan, Skel, sat bolt upright in his bed, panting heavily as if he'd been running. For a flickering second, the nightmare's grip persisted and he stared fearful into the darkness, expecting to see his father's hideously leering face.

But no one stared back at him in the intense Vulcan darkness; there was no one, nothing at all before him except his own hands, raised as if to ward off danger. With unutterable relief, he studied them. They were the broad large hands of a middle-age Vulcan male—slightly lined and laced with prominent veins, fingers spread wide.

And these were his quarters at the Vulcan Science Academy, the same quarters he had slept in for the last twenty-five standard years. Skel immediately lowered his hands and reigned in his dream-induced panic, slowing his heart rate, lowering his blood pressure, coming back to the present. He was no longer a child of ten prone to irrational night terrors, but a scientist of ninety, a master of physics, a respected researcher. Automatically, he assumed his normal meditative position—cross-legged, spine straight—but could not achieve the passive state he needed to quiet his mind.

Finally, his comm beeped softly in the dark room. He sighed.

It was embarrassing enough to suffer a relapse of his emotion-laden nightmares; to rouse others because of his psychic emanations was humiliating.

He composed himself, then fingered a control on the comm console. "Yes, Healer T'Son."

The screen filled with the placid face of his personal physician, every jet-colored hair of her elegant braid perfectly in place, her clothing as professional and crisp as if it were two hours past sunrise, not three hours before it. "Skel, I sensed your dream. Are you well?"

She had worked with him for years to rid him of these nightmares. They were mentally linked; there was no logic in being evasive.

"I am . . . managing. It was particularly vivid. It has been years since the images were so strong. But I am all right now. Thank you for calling me."

"I am your healer," she reminded him—a gentle chide that it was not logical to thank someone for doing their job. "You have been working long hard hours. Your sleep patterns have been disrupted. You have neglected your nutritional requirements. And you are striving to complete a difficult task before the Federation's TechnoFair. These factors, no doubt, have triggered the resurgence of your dreams."

She was gently trying to tell him he was too concerned about his work and the upcoming deadline. She was reminding him that it was unseemly for a Vulcan to feel such emotional pressure. She would have been correct, too—for most Vulcans. But in Skel's lifetime, the unpredictable return of his childhood fears often presaged danger, either for him or for those near him. It was as if his mother's mindtouch could reach beyond the grave and still protect him, even though her katra had been lost, loosed upon the wind. Healer T'Son found no logic in this explanation, preferring to focus on more rational explanations when his dreams resumed. Her steady reliance on reason and science helped Skel through the chaos of his nightmares. With T'Son's help the dreams had become rare. Which made it even more disturbing to Skel that they should recur *now.*

As if she understood his mixed feelings about his problem, she reminded him, "I understand how your history might affect your regard for your work. And I understand how important it is to you. Because of your special circumstances, we must take extra care to ensure your health."

Your mental *health* is what she meant, but she was too polite to say that.

"Of course, you are correct, Healer," he agreed, feeling calmer. It always astonished him how merely talking to her could reassure him. It was one of the reasons she insisted they link telepathically. She did not feel that she could be as effective hearing about the dreams hours after they had occurred. It had been a good choice of therapy. T'Son had been a great help to him over the years.

"Remember, Skel, you are not the only Vulcan that lived through the madness. There were many affected—the survivors all have difficulties. That is why healers share our knowledge of these experiences, to help our patients restore the balance in their lives, and regain their logic and stability."

"Yes, of course, Healer. I will remember." How could he forget? As a young man, he'd spent years talking with groups of others like himself and their healers, trying to recover from the terrible memories, the horrifying experiences. The memory of his mother's screams, her savage, sadistic murder at his father's hands—his father, who had been the gentlest, most logical of men. His father had never recovered from the responsibility of his actions after the madness was cured. He had died young, broken by guilt.

"Please, come by my office before you begin work this morning, Skel," T'Son said calmly.

He stiffened, anticipating her request.

"It is best if we meld," she told him, "so that I can try to remove the most difficult dream memories. Many healers believe this prevents the same dream from recurring repetitively."

He swallowed, but said with the same calm as she,

"I will do that, Healer. In your office, before I go to my laboratory."

"Try to sleep, Skel. You have not rested enough over the past few days. If you can't sleep, take one of the herbal sedatives I've given you."

"Yes, Healer," he promised.

She nodded, and the screen went dark.

He stared at the blank screen a long moment, knowing sleep was impossible for him now. He should take the sedative. He should do as she suggested. It was the logical choice.

But he could not shake the sense of danger the dream had evoked. He moved to his dresser, removed his night clothes, and donned his normal attire. There would be few in the laboratory at this hour. While the Vulcan Science Academy normally employed few security devices, the work he was doing was always tightly secured and restricted. He could check the security system and all the forcefields. It would only take a moment. Perhaps, having reassured himself, he could then sleep. It was not logical, but he would do it anyway, for he had learned as a child that reassurance was the most efficient strategy for dealing with irrational fear.

Then he would be rested before he went to T'Son's office. Before he had to meld.

As he left the living quarters and moved silently through the nearly empty stone hallways of the Vulcan Science Academy, he tried not to think about the upcoming appointment. It was illogical to dislike the meld—dislike of anything was illogical by its very nature. Nevertheless, he hated melding after his nightmares. It brought all the terrifying images to the surface and made him relive them again, even though, afterward, he rarely suffered from the exact same images.

It just meant his memories—his mother's warning—had to take different paths to break through to his dreams.

The sensors turned the lights on in his lab as he entered it. All seemed as it had been when he left but a few hours before. He swallowed and forced his mind to be calm. He reminded himself the lab was often disturbing to him after a dream. Even the healer recognized that there was a certain logic in that.

He walked over to the containment area and checked the computer console that managed his experimental subjects. The multiple forcefields were all in place, under complex codes that only he and two others knew. Everything was as he had left it. He stared at the console. No, not quite everything.

A telltale was out. His fingers flew over the controls. A routine cell replacement was necessary. In fact, the telltale had already been reported and a security maintenance worker had taken tricorder readings, no doubt to effect the correct repair. It was a minor matter—not enough for him to have been notified. Could his dream have been triggered by something so trivial? T'Son would dismiss this as coincidence, and no doubt, she would be right.

Skel noted that the maintenance worker had not left an identifying code. That was contrary to regulations, and he would have to look into it. This area was off-limits to all but the most experienced technicians, as it was too risky to have insufficiently trained workers in this laboratory. Perhaps the senior technician had been on a more significant emergency. He would check into it. He was rigid about security; the very nature of the project demanded it.

He moved away from the console, going now to the observation port where he could view his subjects as they lay passively behind multiple Vulcan forcefields.

Such innocent-looking things they were, these elliptical containers small enough to be held in the palm. They always reminded Skel of a beautiful creature he had once seen while visiting a Terran beach—an oyster, for though they were onyx in color, there was a prismatic, mother-of-pearl sheen to them, glints of metallic blue, green, and rose that shifted constantly like a tide. Even after a lifetime of studying them, Skel found it hard to believe such simple, elegant objects held such a terrible force; in truth, these two small objects contained a peculiarly vicious disease, a murderous madness that had infected the cities of Vulcan eighty years before. The disease had been cured, but its legacy remained. Survivors, like Skel and his father, had been forced to continue with their lives despite the horrible consequences of the disease. Many of them, like Skel's father, never fully recovered. Many, like Skel, were still recovering.

Part of Skel's therapy had been to assume the work of his predecessor twenty-five years ago. And in spite of well-supported research and some of the finest minds of the Vulcan Science Academy, little had been learned of these objects—objects that generated their own impenetrable forcefields without any perceivable power source or mechanism. Though, lately, Skel believed he might have unlocked one secret of the fields. It was a discovery he wanted to share with other Federation scientists. Together, they might harness this advanced technology to serve the Federation as a defensive protection against more aggressive species such as the Romulans.

It had been driving him for years, the need to derive something, anything, positive from these terrible alien artifacts. He blinked wearily as he stared at the beautiful, deadly containers. He would have years to study them yet, learn of their origins, determine who their creators were. Years. But not if he did not sleep.

He signaled the sensors to dampen the lights, watching the glow his subjects radiated on their own. As he did, he heard the warning clearly, unmistakably in his mind:

RUN! RUN, MY CHILD, RUN! NOW! RUN FOR YOUR LIFE!

Wearily, he shut his eyes. Would the memory of T'Reth's voice finally drive him mad?

Mother, please! You are gone, your katra scattered to the winds. Do not torture my sleep, my waking hours. There is no logic to your warning. There is no danger here. There is only your son, an aging scientist worrying about his own deadlines and the inexorable march of time.

The frantic voice faded to a whisper and was gone. Skel was turning to leave the lab and return to his bed when his sensitive hearing detected the slightest of sounds—a faint rustle of cloth.

Freezing in place, he fought the urge to flee as his heart rate accelerated and his body prepared for conflict. Who would be here, in his laboratory, at this hour—hiding? There was nothing of value here. Nothing but . . .

His eyes moved back to the alien containers. Certainly, no one would be so foolish as to attempt to—

The thought was interrupted by sound and sensation: the sound of a light footstep, so swift that Skel had no time to turn and face its perpetrator, and the sensation of something hard, cold, and metal being shoved against his lumbar spine.

A weapon, he knew immediately, though his experience with weapons was limited. From the feel of its muzzle against his back, he judged it to be a phaser; from the diminutive height of the individual wielding it, he judged his visitor to be of Ferengi origin.

"Master Scientist Skel," came a faintly high-pitched, nasal voice which confirmed the Vulcan's hypothesis, "this is an honor. Your assistance would be most appreciated."

"Who are you?" Skel asked, studying the distance between his left hand and the computer's emergency response button, and contemplating whether he would be able to reach it before his visitor fired the weapon.

"Consider me . . . your business partner. There are things you will share with me that will profit us both." The weapon dug deeper into Skel's back.

"If you leave now," Skel said, modulating his voice into the calmest, most emotionless tones, "you will be able to successfully make your escape. No damage has been done. I give you this opportunity."

"There are opportunities unlimited in this room," the intruder hissed. "And you will give them all to me."

"I will not assist you," Skel informed the stranger. He had never meant anything more sincerely in his life. He had already faced a greater fear than most sentient beings would ever know. There was nothing this intruder could to do coerce his cooperation.

"Oh, you will, Master Scientist. You will assist me in all that I wish . . ."

Skel felt the power of the blast envelop him, felt his body lose control, felt himself falling like a stone to the floor. And then, blessedly, he felt nothing at all.

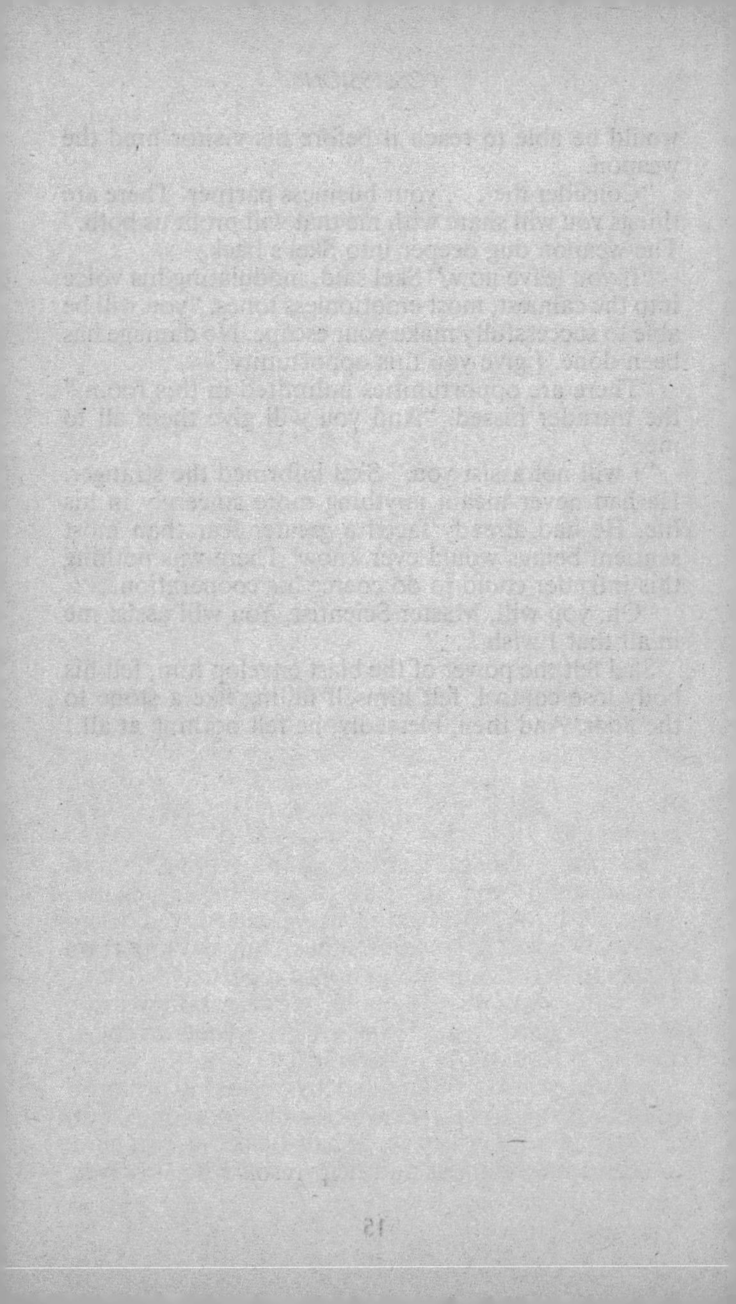

Chapter One

SHIP'S COUNSELOR DEANNA TROI stood uneasily in Captain Jean-Luc Picard's ready room. She'd placed herself almost directly between the captain, who was seated behind his desk, and the chief medical officer, Dr. Beverly Crusher, who stood, arms crossed, several meters away.

"Doctor," Picard insisted, in his clipped, most precise tone, "you have yet to answer the singular question: Why?" His hazel eyes were narrowed disapprovingly not at his medical officer, but at a report on his computer screen—an autopsy report.

"I've told you why, Captain," Crusher said wearily; beneath the exhaustion was a clear undercurrent of anger. "You're just not listening."

Deanna winced, inundated by waves of powerful emotion from these two strong-minded people, but, of course, that was why she, a half-Betazoid, was here: to sense their conflict and help resolve it. However, this time, she doubted whether she had any answers. Death and the raw anger and grief it evoked were, of all things, most difficult to explain.

"It was an *accident,"* Beverly explained again, in a tone so exasperated it bordered on insubordination. She ran a careless palm over her pale forehead as if to soothe the thoughts there, in the process sweeping back a lock of copper hair. "Crewman Janice Ito either forgot—or deliberately disregarded—safety regulations when she went into the power fluctuation in the plasma stream. She went alone, with minimum equipment. No power neutralizers, no safety shields. Just herself, a handful of tools, and a tricorder. She wasn't experienced in working in such a small place with major power conduits, and the shock killed her instantly."

Picard looked up from the report at last and gave a terse shake of his head, as if casting off the very notion that such a thing could occur. "What happened to her *training?* Where was the senior officer working with her? How could an intelligent twenty-year-old ensign, in the top ten percent of her Academy class, do something so damned *stupid?"*

Beverly straightened, bristling—every bit as angered as the captain, Troi knew, by the needless death; perhaps more so, since she had fought vainly in sickbay to resuscitate the young woman. And Beverly's frustration and grief were about to well over and cause her to say something she would later regret.

What is stupid *here, Captain, is your refusal to listen.*

Troi smoothly intruded, before Crusher had the chance to give the thought utterance. "I believe, sir," Deanna said calmly, "that that's why it's called an 'accident.'"

Picard turned his scowl on her. "This is the *Starship Enterprise,* the flagship of the Federation. We're not supposed to have 'accidents'—especially not senseless, fatal accidents with promising young officers."

He rose, straightening his uniform, his actions as taut and precise as his speech, and stepped around his desk. "I will tell you this: there will not be another. I'm ordering a complete shakedown of the crew. I want training sessions reviewed, new officer orientation reevaluated, emergency procedures reconfigured, and the entire drill process reassessed. And when that's done, we'll do it all again!"

Deanna drew a slow, even breath, allowing herself to sense the others' feelings while still maintaining her own inner calm. "Captain . . ." she began gently. "All of that is well-considered, and may even prevent some future tragedy. However, in light of the fact that we're on a tight schedule, the timing of extensive drills could be a problem."

Picard simmered a moment, his lips drawing into a tight thin line as he gave her a sharp glance, then he looked away, down, and sighed, surrendering slightly. "*That* damned thing!" he grumbled.

This was not the time to remind him that he had eagerly volunteered the ship and her crew for "*that* damned thing"—a heavily scheduled transport assignment to support the Universal TechnoFair. The *Enterprise* had been picking up and transporting a major contingent of Federation scientists for at least a week now, and there were still several more stops on the schedule. The TechnoFair would not wait for them—no matter what had happened on board.

"Right now," Deanna continued, in her consummately conciliatory counselor's tone, "both of you need to come to grips with this tragedy. You're both blaming yourselves for something only one person could have prevented—Ensign Ito, who violated procedure and risked herself unnecessarily."

She glanced from Picard to Crusher, but neither officer met her gaze; instead, they each glowered at separate, far-distant points as they pondered her words. There was still anger, yes, but Deanna sensed it weakening. Wisely, she kept quiet until, at last, Crusher broke the silence.

"Janice's Academy roommate is on board," Beverly said, her voice strained, her eyes still focused on an unadorned patch of bulkhead. "She told me that Janice had made some technical blunder right after she'd been assigned here. The senior officer, Lieutenant Singh, handled it properly, but it was the first major error Janice had made in her career. She'd been golden at the Academy—completely unused to failure. Her roommate thinks that she was determined to make up for the perceived screwup, especially in light of our preparations to pick up those scientists. So she took too many risks."

Crusher paused and drew a breath; her gaze seemed to turn inward, toward a painful memory. "I had her in sickbay in seconds. We used everything, did everything possible, but I couldn't stabilize her. She'd suffered so much brain damage . . ."

Deanna herself drew a breath, steadying herself at the wave of sorrow, defeat, and failure that emanated from her friend. She regretted Beverly's suffering; at the same time, she admired the compassion that made her such a good doctor.

"The worst thing about it is," Beverly continued, her voice near breaking, "one of the scientists already on board—a surgeon, Dr. Ellis—has developed a technique for replacing damaged brain cells with synthetic tissue. It's still experimental, but . . . with his technique, it's theoretically possible to stabilize a damaged brain until the victim's own cells can be cloned and specialized. Had I known he was on board, had I known of his work—it would've been a risk worth taking . . ." She lowered her face in a gesture of utter defeat.

"Beverly . . ." Deanna moved to stand beside her friend and put a gentle hand on her arm in support. "There's no way you could keep track of all the people we've been picking up this last week. It's easy to think this doctor might have helped Janice, but there was more than brain damage involved."

Crusher nodded slowly, but her expression remained grim. Even so, Troi sensed the transformation of pure outrage into grief, mixed with the first glimmerings of acceptance—and so she again remained silent for a moment, until Picard sighed, and said, "I had to speak to her parents. Of all the responsibilities that I dread, this is the worst"—he gestured at his computer terminal—"to send my regrets to the parents of that promising young officer." He turned away from the two women to look out at the moving backdrop of stars, his hands clasped tightly behind his back, as if to hold in the surge of emotion.

Deanna felt it all the same. "The entire crew mourns Janice's death," she reminded him softly. "Her body has already been shipped home. But perhaps a memorial service might help those of us still on board to cope with our own sorrow."

Picard turned and nodded quickly. "Of course. Of course. Deanna, may I ask you to organize it?"

"Certainly, Captain."

"And, Doctor," he said, his tone conciliatory, "please don't blame yourself. You did everything medically possible. She could have had no better care."

"Yes, sir. Thank you," Crusher replied, managing a wan smile to match the captain's.

Picard dismissed her with a nod.

Crusher left, and the instant the doors closed over her, Deanna took a step closer to the captain. "You're taking this very hard, sir. As hard as Dr. Crusher. As hard as Lieutenant Singh, Ensign Ito's senior officer. As hard as Commander La Forge, the chief engineer—"

"Shouldn't we be?" he interrupted sharply, meeting her gaze. "She was her parents' only child—the pride of their life. It's an inconsolable loss. Not all deaths are needless; some serve an important purpose. But this . . ." He shook his head.

"I understand your anger, Captain. And your guilt. If Ensign Ito had come to speak to the ship's counselor about her perceived failure, perhaps her foolhardy act could have been circumvented. If I had talked to her, maybe . . ."

Picard drew back in mild surprise at this revelation; his expression softened. "You're right, Counselor. The death of a crew member affects everyone."

Troi did not quite smile. "Yes, sir. And I know you don't really regret involving us in the TechnoFair transport. You've been one of its greatest supporters."

He nodded. "It *is* an innovative idea, gathering so many of the galaxy's renowned scientists together in one place for the express purpose of promoting the free exchange of ideas. But I'm afraid this tragedy has taken much of the joy out of it for me. Perhaps if I hadn't pushed the crew to such spit-and-polish . . ." He trailed off as she cocked her head to one side, ready to remind him that there was nothing they could do to change what had happened.

"I thought," she suggested, "we might have a small service in Ten Forward."

He considered it. "That's sensible." The after-duty lounge had already been emptied of all furniture in preparation for the TechnoFair displays.

"Then, after the service, we can allow our guest researchers to set up their demonstrations, as we had originally planned?"

Picard sighed in reluctant acquiescence. "We must. It's the only way the crew will get to see any of the exhibits, since we'll be too busy ferrying to attend the Fair itself. And . . . life does go on in spite of tragedy, doesn't it?"

She allowed herself an instant of silence, in acknowledgment of her own grief and anger at a Universe that could permit the young and brilliant to die. At last she said, "I'm afraid if death teaches us nothing else, it teaches us that."

"Yes," Picard agreed bitterly, "but how many lessons must we endure?"

"Geordi," Data asked, with the same implacable patience he always exhibited, "even though I have studied this topic thoroughly, I still fail to understand why humans insist that attending memorial services makes them 'feel better.'"

Geordi La Forge, the *Enterprise*'s chief engineer, was busy recalibrating the power conduits that caused the untimely death of Ensign Ito. Now Data, being an android, could recalibrate the conduits, discuss philosophy and the mortal condition, and learn an entirely new violin sonata at the same time—but Geordi was a mere human and, as such, needed to concentrate.

Even more so considering the tragedy that had prompted his task. He hadn't been on duty when Ito had died, hadn't—like poor Lieutenant Singh—heard the hum of the power surge followed a split-second later by the thump of her fall. But his shift had overlapped with hers, and he had called a good-bye to her as he left.

'Bye, Janice . . .

See you later, Commander . . .

She had been leaning over a console, but she had glanced up and turned her head so swiftly that her short, straight hair had swung about in an arc. Then she'd smiled brightly and given him an impish little wave. Swift and bright: those were the words for

Janice. There was a brilliance to her, a radiance that couldn't be captured by any holo. The likeness of her in her Starfleet file showed a plain-looking Asian woman with a broad face, dark eyes and hair; nothing special, nothing exceptional. Ordinary. Until you met her, shook her hand, and were dazzled by the light in her eyes and smile.

As swift and bright and focused as a phaser beam, yet so constantly cheerful, so apparently at ease that the stresses that came with being at the top of her Academy class—and later, the brilliant new ensign aboard the *Enterprise*—never touched her.

Or so Geordi had thought. But *something* had to have touched her, to have rattled her, to have eaten at her, for Janice to have made such a stupid mistake.

If he had only been on duty . . .

He clutched the cold metal calibrator in his hand and stared down at the bright-colored conduits in front of him, imagining how Janice must have looked when Singh found her, with all the light gone out of her.

"Geordi?"

"Oh. Sorry, Data." He returned to the present with a sigh. "You'd just asked about memorial services, didn't you?" His concentration wasn't at its best at the moment, and if he didn't answer Data's question, he'd lose even more time.

He did the sensible thing, and handed the android the calibration device, so that Geordi could concentrate on something less critical while answering the question.

"I thought you had this whole mourning thing figured out, Data," he said, watching the android perform the calculations at a staggering speed. "Wait, wait a minute—don't forget to figure in the power curves. . . . Yeah, that's it."

Data nodded his long, pale face and continued the recalibration work. "As I said, I have analyzed this topic before—when Tasha Yar died, and also when I was planning your memorial service. However, I received mixed messages about the need and usefulness of such a service. I understand that it is intended to comfort the survivors, and yet that does not seem to be the case at all."

Geordi smiled faintly, flattered by the fact that Data liked to discuss things with him, and often let him know that he didn't feel a topic fully explored unless he'd gotten Geordi's opinion. It was one of the things that assured him he and Data were truly friends.

"Memorial services *do* help," Geordi said, thinking of the service for Ensign Ito they had just attended—and how strange it had seemed that Ito herself hadn't been there with them. "They let the people who are grieving bring everything to an end. In a funny kind of way—they *do* make you feel better."

Without a pause in his calculations, Data said, "No one at the service today looked like they felt better. Everyone seemed quite sad. That was true of Tasha's service, as well."

"Well, we were. Losing a crew member in a preventable accident is hard to accept. But having the service reminds us of the value Ensign Ito had, of what a fine person she was. And it reminds us of our own mortality." He fell silent, realizing that perhaps Data had difficulty comprehending the subject because, technically, he *had* no mortality. It was one thing for which Geordi was grateful; here was one friend, at least, he didn't have to worry about losing.

Data continued his work, but the tilt of his head and faintly distant look in his eye showed he was analyzing Geordi's statement. At the same time, the android finished the recalibration figures and handed the palm computer to the engineer to check. Geordi scanned the results and smiled, pleased. It would have taken him more than twice as long to come up with the same results—and he would have had to concentrate.

"So you are saying," Data continued, "that memorial services are not designed to bring immediate relief of sadness. That they mark the beginning of a grieving process for the survivors."

"Yeah, that's the truth. Grief is a process. It takes time for the living to accept and adjust. The memorial service allows us to begin doing that."

Data gave a single approving nod. "A concise explanation. Now, about the concept of the afterlife . . ."

Geordi plugged Data's figures into the main computer and initiated the program. "Hold on, Data. Discussions about the afterlife have been going on for thousands of years. You and I don't have time to explore that right now. We're supposed to help set things up for the TechnoFair scientists. Now that we've got this recalibration going, that's next on the agenda. The afterlife will just have to wait!"

Data drew back with his quizzical "analyzing" expression, which quickly resolved into a look of satisfaction. "Ah! 'The afterlife will have to wait.' Because, of course, that is what the afterlife—if there is one—does. It waits for the living to transcend this life and join the afterlife. Sophisticated humor bordering on pun. Very clever, Geordi."

"Thanks, Data." La Forge took his analytical friend's arm and steered him into the nearest turbolift. "Ten Forward," he told the 'lift, then turned to Data again. "Look, we've got a lot to do. We've got to provide portable power packs for each holo display, make sure each scientist gets enough room for his or her setup, and decide if we're going to have to set up more space in the auxiliary lounge next to Ten Forward."

"I have already arranged for extra power packs," Data answered smoothly, without a shift in tone, as if they had been discussing business instead of the afterlife all along. "And, based upon the information the scientists have offered me, at least eight will need to be set up in the auxiliary lounge."

"Excellent, Data, thanks!"

The turbo doors opened silently onto the large expanse that, a day before, had been the crew's observation lounge and relaxation area; a few hours before, it had been the scene of Janice Ito's memorial service. But the arrangements for the service had been simple and had already been cleared. Now there was nothing but vast open expanse.

"Good thing Guinan stopped off at Andoria to attend that bartenders' convention," Geordi said. "She hates it when they move all her stuff."

"Bartenders' convention?" Data tilted his head and actually managed to look startled. "I though it was a spiritual retreat. She called it a 'relaxation seminar.'"

"Same thing," Geordi insisted with a small smile, as he walked across the vacant lounge, trying to decide who should be set up where. "She said she'd be useless here, since scientists don't believe in being 'off duty.' Well, let's start arranging tables and defining areas."

Data moved to a wall computer and used it to tap into the console in his quarters. "Here is a list of the dimensions of space the scientists have said they will require for their displays. I compiled that information along with the dimensions and parameters of Ten Forward, and the subject matter of the displays, and have come up with a tentative arrangement that best utilizes space and takes topic matter into account."

Geordi grinned broadly for the first time since Janice Ito's death. "That's great, Data. You've thought of everything! That's why I volunteered us for the setup when we could have had a few ensigns do it. I wanted it done right."

To his surprise, Data frowned. "Geordi, I could not

possibly think of 'everything.' That is too broad of a concept, even for me. For example, I am not sure the aesthetics of my arrangement will be satisfying for the less technical crew members. Would it be best to place the display of forcefield technology next to the particle physics hologram, or—"

"Aesthetics be damned, Data," Geordi said, scanning the list. "We're in a hurry. That's something the TechnoFair designers can worry about. Your plan looks fine; I like the way you set Dr. Tarmud between that surgeon, Dr. Ellis, and the ocular specialist, Dr. Dannelke. Their work complements each other's."

Data straightened with something suspiciously similar to pride. "Thank you." He processed for a moment, then added, "Geordi, you seem very eager to meet Dr. Tarmud."

The engineer clapped his android friend on the shoulder. Data worked hard to master the "give and take" of a conversation, and he was doing well with it. On some level, Geordi knew that his compliment of Data's work had triggered a program response that told Data to touch on an area of Geordi's interest. He didn't care. Data was showing he cared, and Geordi was happy to respond.

"You're right about that," he told Data. "I've been wearing his VISOR for a long time." He touched the silvery eye shield that permitted him his own type of vision. "This invention changed my life, and the lives of others like me. It's broadened my abilities and given me more freedom. I can't wait to meet the man and shake his hand! Besides, how many scientists get to meet the actual recipients of their work? He'll probably get a kick out of meeting me, too."

Geordi moved away from the computer and approached the stacked tables and temporary walls they would use to set up the displays. "Come on, Data. We've got work to do!"

* * *

"It's not often I have three handsome men escort me to a fair," Deanna Troi teased her entourage as they strolled down the corridor toward Ten Forward.

Commander William Riker's bearded face broke into a sly grin. "We decided that after wrangling with a cross Captain Picard and speaking at a very sad memorial service, you deserved a night on the town."

"The commander is correct," Lieutenant Worf added in his deep bass voice. His stern tone lacked the good humor of Riker's—and his dark, fearsomely Klingon countenance showed no hint of a smile—but the black eyes beneath his prominent skull ridges contained the very faintest hint of amusement. "Though the best we could do is the impromptu Science Fair in Ten Forward. Still, the displays should be interesting . . . and educational." This last he directed pointedly at his son, Alexander.

The young Klingon/human child glanced up at Troi, whose hand he was holding. "That means *boring* in Klingon," he told her, and rolled his eyes in a purely human gesture.

Deanna and Riker struggled to smother their smiles as Worf growled low in protest. He and his young son rarely saw eye-to-eye.

"Oh, come now, Alexander," Deanna replied, trying to help Worf save face. "You don't find school boring. Your teacher tells me you're in the top ten percent of your grade. She says you're fascinated with physics and calculus and have enough curiosity for five students."

As she expected, the compliment embarrassed the boy; he stared at his feet, his dusky skin tone darkening.

"I guess Alexander knows," Riker added, "that a warrior can't just rely on his strength. He also must be more cunning than his opponent."

"Well said," Worf agreed, mollified.

As they passed through the open doors of Ten

Forward, the adults paused to take in the massive changes to the once-familiar space. Deanna hadn't realized just how many scientists the *Enterprise* had picked up, nor the extensive scope of their work.

It was Alexander who put the entire thing in context for them, as he grabbed his father's hand and, pointing with the other, announced excitedly, "Look, Father! There's a holo display of a giant *eyeball!*"

He towed the hapless Klingon over to it.

As Worf allowed himself to be dragged toward a huge floating eye that seemed to be following him and his son, the Klingon studied the human female who controlled the display. She was extremely fair, almost colorless, her skin so pale it seemed translucent—what Commander Riker would no doubt refer to as a "real blonde." Indeed, the hair she'd braided tightly into one long complicated plait was almost white. Tiny tendrils of the fine hair that escaped the braid fell in wisps about a long face that was attractive by human standards, but seemed far too delicate to the Klingon.

"Dr. Kyla Dannelke, opthalmologist," the holographic banner beneath the giant eye proclaimed—and, Worf decided, the face was the only thing too delicate about Kyla Dannelke. For she was tall for a human woman, nearly eye level with the grown Klingon, and when she stood her back was straight and strong. She had good shoulders, too, and large handsome hands. There was a strength about her that Worf found appealing.

Too bad about her face, he thought, peering again at the bright blue eyes, small nose, bland straight teeth, and full lips. But then, human males were far less particular than he.

The woman spied Alexander as the youngster gaped at the large graphic hologram. "Finally! A spectator! I knew my big eyeball would suck someone in." She leaned down conspiratorially to the startled boy. "All the other scientists were only worried that their displays would be accurate. Concise. *Ed-u-ca-tion-al."* She said this last as if it were supremely distasteful, making Alexander grin. "But not me! That's too boring. I went for the sensational—the big eye! The window of the soul."

She fiddled with a remote device, and suddenly the great optical hologram looked down at them and blinked. Suddenly, the eyelid turned into an antique window shade and snapped up, rolling around and around as if broken.

Alexander giggled helplessly, and the happy sound touched Worf in a way little else could. This bright difficult boy was all he had left of his mate, K'Ehleyr; his son's honest laughter was so like hers, it pulled at his heart.

"Now, watch this," Dannelke said, and made another adjustment. The display above their heads shifted as the great eye became translucent. Even Worf's lips parted in amazement as the blood vessels feeding the organ pulsed and throbbed.

"Wow!" Alexander breathed. "You can see all the rods and cones." He pointed up at the eye. "And look—there's the lens inside, and way in the back, the optic nerve!"

The scientist smiled in surprise, pale pink lips stretching wide to reveal white even teeth. "Hey, you know a lot about this."

"He took top honors in his elementary anatomy class," Worf said, trying not to sound too proud. "They covered four species."

Dr. Dannelke looked at Worf squarely for the first time, and the Klingon had the uncomfortable sensation that she was eyeing him as blatantly as he had her not a moment before. Then she bowed her head in Alexander's direction. "Pretty impressive. You should be running this display, not me. Come over here."

Alexander glanced at Worf for approval; when his father nodded, he hurried over to the scientist. She handed him the remote and said, "Okay, let's see what you can do with this."

As the boy studied the small device, Dr. Dannelke turned to Worf and said quietly, extending her hand, "Dr. Kyla Dannelke."

Worf took the hand, careful to hold his strength in check. Her grip was weak—for a Klingon's—but impressively strong for a human female. "So I gathered," he said, nodding at her name on the holo display. "I am Lieutenant Worf. And this is my son, Alexander."

She nodded, glancing back for a moment with unfeigned pleasure at the boy, then turned back to Worf. "When I realized how few of my colleagues were interested in appealing to the children on board, I decided my work was a natural. His obvious interest is quite a reward! Is he really good at the life sciences?"

"When he applies himself," Worf said honestly. "But I think his central interest is in physics. He wants to know how starships fly. I don't have to prod him in that area."

"Physics?" She turned to study Alexander with amazement.

The boy was in complete concentration, his tongue tip peeking out between his lips as he carefully used the remote to display the layers of connective tissue that surrounded the eye.

"That's wonderful," Dannelke said, but there was a note of clear disbelief in her tone.

"Pardon me, Doctor," Worf said, "but you sound inordinately surprised."

Her pale skin flushed—a reaction that distracted Worf, as he watched capillaries bloom, spreading flame across her white cheeks and neck. "Well, it's just—I mean—" She stammered, then stopped, clearly reconsidering what she had been about to say. "Forgive me, but I've had only limited exposure to Klingons. I would have thought his interests would be in the . . . less abstract sciences. And perhaps in contact sports."

Worf pressed his lips tightly together as he felt his temper climb, but controlled it with the ease of long practice. He drew a long even breath and said, "It is true that Klingons excel in those areas. However, we have specialists in all fields of science, as must any race who would maintain its technological expertise."

Something about her direct eye contact unsettled him, and with a sudden flash of insight that came from being raised by humans, he realized she was attracted to him—and growing more attracted as his temper flared. The reaction was something he would have expected only from a Klingon female, and it startled him.

"I'm sure that is the case," Dr. Dannelke agreed smoothly, her strange blue eyes focused directly on his, her lips quirking faintly upward in a coy half-smile. "However, no Klingon scientist agreed to join the TechnoFair."

Worf felt blood rushing to his own face. "You misunderstand. To a Klingon, revealing scientific findings to the public at large grants knowledge to friend—and foe—alike. The Klingon High Command considers participating in the TechnoFair a security risk."

"Of course," she agreed—too easily. "And the science that is *your* area of expertise?"

He swallowed, realizing he'd been trapped into fulfilling her stereotyped view of Klingons. "I am in charge of tactical on the bridge. I am chief of security."

"Well," she said, still with that faint little half-smile, "I'm sure no one would even dream of violating the rules around here, knowing who would come to escort them to the brig!" She paused. "Does Alexander take after his mother?"

They both glanced at the child. For one split second, Worf was caught off-guard by the apparent non sequitur—and then it occurred to him: Alexander's ancestry was visible even to this stranger's eye. The boy was paler, smaller, more delicate than his father, with less well-defined skull ridges that betrayed his human blood.

Worf's eyes narrowed and he breathed slowly through his nose. It was not the first time he'd heard the kind of veiled innuendo he detected in this woman's question. He'd heard it all through his childhood, all through his years of study in the Academy, even as he came up through the ranks. He was no longer used to it, though; he had certainly never heard it since he'd come aboard this ship.

In the quietest voice he could manage, he murmured, "Dr. Dannelke. Are you implying that, as a full-blooded Klingon, I am incapable of passing on to my son the *intelligence* he needs to study the sciences?"

Her eyes widened sharply, but at the same time, she gave the impression of being secretly—and vastly—amused. "I wouldn't have the nerve, Lieutenant."

Before Worf could think of a response, Alexander interrupted, crowing, "Look, Father! Look what I made it do!"

Both adults glanced up at the hologram as the giant eyeball slowly blinked, then began to melt, dripping green and red ooze as the eye stared about itself in horror.

"Yes, I'd say he was your son, all right," Dannelke said, grinning.

Swallowing a Klingon expletive, Worf grabbed the

boy's arm. "Come along, Alexander. There are many more displays to see."

His son handed over the remote and thanked Dannelke politely; as Worf hustled the youngster away from the stand while unsuccessfully struggling with his resentment, Alexander looked up at him and said happily, "That was fun, Father! I'm glad we came. And you know what? I liked that lady! She kind of reminded me of Mother."

Worf could only swallow his outrage at his son's innocent statement. As calmly as he could, he growled, *"That* woman is *nothing* like your mother!"

Moments earlier, as Worf and Alexander left to explore the fascinating hologram, Deanna suddenly felt Will's hands on her shoulders. He leaned down to murmur softly, "Are you all right?"

She looked at him quizzically.

"Do you think you're the only one who can sense things?" he teased. "I've known you a long time, Deanna. I can tell when you're troubled. Let me counsel the counselor. What is it?"

She patted his hand. "You're a good friend, Will. Thank you for noticing. The last few days have been trying. The sadness aboard the ship, the tension of maintaining our schedule, the captain's unhappiness with Ensign Ito's accident, the scientists' anxiety about their projects and displays . . ." She sighed wearily. "I found myself wishing I could have gone with Guinan to that relaxation seminar."

"The bartenders' conference?" he asked in amazement.

Deanna grinned and lowered her voice confidentially. "She told me there would be an entire day devoted to nothing but the 'Use of Chocolate as an Entertainment Consumptive!' "

Riker looked suitably impressed. "Look, why don't

we just skip this carnival and go relax in private. We'll pull something nice out of the replicator, maybe watch a holo play. Some hot chocolate. A leisurely back-rub . . ."

To another woman, it might have sounded like a planned seduction, but Will was simply offering Deanna her favorite forms of relaxation. "I don't dare. Not after I made the captain go through with this. I'll be all right. But I'll hold you to that back-rub when this is over!"

He smiled warmly. "It's a deal." Sensing a touch of anxiety and heightened anticipation, Troi spotted Lieutenant La Forge. Beside him stood Commander Data. She moved toward them, with Riker following. "I must compliment you both on the setup of this mini-fair," she told them. "It's laid out very well. It must've taken a lot of planning."

Geordi merely glanced at her, smiling distractedly as he scanned the room, confirming what she'd sensed.

"Thank you, Counselor," Data said. "The physical setup took a great deal longer than either the planning or the design. It only took me three-point-five seconds to compute the room's layout; however, the design took a good twelve-point-three—and I am still unsure that it has the correct appeal."

"Data's thinking about a new career," Geordi teased. "Convention design coordinator. But he's torn between that and furniture mover, since he excels at both."

Data tilted his head and gave his friend a perplexed glance; he appeared to be about to correct the engineer when Riker interrupted. "You both did a superlative job in here. I'm sure the captain will be pleased."

"Thank you, Commander," Data replied. "It would be nice if our endeavor aided in improving his humor. Are you sure he will attend?"

"He'll be here," Riker promised, just as Picard and Dr. Crusher came through Ten Forward's doors. Spying Riker's tall form above the rapidly growing crowd, the captain approached his first officer, as Beverly accompanied him.

"Number One," Picard said. "Counselor. Congratulations Mr. La Forge, Mr. Data. Excellent job on short notice." But even as the captain mouthed the pleasantries, Deanna sensed his distraction, as he coped with his own anger and grief over the lost crew member; the painful conversation with Ito's parents still weighed on him. "Is there some reason you're all milling about here at this closed pavilion?"

"We are awaiting the arrival of Dr. Tarmud," Data informed the captain helpfully. "He is the inventor of Geordi's VISOR."

"Ahh," Picard murmured, in partial understanding, as he raised an eyebrow in curious amusement at the others. He glanced over at the adjoining display, with its rotating eyeball hologram that continued to fascinate Worf's son, and caught sight of the stately blond woman attending the booth.

"That must be Dr. Kyla Dannelke," Crusher commented softly to the group, as she nodded toward the fair-haired female. "She's one of the most foremost scientists in the field of reconstructive opthalmology. She's currently working with a Vulcan expert on the development of personal forcefields that would be directly linked to ocular control."

Picard seemed impressed. "Very interesting research. Could be breakthrough technology, especially useful to away teams, eh, Number One?"

Riker nodded, looking with increased interest at the display—or was it the scientist herself he found so fascinating, Deanna wondered, amused. She resisted the urge to scan his emotional level to be sure.

"She's also working with Dr. Tarmud on some of his current research," La Forge advised the Captain.

"Really?" Picard said, no doubt surprised that his chief engineer was that up-to-date on this particular branch of science. "Well, she's certainly made an impression on Worf's boy."

The entire group watched, amused, as the attractive scientist entertained the Klingon youngster with her attention-getting holo display.

"Who ended up being responsible for the refreshments?" Picard wondered, glancing at the perimeter of the mini-fair. Deanna sensed that he'd just realized he hadn't eaten all day.

"Ensign Alvarado," Riker offered. "Her parents are professional caterers. She volunteered for the assignment."

That seemed to mollify the captain, as he said irritably, "Guinan picked a damned inconvenient time to go on a religious retreat."

The officers all exchanged guilty glances, but when Data began to interject a comment, Geordi nudged him, and the android closed his mouth. In the next second, the engineer grasped his android friend's elbow and nodded toward the entrance of Ten Forward. A tall, well-built, middle-age human entered the room and approached the covered display they stood near.

"Well, hello there," the sandy-haired stranger announced cheerily. He had a pronounced widow's peak and an open pleasant face.

Deanna recognized his accent as originating from the part of Earth still incongruously termed New England. He'd turned the word *there* into a two-syllable construct that sounded more like "they-uh." The diversity of accents from her father's planet always amazed her.

"Are you all waiting for me to start my display?" the stranger asked the group. "I didn't mean to be late." He was only a little shorter than Will; he had friendly, bright, hazel eyes, with a strong nose that gave his face an attractive character. He turned on his display equipment and prepared his booth.

"Well, if you're Dr. George Tarmud," Geordi said softly, *"I've* been waiting for you."

The fiftyish scientist turned to the chief engineer, raising his eyebrows expectantly. "Have you been reading my latest papers?"

Deanna sensed Geordi was a little nonplused. He touched his VISOR self-consciously. "Actually, sir, I just wanted to talk to you about *this.* The VISOR. You *are* the George Tarmud that invented the VISOR, aren't you?"

Tarmud startled them with a full-bodied, hearty laugh, and he clapped a friendly hand on Geordi's shoulder. "Oh, *that,"* he said, smiling. "I came up with the design for the VISOR a long time ago, my friend, right after I'd finished my post-graduate work. It was just the beginning of my *real* work, barely the start. It was actually an undergraduate student of mine that finished the practical design of the VISOR that you're wearing. So, I stopped thinking of it as *mine* a long time ago."

It didn't take an empath to realize how startled Geordi felt. He frowned, then finally said, "Well, since I'll never meet that student, Dr. Tarmud, I *had* kind of hoped I could express my appreciation to you."

"I'm certainly happy someone's getting some use out of that pilot research," Tarmud said cheerily. "But there's no reason to thank me. The VISOR was just the first step in a very long journey." He turned on his displays, a wraparound visual board with multiple screens; the sophisticated imagery included graphs and filmed sequences. Tarmud cocked his head to one side and eyed Data speculatively. "A journey that, I hope, will help me tread some of the same paths as that eminent scientist, Noonian Soong. I believe you must be Commander Data."

Data glanced at Geordi and blinked too rapidly, a reaction that indicated momentary confusion, Deanna knew. In spite of the fact that the android was the one individual aboard the ship she could not sense, like most of his crewmates, Deanna didn't find Data hard to "read."

"Yes, that is correct," the android told the scientist quietly. He gazed at Geordi again, his face registering bafflement. "But I am afraid I do not understand your reference to Dr. Soong."

"As I said, it's a long journey, but at its end, I hope to design a construct as physically capable as *you,* Commander." He touched one of his display screens, and each one blinked in turn until they were all showing the same image—a blank, colorless, featureless humanoid form rotating in space, then standing erect, then slowly walking.

Now everyone seemed cautiously interested.

"You're researching the development of androids?" Beverly asked as she followed the images on the display screens.

"In a manner of speaking," Tarmud told her. "I hope to make a functional humanlike android that could be used to house the mental engrams of a living person."

As he said this, the screens changed, showing scientific overlays of the human brain, the pattern of engrams, and a complicated schematic for an engram-transfer device. The scene shimmered, changing to an animated sequence of memory engrams being transferred to the featureless humanoid form.

The officers stood in silence for a moment, then Crusher finally asked, "For what purpose?"

"Why, to defeat death, of course," Tarmud told her, smiling.

Deanna nearly staggered from the collective reactions of her friends. His statement shocked them, making them all relive their grief at their crewmate's recent death. She had to blink and take a deep breath to get a grip on their feelings.

She looked up to see that, eerily, the face of the android in the film sequence had begun to change as the engrams were transferred into its "brain." Its features went from bland to animated, lifelike. It opened clear human eyes—not like Data's, but true eyes that showed emotion—and smiled at Deanna as if it knew her, knew everything about her. She felt herself shiver and rubbed her arms.

"If I can perfect an android as sophisticated as Soong's," Tarmud continued, nodding again at Data, "with all the physical capabilities and functional brain that his androids had, but *without* its own personality, and use that android to house the mind—the *soul*—of a human, then that human can be spared death. Instead, after a full life, when the body begins to decay, that mind can be saved—*transferred,* if you will—into an immortal, indestructible shell."

"Ah," Data said. "Then you are attempting to build on the work of Dr. Roger Korby—"

Tarmud banished the thought with an impatient wave of his hand. "That was almost a century ago; Korby's androids were crude, incapable of the level of sophisticated sensory input *you* experience, Commander, and prone to eventual decay and obsolescence after a few hundred years. I'm speaking about bodies such as yours: self-maintaining, self-repairing—truly immortal."

For a moment, no one spoke, then Beverly asked, "How close are you to finalizing your research?"

He gave another of those hearty laughs and said, "Not nearly close enough, I'm afraid. The VISOR was one of my first studies, to help me develop artificial sight for the android and work out certain neural sequences. I've got a fairly functional body now—admittedly not quite as good as Soong's, but getting there—but I'm having some problems with the brain. And, of course, the engram-transfer technology is still in the planning stages." He eyed Data again covetously. "Oh, what I wouldn't give for a few months to spend with you, my friend. A few months in my lab—I could learn so much, and shave years off my work."

Deanna almost smiled as the group clustered around Data, Geordi actually standing protectively in front of his mechanical friend.

"We don't exactly consider Commander Data a research subject, Dr. Tarmud," Geordi said softly. "He's a senior officer of our crew."

"Oh, I'm well versed in Mr. Data's career," Tarmud assured him. "And I meant no offense. But for me as a scientist, the commander represents the pinnacle to which I aspire. You can't blame me for my curiosity."

Deanna looked at Crusher, who, she realized, was still reacting to Tarmud's desire to defeat death.

Troi was about to say something to her when Captain Picard said softly, "That's an interesting theory, Dr. Tarmud. And, of course, every *medical* doctor fights to defeat death every day. However, as much as we might hate it, death is a part of life. If everyone knew there was an immortal android waiting to spare them their inevitable end—it might change humanity completely."

"Of course it will change humanity," Tarmud agreed brightly. "For the *better!*"

"I hardly think—" Picard began, but Tarmud interrupted heatedly.

"Captain, your reaction is typical—and, if you'll forgive me, almost medieval in its superstitious insistence that we must yield to death because that's the way it's always been. Why? Why yield to such a curse, any more than we should yield to disease, to suffering, to poverty? Our greatest thinkers could be preserved to serve the Universe forever! Each of us could fulfill our destinies without the endless ticking clock that follows our every hour. Young victims of accidents could be saved to live out the life they were intended to."

As a second wash of emotions buffeted Deanna, Beverly made a slight strangled sound, then spun on her heel and left the area before Troi could speak to her. Picard's reaction, likewise, was so strong that the Betazoid moved toward him, trying to think of something, anything she might say to help him resolve his anger over Ito's death. But one look at his face told her now was not the time.

"I'm sorry," Tarmud said, visibly confused by everyone's reaction. "My intent was only to make you think about your prejudices, not to upset you."

"The crew has suffered a recent loss," Deanna explained gently. "Our memorial service was just a short time ago in this very room. I'm afraid it was a needless death."

"How tragic," Tarmud commiserated, his emotions clearly sincere. "But, really, Counselor, *all* deaths are needless."

Troi glanced at Picard, saw him visibly struggling to contain his anger. His jaw worked, then he said in a low voice, "Excuse me, *Doctor,* but I can think of at least two *Enterprise* captains who would have disagreed with you."

Before the scientist could respond, Picard's communicator beeped. He slapped the device on his chest harder than was necessary and growled, "Picard here!"

"Sorry to disturb you, Captain," said a female officer from the bridge, "but there's a priority message coming in from the planet Vulcan."

"Send it to my ready room. I'll be right there. Picard out." Then he pivoted, spine rigid, and strode away.

Geordi and Data sidled away from the display uncomfortably as Deanna turned to her tall escort. "Will, I think I'll take you up on that offer now. Take me out of here, please."

Riker nodded and escorted her away from the man who was determined to defeat death.

Chapter Two

As Picard entered his ready room from the bridge, he straightened his jacket and checked his appearance before calling for the message from Vulcan. He wanted to be sure his exterior wasn't as ruffled as his interior felt. Dr. Tarmud must think him the most irascible captain he'd ever met, but, frankly, Picard didn't care about that right now.

Assured that he appeared as captainlike as usual, he placed himself before the small viewscreen and signaled for the call.

The screen went black. The starkly simple logo of the planet Vulcan appeared a scant moment later, then was abruptly replaced by the austere features of an aged Vulcan male.

Master Scientist Skel? Picard almost said, assuming that his soon-to-be *Enterprise* passenger was contacting the ship to confirm the pickup arrangements.

But before the words could pass his lips, the white-haired Vulcan—clad in somber aubergine robes that marked him as a government official—lifted his gnarled hand in the classic Vulcan salute. "Captain Picard. I am Senat, chief of planetary security. You were scheduled to pick up the scientist, Skel, from the Vulcan Science Academy tomorrow at 0300."

Picard scanned the schedule for the next day on a small screen by his hand, checking the hour and location. "That's correct."

"It is because of Skel that we have sent this emergency call. He is missing; we believe he has been abducted and removed from Vulcan."

Picard frowned in confusion. "I don't understand. Who would do this? And why?" *And why am I being told about a lone missing scientist by the chief of planetary security?*

The Vulcan paused as if considering how much to reveal. "Skel's work on forcefields was a sideline of his original research; his primary field of investigation was the study of alien artifacts discovered by a Vulcan research team over eighty years ago. Those objects exposed members of that team, and subsequently, the population of this planet, to a deadly disease which caused insanity, chaos, and often death. We still do not understand how the disease was spread, what the agents of infection are, or how to control it once it is released. Once the disease was conquered, the objects were secured in a safe facility and have been the subjects of study for eight decades. Skel has been doing research on these agents and their containers for over fifty years. His predecessor studied them for thirty prior to his involvement. We maintained strict security at the research lab that held the devices—however, the origins and the danger of the artifacts have become obscured over the years. The information I have given you I learned myself only a few hours ago. The security around the artifacts became more and more localized, and eventually geared toward the general population. Obviously, securing anything from Vulcans is quite different from securing it against unscrupulous outside forces. Now, Skel—and the objects he studied—are gone."

Well, that explains your involvement, Picard thought wryly. *Nothing like securing the barn afterward.* "You're sure it was abduction?"

"He had an appointment with his healer and never arrived. He has never missed one before, never even been late. She immediately initiated a search. There was no trace of him to be found—except for the lingering residue of a phaser blast in his laboratory, which was picked up by our tricorders."

"Do you think he was killed?"

The Vulcan shook his head slightly. "No, there was not enough residual energy to account for it, and his healer, with whom he was mentally linked, reports no sense of his death. That is why we believe he was taken. In his childhood, Skel was one of the original victims of this disease. His knowledge of these objects is invaluable. It would be logical for whoever wished to steal the artifacts to take the galaxy's sole expert on them as well."

"Do you have any suspicions or leads?"

"Only that they carried Federation phasers."

That wasn't much to go on. Phasers were no harder to obtain through illegal means than any other type of weapon.

"And," the Vulcan continued, "only five ships left Vulcan during the time frame of Skel's disappearance. A Federation starship, two Vulcan science vessels, a robot supply barge—and a small Ferengi runabout."

Picard nodded, not liking the probable scenario. "Any scheduled flight plans from that runabout?"

"No, but we have been able to trace its ion trail until it left the system. I will send you the coordinates, of course. I will also send you all the information I have uncovered about Skel's artifacts. However, most of the original information was taken along with the objects. After eighty years, the duplicate material has become archived and hard to retrieve."

The captain frowned, but he wasn't surprised. Even meticulous record keepers like the Vulcans could become buried in data after all that time. In the meantime, the crew would be able to grid a probable route for the Ferengi ship and start searching. He considered communicating with the Ferengi homeworld, but decided against it.

"As soon as we receive your information," he told the Vulcan, "we'll start looking. I'll keep you informed."

"As I will you, Captain, if we receive any new word, or ransom demand. Another thing," the Vulcan said as Picard prepared to sign off. "The Federation has a top-secret file regarding those artifacts. I have requested that they transmit it to you for your perusal. We are hoping the information in it will help you should you find Skel's abductors and his research subjects. However, the disease outbreak had a far less significant impact on the Federation. They are having similar problems retrieving their files and, I suspect, may not add much to our store of data."

"Thank you, Chief Senat. Any information anyone can give us on this problem can only help us. Live long and prosper." He returned the Vulcan salute that began their conversation, and the transmission ended.

Skel fought the healing trance. His brain struggled to keep his consciousness submerged so that his muscles and the connective tissue surrounding his skeleton could recover from the terrible force of the energy blast he had absorbed from point-blank range, but the Vulcan could not wait—dared not wait. The urge to run, to flee, was more powerful than his body's need to recover. Even now another part of his mind gave warning.

BE CAUTIOUS. MOVE SLOWLY. YOUR ENEMY IS NEAR.

His mind tried to lure him back into the healing trance, but he could no longer submit to it. He needed to know where he was, who had taken him, why they had done so, and—most importantly—where they had taken the artifacts.

He opened his eyes the merest slit, so much like the boy who'd peered through the narrow opening in his bedroom doorway that the analogy rattled him. His vision was blurred, too blurred to make sense of the alien setting.

"I see you are back with us again, Master Scientist Skel." That annoying voice was the one familiar thing in this whole tableau; it was the same grating noise he'd heard just before he'd been rendered unconscious.

Skel blinked as his vision began to clear and slowly turned his aching head in the speaker's direction, first taking the time to scrutinize his surroundings. This was no doubt the interior of a small space vessel: aging, ill-kept, but in warp drive, judging from the hum vibrating through his body. A Ferengi runabout, Skel judged, given the fact that his calves, ankles, and feet hung off the edge of the uncomfortable rank-smelling cot.

The planetary origin of his abductor was confirmed when his gaze tracked to the left and settled upon a lumpish meter-high figure that coalesced into an adult male Ferengi. A Ferengi, Skel noted with a distant trace of alarm, gripping a phaser. At the sight of his waking captive, the Ferengi growled threateningly and raised the weapon. Skel immediately lowered his gaze.

Never look into their eyes, my child . . .

But he dared an utterance. "I assume we are no longer on Vulcan."

"Very logical," the Ferengi taunted in his grating, nasal voice. The modulations of this species' language had always irritated Skel's sensitive hearing—made doubly sensitive now by the effects of a full phaser strike. "*Very* scientific. And very correct: We are no longer on Vulcan. And *you* are no longer in control of what may be the most *valuable* pair of objects in the galaxy."

The weapon wielder moved away from Skel toward a Ferengi-size console where another, even shorter male stood. Skel blinked, forcing his mind to wake up and perform its job, demanding that his body respond to whatever the brain might order it to do. But he had not had enough time to heal. He gazed at his two captors, realizing that he was quite helpless. At the moment, escape was logically impossible.

"Your research," the taller Ferengi prodded. "It appears to have been going quite well."

Skel merely gazed silently at them; the Ferengi took his silence as confirmation and continued.

"You will explain to my brother, Nabon, and myself—Dervin, the DaiMon of this ship—about this forcefield research," the Ferengi said sternly. "You will explain everything. And then we will be *business* partners."

"If you have kidnapped me to learn of my research," the Vulcan said tiredly, "you have planned poorly indeed. I would have revealed all my pertinent discoveries at the TechnoFair. You had but to come and you would have learned all you wish."

"But then we would have to *share.*" The Ferengi spat the word out as if it were the most loathsome concept. "No, Master Scientist, that is not our interest. You will give your research to us alone. We will be *partners.* Consider this an opportunity for your species to learn more about the philosophy of *profit-making.*"

"That is not possible, as you well know. My research is for the advancement of knowledge, of understanding . . ." He trailed off. *Of understanding the small compartments, the artifacts that hold the deadly disease. The artifacts . . .*

Skel sat up smoothly, in one swift move, startling both Ferengi. Dervin, the armed one, straightened as he clutched the phaser more tightly and moved shoulder-to-shoulder with his brother. It was a simple matter to ignore pain, even disorientation, once one could focus on something significant. Skel was focused now, and the two Ferengi must have realized it, because they both seemed much more wary. Skel was physically more imposing and a great deal more powerful than either of them.

"What have you done with the artifacts?" He asked calmly, softly, rationally—but the Ferengi heard the subtle undercurrent of danger in the question and aimed the phaser at Skel's heart.

"The artifacts? You mean, your treasures? Why, they are as safe as can be, Master Scientist. Where could they be safer than in your presence?"

The two aliens stepped away from each other to reveal two palm-size black receptacles lying on the console—unshielded, exposed for the first time in almost a century to the open air.

To unwitting victims.

Only ninety years of discipline and training in Vulcan philosophy kept Skel from gasping aloud in terror as he stared at the objects of his research for the first time without the protection of multiple fail-safe forcefields. How benign, how passive, how insignificant they appeared—and yet how elegant and lovely in their simplicity: the dim flickering light inside the Ferengi vessel reflected upon them, causing a shimmering play of rose and turquoise mother-of-pearl highlights to dance across their shining black surfaces.

Skel immediately clamped down on the surge of powerful emotion. He was a Vulcan. He would handle this logically, emotionlessly . . . for only through calm thoughtful logic could he solve this problem. And the galaxy was depending on him to solve it here and now.

"It is totally unsafe to house the artifacts as you have them," Skel said in the most rational of tones. "To expose them to a normal environment, without protective forcefields around them, will cause them to degrade. In only a few hours, they will deteriorate completely and be worthless. They must be protected if they are to maintain . . . their value." He did not look at the Ferengi as he said that, because to look at them would be to see the artifacts so close by . . . to see his father's grinning face.

"I *told* you, Dervin," the smaller Ferengi, Nabon, hissed at his brother. He was speaking softly, but Skel heard him clearly. "I told you they kept these behind forcefields to *protect* them."

"To protect them from *theft,*" Dervin said, sneering, "as though any Vulcan would have the sense to steal them. He's just trying to keep us away from them. Keep us from finding out what secret they hold inside."

Dervin was indeed correct about that, Skel mused. He would do anything to protect these aliens from what was inside those artifacts; he would even give his life. But the cultural perspective of the Ferengi would never permit them to believe that.

"You could be correct, DaiMon," Skel said with the same calm tone, "but if you are wrong, you could be destroying the very treasure you seek."

Dervin's face ran a gamut of repellent emotions as the Ferengi tried to rationally work the problem out. Instead of coming up with an answer, though, he merely fired more questions at Skel. "The Vulcans have less security than any other race. So *why* are these small things so jealously guarded? Tell us that, *Master Scientist.* If you do not, I will let them deteriorate—if that is in fact what they will do—and watch all your years of study go to waste! What is in these containers?"

"Brother, listen to me," Nabon implored. "If the Vulcans saw fit to keep these things secured, they must be dangerous. The Vulcans have no interest in profit. They must have been safeguarding the objects, either to keep them safe from their world, or to keep their world safe from the objects. It can do no harm to secure them. It will even prevent the Vulcan from trying any mind-trickery on us to try and steal them back."

How eminently logical, Skel thought, admiring the smaller Ferengi's rationale. Interestingly enough, Nabon seemed terrified of the objects, as if he already suspected the danger they presented.

Dervin considered his brother's words, but only for a moment. Impulsively, he grabbed one of the containers with his free hand and brought it up to his face, staring at the alien script engraved across it—writing the Vulcans had yet to translate, except for a short phrase that told them little. Baffled by the alien language, Dervin shook the palm-size object, holding it near his ear. It took all his Vulcan control for Skel to hold his ground and not lurch forward to wrest the shelllike object out of the Ferengi's abusive hands.

"Dervin!" Nabon protested. "What are you doing?"

"I hear nothing inside," the DaiMon insisted. "This thing could be part of some bizarre Vulcan ritual, and hold nothing of value at all. We must see what is inside, Brother!"

"Stop this at once," Skel insisted. "You will harm—"

"Harm what, Vulcan?" Dervin demanded. "This trinket?" While still holding the rifle in one hand, the angry Ferengi used his free hand to try to pry open the two halves of the artifact. "Damage this toy? This religious object?"

Skel contemplated tackling the Ferengi then, but the muzzle of the energy weapon was still aimed directly at Skel's heart. If Dervin's reactions were good and he managed to kill the Vulcan—then the receptacles would be left in the fumbling hands of these two ignorant thieves.

"Dervin, stop!" Nabon insisted. He reached out and grappled with his brother, frantically trying to wrest the artifact away. "There's no point in damaging it! We must make him tell us how to operate it!"

Skel watched, waiting for an opportunity to join the melee without risking his own death, as the two Ferengi wrestled for the weapon and the artifact at the same time. *Why doesn't it open? Why doesn't it release its deadly cargo?*

Yet as the brothers struggled, Skel realized that their warring forms were limned by a faint unearthly light: beyond them, lying placidly on the console, the untouched artifact had begun to glow from its own internal light—a light that grew brighter and brighter as a seam of brilliant color gleamed from the slowly parting shells.

RUN! RUN, MY CHILD, RUN!

The voice was stronger than at any time in his life, but this time he could not obey. *No, Mother, I cannot run. For I am in space, and there is nowhere to go.*

As the small inconspicuous artifact slowly opened, Skel averted his eyes and seized his most desperate opportunity, lunging for the battling Ferengi and the weapon they held. As soon as his hands closed around the phaser, the high-pitched whine of its discharge sang through the small area. The blast scarred the ceiling, shattering a light fixture, charring tiles, then swung wildly and hit the control console, exploding it in a dangerous shower of sparks and metal debris.

The errant phaser beam streaked across the cramped quarters, searing a black diagonal across Skel's cot, bisecting a chair whose two halves clattered to the deck. Alarms blared; the Ferengi shrieked, all against the pulsating glow from the opening Pandora's box. Yet no warning sounded louder than that which shrilled silently in Skel's brain:

RUN, MY CHILD! RUN . . .

On the *Enterprise*'s bridge, Geordi La Forge decided that the only time he really appreciated the vastness of space was when he was forced to search for something in it. The enormity of the task was punctuated by the diminutive size of the sought-after object: a Ferengi runabout. The ion trail the ship had left after departing Vulcan indicated the general direction of its flight, and Picard had them plotting search patterns around the focus of that trail; they'd been scanning for hours.

"Any progress, Mr. La Forge?" Picard asked behind him.

An improvement, Geordi thought; this time, Picard had waited almost half an hour before repeating the question. The engineer glanced at Data, who sat beside him at the console they shared, as together they adjusted the scanners, trying to pick up something—anything—that might be out there. But the android could only offer a short shake of his head.

La Forge sighed. "Sorry, sir. We're still scanning. It may be best to move the ship again. Maybe keep moving along at impulse and extend the scanners as far as they'll go. We might miss something that way, but it'll give us the best range."

Picard turned to the helm. "Make it so, Mr. Braxton."

"Aye, sir."

Geordi doubted this new move would make any difference; his normal optimism was fading fast.

"Captain," Commander Riker interjected, "it's pretty late. This crew has already worked a double shift, and between the memorial service, the TechnoFair in Ten Forward, and this ongoing search, I think they've been stretched pretty thin. I'd like to suggest a change in crew, so that the senior staff can get some sleep."

Picard considered it, scowling. In times of crisis, Geordi knew, the captain preferred to have his most experienced crew around him, but Riker was right. They were all dead on their feet.

Before Picard could respond, Worf interjected, "Excuse me, Captain. I believe you should see this. We are getting an unusual reading at the periphery of our scanner range."

Picard moved at once to the Klingon's tactical station as Geordi and Data both brought up Worf's readings on their screens. "Is that a distress signal?" La Forge wondered aloud.

"Not precisely," Data replied. "It is an energy pulse—perhaps a tractor beam or something similar—that is cycling on and off." He frowned. "But it is definitely coming from a ship."

"Could it be a code?" Picard asked, as he squinted at Worf's tactical screen and lightly fingered the controls.

"I have already cross-referenced the pulse pattern with all known codes, sir," Data said, "but there is no match. The computer suggests that it is a malfunctioning generator."

Picard glanced over his shoulder at Geordi. "Can we pinpoint the location of those pulses?"

"Already done, sir," La Forge assured him. "I've sent the coordinates to helm. Whatever is sending that signal is still moving, but we'll catch up. We should be alongside in less than an hour."

"Very good." Picard moved back to his chair. "Let's keep our position onscreen, and as soon as you can get a make on that ship, I want to hear about it. With the way our luck's been going, we'll find ourselves chasing a broken-down robot barge with a faulty tractor beam."

La Forge and Data exchanged another glance, then went back to adjusting their scanners.

Nabon's sensitive ears ached from the scream of the alarms as the ship attacked smoldering bits of debris and extinguished the many small blazes. The noise, smoke, and confusion grew too much for the younger Ferengi, who suddenly lost his grip on the phaser and his courage, all at the same time.

He scrambled out from under the melee and dashed for cover as his brother and the Vulcan continued to fight for the weapon and the small alien device. As he crouched behind the surviving chair, Nabon realized that the second device, the one sitting on the counter, was almost completely open. He stared at it in terror. He could see the glow of power coming from within the small shell-like container. It pulsed as if alive. Without realizing he was doing it, he crept closer to the container. When he was close enough, he peered inside the strange thing.

POWER.

A purely electrical jolt of power surged through his body, causing him to cry out—a sound that was lost amid the tumult. For the briefest of instants, pure horror overwhelmed him—the horror of a mind, a soul, consumed by something greater than itself, followed by a hellish hunger that could never be sated.

Abruptly, the terror and craving subsided, entirely forgotten. In its place was contentment, belonging, peace. Nabon stared into the heart of the shell and saw only a lovely swirling mist, brightly lit from within, as though the mist surrounded a source of power. Why had he feared such beauty? He looked closer. The colors of the pulsing power were enticing, almost hypnotic.

Both his brother, Dervin, and the Vulcan still struggled for the energy pistol, but Nabon knew that the only reason the Vulcan hadn't succeeded in pulling it away from his brother was because he was concentrating on saving the artifact from damage. Dervin was right; the alien devices must be both valuable and powerful, but Nabon sensed the Vulcan was right, too. They would bring no profit to them, only grief.

(No, no—the artifacts must be protected at all costs . . .)

Nabon shook off the oddly intrusive thought and continued his original reverie: he had begged his brother not to pursue this theft. But once Dervin had uncovered the old data on an abandoned vessel they had salvaged, an ancient report that referred to the valuable artifacts brought to Vulcan, he would not be swayed. Nabon didn't want to think about how much latinum had been spent to enable them to get past the Vulcan security devices that had guarded the artifacts, nor how many months of planning. Dervin's ambition was powerful; it was possible he would fight to the death for these artifacts, and bring nothing but ruin to them all. But if Nabon could get the devices away from him, put them in an airlock, send them into the vacuum of space—

(No, never. They must be cared for, like the jewels they are . . .)

His brother would hate him, disenfranchise him, but they would live. Nabon was willing to risk anything, even poverty, if it meant he might save his and his brother's life.

Nabon crept over to the command console and reached into a compartment beneath it. Pulling out another hand-held phaser—which, like the first, had been stolen at great risk from a poorly guarded Federation cache—he carefully set it to stun . . . then reconsidered. Vulcans massed so much more than Ferengi; would the same blast that could render his brother unconscious fell a mature Vulcan male—or merely remove his logical inhibitions and give full rein to his anger?

Dervin must've seen what he was doing, because he shouted, "Hurry, Nabon! He has the artifact! Fire the weapon! Kill him if you must!"

At that moment the Vulcan turned his head, staring directly into Nabon's eyes, and what the Ferengi saw there chilled his blood. Skel's dark slanted eyes bore into him with fearsome intensity.

This must be Vulcan rage. This must be what happens when they lose their precious emotional control. . . .

"No!" Nabon shouted, unsure of what he protested. "No! You won't! You will not!" He squeezed the trigger.

A bright eye-paining blast engulfed both the Vulcan and Nabon's brother; for a bright millisecond, both turned to regard him in surprise. Dervin fell to the deck first, followed—a harrowing second later—by the Vulcan.

Both had gripped the rifle, which clattered to the deck beneath them. Nabon darted over and, gasping, dug the weapon out from under the unconscious bodies. But the small black shell was still gripped tightly in the Vulcan's hand.

Nabon pried the artifact from him, painfully extracting the thing finger by finger. Then he turned, ready to slam the lid down on the other and take that as well. To his surprise, the artifact on the counter was closed again and sealed, showing no signs of inner light. He grabbed it and shoved it in his pocket with the other one, then leaned over his brother.

Dervin was alive, facedown, breathing easily thanks

to the prop provided by his prominent orbital ridges. Oh, he'd be furious by the time he came to, totally furious. Nabon shook his head at the prospect of facing his brother's wrath—but he knew he was doing the right thing. He would save them from his brother's insatiable greed and poor judgment.

A sudden spasm of hunger shook him—a hunger such as Nabon had never felt, one that tormented not his belly but his mind. For the most fleeting of seconds, a sudden image crossed his mind: himself, standing over his unconscious brother with the phaser, lifting it high above his head, bringing it down on Dervin's thick stupid skull again and again and again to the spattering of blood and brain . . .

"No." Nabon wheezed, his entire arm trembling as he suppressed the urge to lift it and the rifle high. "He is my *brother . . ."*

The sensation passed as abruptly as it had appeared; Nabon opened his grip and let the weapon clatter to the deck. At the same instant, the Vulcan moaned softly and stirred. Nabon swallowed back the panic and, clutching the phaser, backed away quietly as the alien pushed himself into a sitting position. Blinking, the tall Vulcan peered around, obviously searching for the only thing of any importance to him.

The Vulcan turned his head, once more staring into Nabon's eyes. "Bring them back," Skel demanded, his lower lip curling in a most un-Vulcanlike fashion. "Give them to me. They are *mine."*

(Yes, give them back.)

(We must be protected at all costs.)

"No," Nabon whispered. "This is a trick. A Vulcan telepathic trick! Get out of my head!"

Shoot him, Nabon, he urged himself. *You have the phaser, you have the opportunity—use them! Now! Kill the Vulcan!*

(The Vulcan must not be harmed.)

Yet, try as he might, he could not change the setting from *stun* to *kill,* could not even manage to squeeze the trigger—as if the Vulcan gripped him even from this distance. With a terrified yelp, he spun on his heels and raced for the nearest airlock. Even as he fought with himself to increase the *stun* setting on the phaser, he could hear the quiet sounds of the Vulcan scrambling to his feet and setting off in pursuit.

"It's true we're well within scanner range now, sir," La Forge admitted, "but I can't really tell you what's going on. The readings are chaotic. There are two Ferengi and another reading that I'm pretty sure could be Vulcan. But there seems to be complete confusion on board! It looks like the ship is just moving along on a preset course—to where I can't say—while at least two of the people on board are running all over the ship!"

Picard considered that for a moment. "Any chance of beaming the Vulcan out of there?"

"Not at this range, sir. We'll have to get a lot closer."

Picard nodded. "Increase speed to maximum."

"You think they might have been exposed to the disease?" Riker asked softly.

Picard turned and gave him a pointed look. "We don't know enough about it. The Ferengi are . . . an excitable people. Anything could be going on. The Vulcan could be fighting them for possession of the artifacts. We'll just have to wait until we're closer."

As he huddled in a storage closet, Nabon reflected sourly on the amount of damage a few phaser blasts had done to the workings of their small ship. The random shots had hit the engineering control panel and disrupted almost every single function of the ship. Only with enormous physical effort had he managed to get one airlock open and send the gleaming ebony shells out into space. Communications were dead. The tractor beam—one of their most valuable assets in their salvage operations—was pulsing wildly for no reason, draining their batteries of power. Not that it mattered: The engine controls were dead, and the ship was traveling on sheer impulse and would continue to do so until something or someone stopped her.

Nabon lapsed into fantasy: hundreds of years from now, an unknown alien race would come upon their ghost vessel, where his essence would still be racing through the corridors, hiding from a deranged Vulcan who, if he ever caught him, would surely kill the young Ferengi who helped bring him here.

He'd managed to elude Skel long enough to get to an auxiliary control panel. But there was no hope. Nabon could not override the huge amount of damage that had been done by the phaser blasts. Why had Dervin turned the setting so high? Did he believe it took that much power to control a Vulcan?

Nabon touched the pocket that held the alien artifacts, the objects that had caused this disaster . . .

And a fresh surge of terror washed over him. The artifacts! Hadn't he just jettisoned them out the airlock? If so, what were they doing *here* in his pocket?

And if he hadn't gotten rid of them, then what *had* he shoved into the airlock?

With sickening dread, he looked about him and realized that he no longer clutched the phaser. Had he been so crazed by panic that he'd mistakenly jettisoned it? What had possessed him to make such a deadly mistake?

Fear left him nauseated and lightheaded; in desperation, he pulled the contents from his pocket to study them, to verify with his own eyes the objects of his doom.

There they lay in his palm: cold and smooth as polished metal, dark as night, yet glittering like prismatic jewels. It was so simple, so simple: If he would only turn them over to Skel, this whole nightmare would be over. The Vulcan would leave him alone then, and he and his brother could spend the time they needed to make their ship functional once more.

As he stared at the coveted articles, the small lids began to rise. This had become his favorite part, to watch the tops lift up and the strange pulsating rainbow light grow from within. It was calming, relaxing . . . but he couldn't imagine what possible value that little trick could have to anyone.

He had failed to shove them out the airlock, but he *could* send them down a refuse recycler. However, it was obvious the devices had their own inner power, a force he still didn't understand. If their energy was stronger or incompatible with the recycler's, it could cause a power surge that could lead to an explosion.

He blinked, staring at the shells. An explosion. The idea began to excite him. He imagined the clashing forces of the small ship's tiny generators ripping it apart, the terror, the pain, the surprise of it as his foolish brother and that horrible Vulcan were ripped to shreds right before his eyes.

Not the Vulcan or the artifacts. Never the artifacts. The artifacts must be safe . . .)

"But someone must *suffer,"* Nabon said gleefully, then broke off with a gasp at the sound of his own words. What was this insanity? *He* would be killed as well in any such explosion.

He glanced up swiftly from the closing shells as his sensitive hearing picked up a sound. A footstep? He'd stayed here too long. Pocketing the devices, Nabon bolted from his hiding place, even as his subconscious came up with several interesting ways of destroying the ship—if he ever had the time.

* * *

"It is traveling under inertia," Worf told his captain as they drew closer to the object of their pursuit. "The shields are down. Its tractor beam is still pulsing, but we can easily stay out of its path."

"Well, it's certainly a Ferengi vessel," Picard remarked, pondering the ship's odd situation. He wished he knew more about the complexity and danger of the disease-harboring artifacts. He didn't want to risk his crew unnecessarily, but neither could he leave those deadly objects with unscrupulous Ferengi thieves.

"It's also the same vessel that left Vulcan after Skel's disappearance," Riker told him. "The markings on the vessel match the information the Vulcans gave us."

"Mr. Worf, why isn't the ship using power to travel?" Picard asked.

"Unknown as of yet," Worf replied. "According to scanners they have power to spare. There has been serious internal damage, possibly from phaser fire. Life support is functional, but everything else is either off line or marginal."

"How many on board?" Riker asked the Klingon.

"There *were* two Ferengi, but one is dead. The other is alive and on the move. Several areas of the ship are sealed off. There is one Vulcan."

"Alive?" Picard wondered aloud.

"Alive and conscious," Worf confirmed.

"A Vulcan could've easily killed that Ferengi to save his own life," Riker surmised, "or to protect the artifacts."

"Could have," Picard agreed, "but—would have? I don't know. This is a scientist, Number One, not a Starfleet officer." Picard turned to the ship's counselor. "Thank you for joining us, Deanna. I know it's been a very long day for you. But can you sense anything aboard the ship?"

The Betazoid stared at the drifting ship for a long

quiet moment. "Terrible confusion. Fear. The gamut of emotions is nearly chaotic. Of course, the Ferengi are an excitable people, but this is a magnified emotional outlay even for one of them."

"Can you sense the Vulcan?"

She nodded. "He's there; I sense his calm, his sense of purpose, his center of logic. It's as if he's in the eye of a hurricane of emotion. It must be terrible for him."

Nabon rubbed his face roughly. It was covered with sweat, even as he shivered with the cold. He was sick, he knew—sick at heart. Sick in his soul. But he now understood the value of the artifacts. They had infected him somehow, given him some disease. He was thoroughly confused. The Vulcan Skel had supposedly been working on forcefield technology, not bioagents, but the little shells had given Nabon some ailment. Could it be fatal?

He trembled. It didn't matter; Dervin—his brother, his friend, his DaiMon—was dead.

In his flight from Skel, Nabon had circled completely through the small ship, barely staying ahead of the crafty alien, frantically trying to seal him behind bulkheads. Every time, the being who had once been their prey escaped.

And now Nabon was back in engineering, standing over the cooling body of his brother. When he first touched him, Nabon feared it had been his phaser shot that had somehow ended his brother's life, since Dervin lay facedown on the deck, almost exactly where Nabon had left him.

Then Nabon had gently turned the corpse over—and seen the savage bruising that covered his brother's face, chest, and lower body. Every inch of Dervin's face and frontal lobes had been crushed as if struck repeatedly with a heavy blunt object.

A phaser?

No, no—I never would have harmed my own brother. . . .

But then, he had at first thought he'd shoved the artifacts out the airlock.

No. No. This murder had been carried out by someone physically stronger. Dervin's savaged body told him the frightening truth: Whatever disease was carried by these strange shell-like objects, they had infected the Vulcan. Skel was mad, rampaging around the ship, no longer interested in retrieving his precious artifacts.

All he wanted to do now was indulge his dark fantasies on Nabon.

It was a horrible disease indeed that could turn a peace-loving Vulcan into a crazed killing machine. No one deserved to die like this, not even his beloved brother. Soon, Nabon knew, he would be as crazy as the Vulcan, and he would no longer have the sense to run from his inevitable fate. The lapses into violent fantasies were becoming more frequent—soon they would overtake his conscious mind completely.

He looked at Dervin's destroyed face again, and instantly images of the Vulcan pounding the life out of his DaiMon came unbidden to his mind. Images so real, so intense, he shuddered from the brutal force of them—despite the simultaneous thrill of pleasure that arose in him.

This was too terrible a disease to foist on any people, even your enemies.

It was good, Nabon reflected, that they would all die here and no one would ever be exposed to it again.

Picard frowned at Counselor Troi's report; he didn't like the way things sounded. Still, the Vulcan seemed normal. And who knew about the Ferengi? Troi might sense that kind of chaos from them over a business deal. He didn't say anything to the crew, but

Picard decided that if the disease had already spread aboard the Ferengi vessel, he'd destroy it with all hands aboard—including the Vulcan scientist—to prevent infecting the *Enterprise.* The political repercussions would be horrendous, but he couldn't worry about that in the face of a disease that hadn't been cured in eighty years.

"What about an away team?" Riker, standing at Picard's side, asked.

"Let's wait," Picard decided. "I don't want to risk exposing our people to danger or disease. We will not bring the ship aboard for the same reason. Mr. Worf, get a tractor beam on that vessel and slowly bring it to a halt." He touched his comm badge. "Picard to Crusher."

"Here, Captain."

"Make sure a quarantine unit is available, Doctor. We may have to beam several patients into it."

"Aye, Captain. We'll be ready."

"Mr. La Forge." Picard turned toward the engineer. "Do we have the isolation units ready for the artifacts?"

"Yes, sir," La Forge assured him. "Coordinates are in the computer. All we need to do now is find them."

That, at least, was reassuring. The medical quarantine units should be able to safeguard the rest of the crew from any infectious agents. And the isolation units for the artifacts were doubly secured.

"Captain," Worf interjected, "the Ferengi vessel is now stopped. And I think I have managed to establish a communication link with it. Their communications are damaged, but I have routed a message through some auxiliary boards at their comm station. What I do not understand is why they did not take the time to do it themselves."

"Perhaps we can ask them that, Mr. Worf. On screen, please."

* * *

Nabon turned as he heard the sound of an override sequence click and engage; the doors to engineering opened narrowly, then halted. But the crack was wide enough for a slender Vulcan to step through. As soon as Skel set foot on the bridge, the partially opened doors sealed shut behind him.

Nabon edged away from the battered body of his brother until his back pressed up against the cabinet that supported the damaged control console. Terror surged through him, a terror like none he'd ever known in his short profitless life. The Vulcan seemed abnormally tall and severe in his black tunic. His hands clasped a small device—a weapon, Nabon thought at first until he recognized a small stasis chamber from the runabout's storage.

To his surprise, the Vulcan stopped and remained near the doorway. "There is nowhere else to go," Skel said quietly, logically. "There is no reason to continue the chase. Give me the artifacts, and it will be ended."

Nabon trembled. *All ended for me, as I join my brother at your killing hands.*

"Give them to me, Nabon," the Vulcan said, his tone all too normal, even kindly.

(Yes, give them . . .)

The Ferengi's tortured mind worked furiously. *If I do what he wants, he will be distracted. Then I might escape.* It was madness to think that, but he *was* mad now, wasn't he? He reached into his pocket and pulled out the two artifacts, once again tightly sealed. He placed them on the floor and pushed them to the middle, then retreated back to his brother's body where it lay beneath the console.

Cautiously, the Vulcan approached the artifacts, then picked them up and returned to his place by the doors, as if he feared Nabon as much as the Ferengi feared him.

Skel studied the artifacts. "They are still sealed," he said, and his voice sounded relieved—if a Vulcan's voice ever revealed such feeling. He opened the small stasis chamber, placed the shells inside, then activated the device. The energy field awoke with a hum—at which point, Skel released an audible sigh.

If my foolish brother had only done that simple thing, Nabon thought sadly, *he might still be alive. But now it is too late to secure the monster. He has his treasure. There is nothing now to stop him from killing me.* Desperately, Nabon hunkered under the console and thought of himself battling the Vulcan hand-to-hand. The ridiculous image provoked a sudden edgy giggle. If he were still alive, Dervin might have attempted such foolishness, but Nabon knew his limits.

"There is no need for you to hide from me, Nabon," the Vulcan said calmly. "The artifacts are contained. We are safe again. Together we can effect repairs to the ship's communications relay and send a distress signal so that we might be rescued."

Nabon blinked and tried to concentrate. What kind of trickery was this Vulcan up to now? His father had always said they were the most foolish of people, having no interest in profit, warfare, or even mating. Nabon could never figure out why they bothered living if they cared for none of those things. Skel had not left his position by the door, which puzzled Nabon. It was as if the Vulcan were being deliberately nonthreatening.

"You don't want to repair the ship's communications," Nabon grumbled. "You just want me to come peaceably—to my death!"

The Vulcan paused, and Nabon flinched, fearful that some incomprehensible mental probe would snake into his brain. "Why would I kill you, Nabon? I only pursued you to obtain the artifacts that are my research. There is no logical reason why I would attempt to harm you, except self-defense."

Nabon's head pounded. What was he talking about,

logic? The Ferengi lifted the body of his brother, still lying facedown on the deck, and pushed it over on its back so the Vulcan could see the smashed face, the broken skull. "Where is the logic in this, Vulcan? Yet here it is. My brother. Dead—*murdered* at your hand!"

Skel took a short step back, as if the sight startled him, even with all his discipline. "Nabon. I assure you. I am not responsible for this. I left your brother here to pursue you through the ship. You saw me gaining on you, and fled. When would I have had time to do this? There must be someone else on board. Unless *you* did this."

Nabon's eyes widened as he stared horrified at the Vulcan. *"Me!* Why would I do this to my own brother, my DaiMon?"

You threw the rifle out the airlock, remember?

Remember?

No! Nabon cried out silently at the intrusive thoughts. *I* can't *remember. . . .*

"I do not understand the causes of violence among people so accustomed to strong emotions," the Vulcan was saying. "But it was clear to me you were furious with him. If there are only three of us on board, and I did not kill him, then logically—"

Nabon shook his head woefully. "You killed him. My only brother. My DaiMon."

Skel had opened his mouth to counter the charge when a hailing whistle sounded loudly in the stillness, making Nabon jump. For a second he thought, *The Vulcan is right, there is someone else on board!*

But then he realized what it was as a computerized voice interrupted: "You are being hailed by the Federation *Starship Enterprise.* Please reply."

We are saved! Nabon thought hopefully. Then, immediately after, he thought, *The disease! That ship will hold hundreds of beings, families, children. . . .*

They will be exposed to insanity and terrible death. He gazed at his brother's brutalized body. *I cannot allow that to happen. Not even to a Federation ship.*

(But the artifacts . . . the artifacts must not be harmed. . . .)

The automated hail answered again while Nabon's brain warred with itself between self-sacrifice and self-survival.

Picard turned to his viewscreen as the image of the drifting ship blinked off and a static-filled picture of an unstaffed Ferengi control room appeared. He had Worf end the automated hail and stepped forward to address the crew himself. "This is Captain Picard of the Federation vessel *Enterprise.* Is there anyone who can acknowledge our hail?"

There was only silence and the eerie image of the vacant cabin.

"According to scanners," Data said quietly, "everyone aboard is within range of that screen—the surviving Ferengi, the deceased one, and the Vulcan. Also, scanners indicate that there is a small stasis chamber out of camera range, with two small objects in it."

"The artifacts?" Picard wondered aloud. Had Skel convinced the Ferengi to contain them properly? A stasis chamber was hardly adequate, but it was better than nothing.

But none of that could be seen in the camera's view. The image was small, almost claustrophobic. All they really could see was the area immediately around the console. The console was severely damaged, with charred areas and a devastated control panel. Normally, he suspected, an officer would be manning the station, with the screen's camera focused on his face. He wished he had a better view of the rest of the area.

"Anybody home?" Riker asked as they all peered at the strange sight.

"Mr. Worf," Picard began, "get a lock on the Vulcan, and that stasis chamber. Be prepared to beam them up on my word."

"Aye, sir," Worf assured him.

"If the Vulcan scientist Skel is close enough to hear me," Picard announced to the other ship, "be prepared to be beamed aboard the *Enterprise.* Now, Mr. Worf."

"Energizing now, sir," Worf said quietly.

As soon as they heard the whine of the transporter beam on the deck of the Ferengi ship, the survivor suddenly popped his huge head up over the console, as if he'd been down on the floor, and nearly leapt at the screen. The Ferengi's huge ears and multilobed skull filled the viewscreen so rapidly that the entire crew drew back in surprise.

"Federation Captain!" the Ferengi shouted in a panic, "do not take the Vulcan aboard your vessel! You must leave this area! Get away! Get away! You are not safe! None of us are safe! He's a madman! My brother—"

Picard signaled Worf to cut the audio on the ranting alien and turned to the counselor for an interpretation.

"He's terrified," Deanna told the captain. "He fears for *us.* For our safety. But he is so hysterical, I can't get anything more than that."

Picard turned to Riker.

"Do you think he knows about the threat of the disease?" Riker speculated.

"Do you think there's a chance he *has* it?" Picard shot back. He touched his comm badge. "Dr. Crusher, do we have the scientist Skel in the quarantine unit? And if so, what is his condition?"

"He's here, sir," came Crusher's assuring voice. "His research artifacts are safely contained in the lab and seem undamaged. And except for a bit of wear and tear, Master Scientist Skel appears in perfect health. The biofilters found nothing, and intensive scans reveal nothing, either. He's lucid and calm, if a little tired."

Picard glanced at Troi.

"I sense nothing but normal Vulcan composure," Deanna said.

"Do we have another quarantine unit available, Doctor?" Picard asked Crusher. "We have a Ferengi aboard the vessel who is in questionable condition."

"Another unit is in place, sir," Crusher told him.

"Mr. Worf, restore audio, please," the captain requested.

"—not listening to me, Federation Captain! You don't understand the danger! You don't know about—"

"Thank you for your warning," Picard said forcefully, interrupting the Ferengi's diatribe. "We would like to beam you aboard our ship, to determine the status of your health. We will beam over your deceased crewmate for an autopsy."

The eyes of the wild Ferengi opened even wider. "No! No, you mustn't beam us over! And you must return the Vulcan and his artifacts! You cannot—"

Picard was about at the end of his patience. "Now listen here—we are going to beam you onto our ship, whether you come willingly or not. Once you are aboard this vessel, you will be placed under arrest for kidnapping, theft, violation of interplanetary treaties—" Picard ground to a halt as the little alien suddenly plunged his hands into the battered control panel and began working furiously. "Lieutenant Worf, what is he *doing?*"

Worf paused for a second, then said, incredulously, "He—he's opening the plasma conduits of his batteries, and flooding the battery storage area with an incendiary gas!"

Picard turned to the tactical station, but before he could bark an order, Riker shouted, "Disengage tractor beam! Shields up!"

The captain was peripherally aware of Data, La Forge, and Worf working in concert to obey that command, just as the Ferengi bridge still pictured on their viewscreen turned into a fireball of light so brilliant that Picard raised a hand to shield his eyes. He realized that the tractor beam had been disengaged, and the shields engaged at precisely the right moment, as the ship rocked from the small explosion happening so close to her, but was unharmed. A second later, there was nothing on the viewscreen but the image of space, and a small cloud of debris.

"The Ferengi vessel, sir," Worf announced, "is no more."

Why? Picard wondered, baffled. "Did you get any clear motivation from him, Counselor?"

She seemed thoroughly shaken by the destruction of the ship; Riker noticed it, too, and took her by the elbow and led her to a chair. She eased herself into it while collecting her thoughts. "His mental panic is hard to describe. There was a flood of images right at the end—his love for his brother, his grief over his death—"

The deceased Ferengi, Picard thought.

"—a residual terror of being pursued by the Vulcan, and a terrible fear of being beamed aboard this vessel."

"He knew he was facing serious charges," Riker rationalized over this last.

But Deanna shook her head. "No. He didn't fear imprisonment. He feared for *us.* At the very last second, there was a surge of emotional outlay—fear, sadness, terror, hatred, violent rage— all of it triggering a sickening pleasure in the Ferengi. But under all that was a core of courage, and the determination that he alone could save *us.* He destroyed the ship to save all of us."

The bridge was silent. Finally, Picard said, "He must have been convinced he'd been exposed to the disease. I can't explain it any other way." He touched his communicator. "Dr. Crusher, are you still convinced that Skel is free of any alien organism?"

"Yes, Captain," Crusher responded. "I've treated him through the quarantine unit for a variety of abrasions and the residual effects of close-range phaser fire, but other than that he is perfectly healthy."

"Can you determine if the research artifacts have been damaged, or opened in any way?"

"According to scanners," Crusher replied, "they are completely intact. As far as I can determine, they have never been opened, and Skel assures me that they escaped damage while in the hands of the Ferengi."

Picard stared at the slowly expanding cloud of debris that had once been the Ferengi vessel. "Dr. Crusher, please keep the scientist Skel under full quarantine until I've had a chance to speak with him."

"Certainly, Captain," Crusher agreed.

Picard turned to his crew. "It's unfortunate the Ferengi officer chose to take his own life before we could learn more about this incident. However, Skel and the artifacts are safe and apparently unharmed. Number One, please effect a change in crew immediately. You all deserve a good night's sleep. Well done, everyone."

Picard started for the turbolift, then had a moment's reconsideration. "Counselor Troi? May I impose upon you?"

Riker stared at Deanna, clearly concerned about her condition. She smiled wanly at the commander, then stood up and moved to join Picard by the lift.

"Of course, sir," she assured him with forced cheer. "I'll be happy to accompany you to interview Scientist Skel."

Picard nodded in gratitude. As they both entered the lift, however, he couldn't help but wonder just what it was he had beamed aboard his ship, and whether he could afford to ignore the ranting of one suicidal Ferengi.

Chapter Three

DR. BEVERLY CRUSHER watched with admiration and concern as, behind the transparent shield of the quarantine facility, the Vulcan scientist attended to his own minor abrasions. Skel had assured her he was well-versed in the use of medi-scanners and tissue regenerators, and the ease with which he used the facility's medical equipment testified to his proficiency. Lean and tall, his dark hair streaked with silver, Skel moved with the serenity and grace typical of his people; yet shadows gathered beneath his calm eyes, and his complexion seemed sallow. He was exhausted, Beverly decided, and her assumption was borne out by the diagnostic readouts on the unit. The scientist was still recovering from the effects of phaser fire, he'd had no nourishment in over twenty-four hours, and he was suffering from fatigue and the effects of extreme stress. Minor stuff, most of it, especially for a Vulcan.

"After the captain talks to you, Skel," Beverly said, "I want you to eat. Then you can rest and let your body take over your healing. There's no reason you can't go into a healing trance for as long as you need."

He glanced in her direction, then lowered his gaze. "I doubt I will have time to do that, Doctor, though I appreciate your consideration. I am still due to present my findings at the TechnoFair. I have colleagues aboard this vessel that I must collaborate with before then. I have lost valuable time already."

Beverly sighed. She knew better than to argue with a Vulcan about putting personal needs before duty. "Well, you can at least spend *some* time—"

In the outer rooms behind them, the doors opened; that would be the captain, Beverly knew. "Excuse me, Skel, there's something I must attend to." The scientist nodded at her, and continued his self-healing.

Picard and Troi met her in her office off the main sickbay area.

"Report, Doctor," Picard said succinctly.

Crusher nodded. "Nothing has changed since I spoke to you on the bridge. Skel has some minor injuries, which he's treating right now in quarantine. I can't find any evidence of a contagious organism either in him or in those containers we've beamed aboard. I've also compared the scanner readings from the artifacts with the scanner readings sent from Vulcan. As far as the computer is concerned, the artifacts haven't been tampered with at all."

"So in your opinion Skel is free from disease, and the alien artifacts have not been breached," Picard reiterated.

"That is my opinion, Captain."

Picard straightened his jacket and gave a short sigh—whether of relief that the disease was contained, or of reluctance to possibly expose his crew to it, Crusher could not say. And then Picard glanced at Troi. Crusher followed his gaze, quizzical about

Deanna's purpose here; no doubt her curiosity showed in her expression, for Picard softly explained, "I wanted the counselor to evaluate Skel as well. From the little we know of the disease, it affects the mind, causing delusions, hallucinations, and madness. If Skel is in the beginning stages of the ailment, it's possible an empath can sense it."

Crusher nodded again in approval; while she might be convinced that Skel harbored no contagion, it was impossible to be too cautious when dealing with such a horrific disease. She turned to Deanna. "Do you want to meet him now?"

"Of course," Troi agreed, smiling. "But first, I must tell you, Captain, that I can already sense his center of Vulcan calm. All the strong emotions I felt coming from the Ferengi vessel are gone. He knows he is safe now, that his artifacts are no longer in danger. His mind is blanketed by that unique sense of logic, that warm containment of rational thought."

As Picard listened to his counselor, the worried crease in his brow slowly eased, then disappeared. "Counselor, if, when you meet the Vulcan, you are as assured of his health and sanity as you are now, I'll order his release from the quarantine. Doctor, do you agree?"

"Most certainly," Crusher said. "I see no reason to keep him confined if he's not ill."

Picard nodded at his two officers. "Well, let's welcome our newest guest properly then."

Troi followed Crusher and Picard into the quarantine area, using the slight distance between them to collect her thoughts. The incident with the Ferengi ship was disturbing to everyone involved, and as tired as she felt, it was hard for her to filter out the rush of emotions of the crew, especially from the people she knew best. The entire day had been an unusual emotional roller-coaster ride, starting with the death of Lieutenant Ito, the pressure of the TechnoFair schedule, and the disturbing incident with Dr. Tarmud. Everyone around her, with the single exception of Data, was still reacting to the difficult events, so much so that it was difficult for her to concentrate on sensing the Vulcan's mental health.

Picard, in particular, was under a very unique emotional strain. In spite of his cool reserve and professional exterior, he was as prone to the same emotional stresses as anyone else. His physical proximity wasn't helping her segregate this one Vulcan over all the other minds on the ship.

She focused as she entered the room, pushing all the other minds and feelings to the outer edges of her senses, leaving herself more open to the one individual she had to analyze: Skel, who sat at a small computer terminal, apparently already attempting to contact his colleagues on board. He was an attractive male by Vulcan standards, with a narrow angular face and sharply sculpted cheekbones and chin; most striking to Deanna were his eyes—bright green irises rimmed with black, emeralds encircled by onyx. Their gaze was so striking that Troi would have liked to have studied them, but Skel almost immediately lowered his lids.

"Welcome aboard the *Enterprise,* Master Scientist Skel," Picard said. "I am Captain Jean-Luc Picard. I truly regret the need to confine you in quarantine." He stood consummately erect, hands clasped behind his back, and while his tone was warm, it was also consciously formal. Nor did he smile, in order to make his guest as comfortable in his presence as possible; his manners were, Deanna reflected, impeccably Vulcan. She took care that her own posture and expression were appropriately reserved.

"It is not logical to apologize for taking a sensibly cautious approach, Captain." The Vulcan's tones were quiet, moderate, and unemotional.

Almost serene, Troi thought, focusing on that voice, opening her mind to him in his clear confined booth. It was in many ways a relief after the intense human emotions she'd recently experienced.

"The safety of your crew is paramount," Skel continued. "I am completely comfortable here, and Dr. Crusher has made available to me everything necessary to heal my minor injuries. I can even sleep here or consult with my colleagues. You have gone out of your way to make the confinement as tolerable as possible."

"The least we can do, sir," Picard assured him.

"Captain Picard, did you beam aboard the Ferengi Nabon, and the body of his brother, Dervin?" Skel asked.

Picard hesitated slightly, then said smoothly, "I'm sorry to inform you, but the surviving Ferengi—Nabon, did you say?—managed to destroy his ship just as we were beaming you, and your artifacts, on board. We were fortunate we were able to get you out of there before Nabon, his deceased brother, and their vessel were completely obliterated."

Troi sensed Skel's surprise, and a strange surge of emotional reaction to the news. The emotions, however, were quickly analyzed and suppressed in the same type of rational pattern most Vulcans employed in emotional control.

"I truly regret hearing that, Captain," Skel said. "While Nabon participated in my capture and the theft of the artifacts, he was quite logical in his handling of the artifacts and tried to keep them safe. I regret the loss of his life; indeed, the entire incident. I will have to reexamine the security situation at the Vulcan Science Academy. I fear that I and my colleagues have become too complacent since the disease last ran rampant."

"Skel," Picard pressed on, "the Ferengi's behavior, in general, seemed quite odd. Do you have any fears that they may have been exposed to the disease? That could account for some of Nabon's reactions, and perhaps, his destruction of the ship."

"I cannot explain the Ferengi's behavior, Captain," Skel admitted. "However, had the disease escaped the artifacts, they would have been left open and powerless, and when I confined them in the Ferengi stasis chamber, they were both still sealed. We do know that contamination occurs when the top shell opens and a victim is exposed to the contents. Once the victim is infected, the shell is left 'empty' and appears dead—powerless."

"When the artifacts arrived in the Ferengi stasis chamber, they were completely sealed, Captain," Beverly assured Picard.

"Can you tell us how Dervin died?" Picard asked softly.

Skel sighed. "No, Captain, I cannot. Dervin was attempting to force open the two halves from one of the artifacts. Fearing he would succeed, I grappled with him, but hesitated using the force necessary to subdue Dervin while he had both hands wrapped around the artifact. His brother, Nabon, eventually stunned both of us, then took the artifacts and ran. I woke up from the phaser fire first, and went to pursue Nabon. At that time, Dervin was unconscious but alive. I circled the entire ship and ended up where we started—the bridge/engineering center—and that was where I found Nabon huddled over the body of his brother. I can only assume that Nabon killed Dervin, possibly over their disagreements about the handling of the artifacts. It is the only way I can account for the elder Ferengi's death."

Picard turned to glance at Troi. He would not insult the Vulcan by asking her to verify his story, but she knew that was the reassurance he needed. By this time, she'd succeeded in suppressing all the myriad feelings from her friends and crewmates and opened herself solely to the mind of the Vulcan before her. She found nothing but the same rational center of logic and serenity. Closing her eyes, she pushed a little deeper:

RUN! RUN, MY CHILD! THERE IS DANGER HERE!

Troi took one staggering step backward, then another, as the desire to flee, to escape, overwhelmed her with a primal terror. She groaned and took another step backward before bumping into Dr. Crusher.

"Deanna, what is it?" Beverly asked, gripping her arms and holding her in place.

Troi's heart rate had accelerated wildly, and she was panting. Picard stared at her, alarmed. She swallowed, stood up straight, and collected herself.

"Counselor?" Picard demanded. He glanced between Troi and the Vulcan suspiciously.

Skel would not look at her. His face was as composed as any Vulcan's, but she knew now he was not like any other Vulcan she'd ever scanned. She turned to him for an explanation.

"Forgive me, Counselor," the scientist said softly. She thought—to her amazement—that he sounded ashamed. "I have never been scanned by a Betazoid before. I was hoping you would not sense it."

"Sense what?" Picard snapped.

Crusher had a medical scanner out and was running it over Deanna, then comparing the readouts with the ones from the quarantine unit. "Yes. I'd like to know the same thing."

Deanna swallowed again, and Picard moved to bring her some water.

"It is my fault, Captain," the Vulcan explained as Deanna drank from the offered glass. "I should have warned her, but I did not think—" He exhaled in a rush and started over. "When the disease caused by the artifacts infected the planet Vulcan, I was a child of ten. My father was infected. He went mad and killed my mother, T'Reth, through brutal torture. Her last act was to save my life, by mentally calling a warning that woke me from my sleep and allowed me to escape. However, the experiences I suffered during that period—seeing my father's madness, sensing my mother's torment and death, hearing her mental screams—have caused me long-term psychological damage. In times of stress, my mother's warning and the fear it induced come to me unbidden, affecting my sleep and my reactions to normal stimuli. Being kidnapped, having my life threatened, fearing that the artifacts might reinfect others again—it reawakened my childhood fears and made them new again. It is as if my mother's voice is running rampant through my mind." He glanced at Deanna, his face somber. "I apologize again, Counselor. I thought I could shield you. I should have warned you."

"I—I'm all right," Deanna told her worried crewmates. "Your explanation puts the raw sensation into perspective. It was just such a surprise. I usually only pick up feelings, impressions. But—it was as if I could hear your mother's voice. That must have been so terrible for you, Skel. I am so sorry that you must live with that difficult memory."

"T'Reth's voice, though disconcerting, has often warned me of imminent danger," Skel told her. "It is not logical to believe so, but over the years, I have come to know it is true. My mother was a brave and courageous woman. I could do far worse than to have her voice in my mind, still warning me, still fighting to preserve my life all these years after her tragic death. I appreciate your understanding."

Deanna realized she'd never given Picard the information he needed, that he was still waiting. "Master Scientist Skel has told us the truth as he knows it. The sense of strong emotion that traces back to his childhood is understandable in the light of his past. He appears to be mentally sound and totally uninfected by any force or organism."

Picard asked pointedly, "You feel it would be safe then to release Skel from quarantine?"

She glanced back at the scientist, at the placid Vulcan exterior, at the calm outer shell. "Yes, I believe it is safe."

"Why take the chance, Captain?" Skel interjected. "This facility will allow me to do my work, and to meet with colleagues. In a few days we will arrive at the TechnoFair. By then you will have your answer as to my state of health. Why do I not simply remain here to be safe?"

Picard looked as if he were seriously considering it, when Crusher intervened. "Captain, perhaps you would feel more self-assured if you viewed the artifacts that Skel rescued from the Ferengi."

"Excellent idea, Doctor," Picard said, as if relieved to have a change of atmosphere. He turned to the Betazoid. "Counselor, are you up to accompanying us?"

"Aye, sir," she said. She looked at the gray-haired Vulcan once more, but could not make herself scan him again. She would do almost anything to avoid reading that terrible childhood memory.

"I appreciate your suggesting the change of scene, Doctor," Picard said, as they entered the primary area of sickbay on their way to the quarantine lab that held the artifacts. "Deanna, are you really all right? You went white as a sheet!"

She placed a reassuring hand on the captain's arm. "I'm quite fine now, sir. It was just the shocking jolt of emotion—a child's emotion, perhaps the strongest there is—and from a Vulcan it made it doubly odd. I was simply unprepared. But his story is clearly true, Captain. You can certainly release Skel from quarantine."

Picard turned to Crusher as if for confirmation of

Troi's story. "The readouts I got from Deanna when she was reacting to the Vulcan's mind matched his so closely," Crusher said, "I knew she was really linked to him. This wasn't her normal Betazoid scan where she picks up feelings or senses an emotional state. Since he's a telepath, yet burdened with these vivid emotional memories, he may have inadvertently augmented her mental scan."

The three continued walking to the quarantine unit. "Well, since you both feel releasing him is appropriate, I'll agree," Picard said.

Crusher took the lead as they entered the lab, leading the others to a transparent container that looked like a miniature version of Skel's facility. In its center sat two innocuous-looking black receptacles. They resembled, Deanna thought, some of the beautiful jewellike shellfish from Betazed; the light caught the artifacts' smooth black surfaces and reflected shimmering pastel colors—yellow, green, blue, pink.

Crusher held a hand out toward the container. "There they are! There are double containment fields surrounding the artifacts on the interior, and a safety forcefield blocking entrance or egress. The forcefields and containment fields have special on/off codes set up by the computer. Only you, Captain, and I have access to the codes."

"You mean," Picard said, incredulous as he stepped up to the field, "all this fuss is over those two little things?"

"I'm afraid so." Crusher gave a gentle shake of her head, clearly as unable as the captain to believe it.

"They look no more imposing than a Terran *clam!*" He leaned down to get a better look.

"That may be so, Captain," Crusher agreed, "but looks can be deceiving. I can't exactly tell you what's in there, but I can tell you it's kept inside by a self-generating forcefield fueled by an unknown power source. It can't be opened from the outside, not with all the force we could generate from this starship. It can only be opened by trigger mechanisms from within—mechanisms still only vaguely understood. We don't have the technology to create anything like this; we can only speculate about the people who did."

"The Vulcans think this was deliberately created, then?" Picard asked. "They don't think it's alive, that it evolved?"

"The current theory is that they may have been a delivery method for an advanced germ-warfare-type weapon," Beverly said.

Picard nodded. "They're quite old, I understand. Have they been able to translate the writing on the shell?"

"Not yet. I think they have a phrase, but that's all."

"Maybe Mr. Data would like a crack at it," Picard mused. "He's got a singular talent for cross-referencing language matrixes. He might have an insight on this that the Vulcans couldn't have. I'll talk to Skel, see if it's all right with him." Picard stood up straight again and turned back to Deanna. "You don't . . . 'sense' anything from them, do you, Counselor?"

"How could she?" Beverly wondered aloud. "They're not intelligent. I'm not even sure the Vulcans consider them 'alive' in any sense."

Deanna had been listening to the two officers as she stared at the small unimposing artifacts. She felt odd watching them like this, as if she were observing a venomous snake caged in a glass tank—a snake that knew it was in a tank and therefore made no attempt to strike. A snake that was content to sit, wait, and bide its time.

"Counselor?" Picard asked again. "Are you sensing anything?"

She heard again that terrible voice, that primal scream of a mother protecting her child.

RUN! RUN, MY CHILD! RUN FOR YOUR LIFE!

Only this time it was her own mother's voice she heard—Lwaxana pleading with her to flee, to get out of there, to save herself . . .

Troi gave herself a mental shake, knowing that she was just reacting to the shocking effect of Skel's memories. Deanna glanced at Picard, then turned back to the artifacts.

Vulcans were primarily touch telepaths, and obviously, with these objects contained behind multiple forcefields and the danger of infection, no Vulcan would ever be allowed to put hands upon these. If there was any chance there was life in these pods, or even, however remotely possible, intelligence, she was obliged to discern that.

Hesitantly, Deanna opened her empathic sense to the artifacts sitting in the containment field.

POWER!

It hit hard, like a blow to the skull, as a torrential flood of sensory input invaded her mind. Her head snapped back as if she had been physically struck, causing her instinctively to hold up her hands to ward off the attack.

"What's happening to her?" she heard Picard demand, worry etched in his voice, but she could not respond to him. She could only fight for her own sanity.

Something was grasping her arms: Crusher, Picard, followed by Beverly shouting, but Deanna could no longer understand the words, could no longer do anything except fall into a maelstrom of emotion, hatred, rage. Dimly, she was aware of Picard lifting her in his arms and running out of the room, as if he could outrace disaster and impending doom.

"Deanna! Deanna!" Beverly shouted, as the empath spiraled down, down, down into hell. "Deanna, break the connection! Break it! You can do it! Come on!"

A slap . . . distant and faraway, a quicksilver glimmer of physical pain like a lifeline in the middle of overwhelming rage, fury, terror, despair. Troi mentally grasped at it.

Another slap. Another, stronger . . .

The blows rocked her; she sucked in a lungful of air like a newborn, at last breaking the connection.

The sensation of normalcy, of freedom from mental anguish, brought infinite relief. Deanna inhaled shakily and examined her surroundings: she lay on a diagnostic bed in outer sickbay, as far as possible from the receptacles, with both Picard and Beverly gazing down at her with expressions of profound alarm.

"Deanna, thank God!" Crusher exclaimed, as she stared at her medi-scanner readout. "You're all right now. But that was close."

Picard turned to Crusher, a mixture of worry, indignation, and the need to know warring on his face. "What happened in there?"

"Her bodily functions were shutting down," Crusher said incredulously, still studying the readout, "while her brain—" The doctor shook her head, struggling to explain. "Her brain was trying to reformat its neural pathways into something completely different! I've never seen anything like it—well, maybe once. Over a century ago on Reydovan Four, there was an unusual virus that reformatted the brain to its needs. The victims were alive but no longer humanoid, trapped in a nightmare world of consciousness not of their own making. That's the only analogy I can come up with. But Deanna's body was dying, even though the brain was showing no response to the organ failures. I don't understand it. Not at all. It doesn't make any sense."

"What did you feel while this was happening?" Picard asked Troi gently.

"What I just experienced," Deanna said shakily, "was a thousand times more horrible than Skel's terrible memories. What is in those containers, Captain, is not life as we understand it. It is something different. It is organized, powerful, conscienceless, rapacious. But it's not exactly life—not a virus, but far smaller than that, and far more dangerous. And its hunger, its needs are insatiable. It is completely, totally *evil.*"

Picard drew back at that final word, then—after a moment's reflection—asked, "Was it constructed, or did it evolve?"

She shook her head carefully. "Perhaps both. The core of it, its essence, is something from nature. Something that, I think, was captured, discovered, then refined to its purest essence—as if you could capture the banshee and put it in a bottle. It was artificially refined, augmented, and improved. I believe the Vulcans are right about its origins: it was designed for warfare."

She closed her eyes, trying not to relive the terrible moment of connection with the unworldly power. "It devoured its enemies and its makers alike . . . until none were left to stop the madness they created."

Worf walked quietly into his son's room. Alexander slept soundly now, but he must have been dreaming earlier, since his covers were everywhere except on his body and his pillow was on the floor. In the corner at Alexander's desk, a holographic eyeball was suspended near his computer station, blinking at Worf as if it were intelligent.

Now, where did that come from? the Klingon wondered. He went over to it, moving to turn it off, but the eye glared at him so balefully that he pulled his hand back. *Of course,* Worf realized, *it is the all-seeing eye of a Klingon warrior!* He chuckled and let it be, amused that the eye would watch over his son all night.

Carefully, Worf picked up the pillow and eased it

under the boy's head, then straightened the covers and tucked the youngster in. Alexander would have been outraged at the tender gesture if he had been awake, but Worf had clear memories of his father doing the same to him when he thought his little son was asleep. Worf loved his child with a warrior's fierce devotion and a father's gentle caring. Few outside of the Klingon family unit ever saw that side of the warriors, but it was there. Worf only regretted having missed the time of Alexander's life when he could have been gently cradled in strong arms as his father murmured stories of glorious battles and ferocious one-on-one combat to his infant son. Alexander would have none of that now.

He bowed over the boy, meaning to kiss his skull plate, when the soft chiming of his door startled him. *Who could be here at this unseemly hour?* If it were ship's business, either the captain or Data, who had the conn on the late-night shift, would have called him on the communicator.

He left his son's room and went into the general living quarters. "Enter!" he called gruffly.

He was stunned to find the scientist Kyla Dannelke at his door. She was dressed now in an attractive, low-cut velvet tunic of sapphire blue, which made her pale eyes dazzling in her unsettlingly pale face, and she had brushed her pale hair out so that it fell, unbraided, on her shoulders.

The sight of her evoked conflicting feelings: Worf's outrage at her prejudice was tempered by her forthright behavior and her clear willingness to change her views.

And, of course, there was no denying the fact that—despite her human features—she was a strong attractive woman.

The mental admission brought forth a surge of guilt, as though he were being unfaithful to his dead mate, to K'Ehleyr's memory.

Yet at the sight of him, Kyla smiled—an expression of such honest, unashamed happiness and appreciation that the Klingon could not entirely resist its charm. He pressed his lips together and permitted the corners of them to quirk a bit; it was the closest he could come at the moment to returning the smile.

But he kept his tone formal, serious. "Dr. Dannelke," he said before she could speak, "it is late. I have just now gone off duty. There is another crew on board that can answer your needs. You have but to ask the computer—"

"May I come in?" she interrupted—and before he could refuse her, she stepped into his quarters far enough to let the doors close behind her. Boldly, she walked about the general living area. "Well, this is not what I expected!"

Worf's lips parted in amazement; never had he seen a human demonstrate such forward, brazen behavior: why, she was behaving like a Klingon!

The thought sparked both guilt and anger, the same anger he had felt when he scolded Alexander: *That woman is nothing like your mother!*

"Dr. Dannelke, I do not know what it is you want but—" He blinked, finally reacting to her last statement. "What do you mean, this is not what you 'expected'?"

"These aren't a *Klingon warrior's* quarters," she announced with a grin. "Klingon quarters are austere. Warriors sleep on slabs of unyielding stone or metal. Comforts are for the *weak*. I looked it up this afternoon, after our talk. I'm right, aren't I? So, what is all this? Pretty cushy place, Lieutenant."

Worf ground his teeth and took a slow calming breath. This was the most *exasperating* female! "I have served aboard Klingon vessels and Federation vessels. When aboard Klingon vessels I have Klingon quarters as you have described. When aboard Federation vessels, I live as a Federation officer. It is practical and makes my fellow crew members comfortable when they visit. *If* it is any business of *yours!*"

His annoyance made no impression on her. "But surely your private quarters—your *bedroom*—is in true Klingon style. Hard slab. No pillow." She moved toward the door that led to Alexander's room, no doubt assuming it was Worf's.

"Wait!" he called out quietly, worrying his son would hear them and wake up.

His hesitation allowed her to step close enough to the doors to open them. Worf drew up beside her as she realized whose room it really was.

"Oh, isn't that sweet!" Dannelke murmured softly, as the Klingon eye glared at her from the computer station. "He sent me a message through the computer after the TechnoFair, along with a program he'd made that would allow him to have a small eye just like the big one I have over my display. He needed some help with it. I cleaned it up and sent it back to him. But he's changed it! Originally it was a human eye, but now it's clearly Klingon. What a clever young man."

Worf felt his anger dissolving as the scientist plainly admired his son. He took her arm respectfully and pulled her away from the room, so the door would shut and allow his son to sleep.

"I thank you for spending the time on his program," Worf said sincerely. "I know this close to the TechnoFair, it was time you no doubt needed for your own work."

"That's a charming kid you've got there, Lieutenant," Dr. Dannelke said. "He's hard to turn down. I notice he doesn't sleep like a Klingon, though." Had there been even a hint of sarcasm in her tone, he would have lost his temper completely; but her comment was simply curious, the comment of one who was sincerely interested in the child.

"Alexander's mother was half human, so he has a mixed heritage," Worf admitted, with no small amount of discomfort. "He is much more like her than he is like me. I am content exposing him to Klingon culture and letting him choose what parts of it he cares to adopt."

For the first time, Dannelke's brazenness faltered; she lowered her eyelids as she glanced guiltily around the quarters. "And Mrs. Worf . . . she's asleep?"

The question's purpose was so blatant that Worf could not resist a faint smile; at the same time, it increased his sense of awkwardness. "Had she been asleep, the scent of an unknown female in her quarters would have brought her instantly awake. No, Dr. Dannelke, there is no 'Mrs. Worf.' My mate K'Ehleyr, Alexander's mother, was killed by an enemy of ours some time ago."

She brought a hand to her mouth as if to contain an expression of surprise. "That's awful. Oh, I'm so sorry, for you, and especially, for Alexander. I've really botched this up, Lieutenant!"

He had no idea what to say; he therefore said nothing, but waited for her to gather her composure.

"I'm here for two reasons," she admitted at last, "but the first and most important one is to apologize. Instead, I've barged into your life, invading your and Alexander's personal space, and bringing up sad memories. I feel terrible." She stepped closer to him, meeting him eye to eye like an equal. It was a bold act, and he couldn't help admiring her for it; most non-Klingons would have never had the nerve. "I wanted to apologize for my behavior earlier. I acted like a prejudiced, backwater ignoramous. I insulted you, and I'm sorry. I have no excuse. I am very ignorant of your culture and your people and have little opportunity to interact with them. I promised myself tonight I would remedy that and have started reading up on these issues, but you have a complicated culture, and we will be long separated before I know enough to keep from making a fool of myself again.

Will you accept my apology for the foolish things I said before—and the foolish things I will no doubt say in the future?"

Worf felt a strange sensation uncurl in the pit of his stomach as he realized, *Alexander is right! She is much like K'Ehleyr!* The realization was like a bitter-sweet knife to his heart. He wet his lips, his mouth suddenly dry, as he searched for the right thing to say.

"Dr. Dannelke, you are an important scientist. It is hardly necessary for you to come to an officer's quarters to make such an open apology for a momentary misstatement."

"You thought it was a lot more than that this afternoon," she reminded him. "Your face was like a darkening stormcloud, threatening to hurl lightning everywhere! But what you're trying to say—politely—is that you think I have ulterior motives for apologizing."

He started to protest, but she held up a hand to stop him. "That's okay. You're right. I *am* really sorry I said what I did. That's the honest truth. But, there is a favor I need to ask, and that's the truth, too."

"And that is?"

"I want to know what's going on!"

"Excuse me?" he said quietly.

"Now, look, Lieutenant. We were on our way to Vulcan to pick up the scientist, Skel, with whom I happen to be working on a very important project. The next thing I know, the stars outside my quarters look funny, and the computer tells me we're no longer on our way to Vulcan, but won't give me any more information than that. We're going to miss the TechnoFair for some Federation emergency, aren't we?"

Worf sighed. He couldn't very well share with her ship's business, but he could reassure her. "Doctor, on my word, you will arrive at the TechnoFair on time."

"How? We're still not heading for Vulcan, and if we don't pick up Skel—"

He supposed it would do no harm to tell her. "Skel is already on board, Doctor. He is currently in sickbay, but as soon as he is free to leave, I am sure he will contact you. I cannot give you more information than that."

"Skel's here? On board?" She let go a breath and almost smiled, making her plain straightforward features beautiful again. "Well, that's a relief. But I can't talk to him?"

Her single-mindedness about her work was admirable, if exasperating.

"Dr. Dannelke, you must trust that our medical staff has Skel's best welfare in mind. It is late. No doubt he will call you in the morning."

"I suppose you're right. Thank you for that information, Lieutenant." She looked at him wryly, a mischievous glint back in her eye—which made him straighten warily. "I really am sorry about this afternoon. There are times when my mouth gets the better of me, when I just blurt the most embarrassing things out. It always seems to happen at the one moment when I wouldn't want it to."

"And when is that?" Worf wondered aloud. *How many TechnoFairs can this woman attend?*

She grinned at him unabashedly. "It just always seems to happen when I meet a man I'm attracted to."

His eyes widened in shock. That was the last thing he had expected her to say. "Dr. Dannelke!"

She moved closer to him again, grinning and narrowing her eyes like a Terran wolf. "I've always had this terrible weakness for tall, dark, handsome men, Lieutenant Worf. And it makes me say the most foolish things. So, do you think there's any chance we could get past the 'Lieutenant Worf–Dr. Dannelke' stage anytime soon?"

Worf found himself working to suppress his own

smile and heard himself thinking that, yes, they might have a very good chance of getting past that stage quite soon.

Deanna stood before the food replicator in her quarters, irritably drumming her fingers. She'd wanted a hot chocolate, but was afraid the mild stimulant in the drink would interfere with her sleep—and if there was anything she needed after this interminably long and depressing day, it was sleep. So she decided that she would instead order a hot milk laced with honey and vanilla—but she really wanted the chocolate. So she found herself locked in indecision, staring at the food replicator as if it were an altar on which she should make an offering. There was too much on her mind, too many thoughts swirling in her brain—particularly the last discussion she'd had with Picard:

"Captain, destroy them. Throw them out an airlock. Send them into space," she'd insisted after she'd come out of the trance the artifacts had produced. *"They're too dangerous to be kept on board the* Enterprise."

"But they don't belong *to us,"* he'd reminded her. *"What effect would that have on Skel's research, if we did such an outrageous act? How would we explain ourselves to the Vulcans?"*

"If you had felt them the way I have, you would understand—"

"Deanna," he'd said patiently, placing a comforting hand on her arm, *"you know I trust your judgment. But you have had two difficult mental encounters after a long day with too much sorrow in it. I don't doubt that the impressions you picked up from those artifacts would've shaken anyone. But we have no right to destroy them. However, I can make arrangements to pass on the responsibility of holding them to someone else. I will ask the Vulcans to arrange a rendezvous with their nearest science vessel. With luck, we can*

unload the artifacts before we arrive at the TechnoFair. After all, Skel's original plans did not call for having them at the science gathering."

It had not been nearly sufficient, Deanna knew, but she'd understood it was the only compromise she would get. And it would have been a fair one under normal circumstances.

"Another thing, Counselor," Picard had said sternly. *"Until those artifacts are off this ship, I want you to stay as far away from them as possible. And Skel, also."*

"Captain?" she'd asked, surprised.

"You've been through enough for one mission. I want you to take a day off and relax. Forget about scientists, artifacts, TechnoFairs, and schedules. Deanna, you need time to recover from the mental stress you've endured today. I'll make apologies to Skel. He's a telepath. He'll surely understand."

"But, Captain, I don't think this is necessary—"

"That's an order, Counselor," he'd announced, ending the conversation.

Now Deanna knew he was right, but she hated to admit that. And in truth, she was grateful not to have anything more to do with the artifacts. If she was being honest, she would also admit that she would be happy not to see Skel again either. What a tragic figure he was; what a burden he had to live with. But if Vulcan healers could not help him, there was nothing a lone Betazoid counselor could do.

"Just water, cool," she finally told the replicator. It obliged immediately, providing a frosted, sweating glass; she lifted it and drained it in a swallow.

Before she finished, a soft chime came at the door.

She glanced at the time, then immediately sensed the scientist, Skel, outside her door. Her heart rate instantly accelerated.

But the captain said—

She took hold of herself when she realized how

upset the Vulcan's presence was making her. She was acting like a child. No doubt Picard hadn't had a chance to say anything to Skel, and didn't think that at this late hour the scientist would want to do anything but sleep. But, of course, Vulcans could do without sleep for days.

What harm could there be in seeing him? she asked herself, but never waited for the answer.

"Come in," she bid, and the doors opened, showing her the scientist she'd already sensed.

"I was not sure whether you would still be awake," he said softly from the hallway. His demeanor was calm, reassuring, gentle. His serene emerald eyes were politely downcast, yet she could not quite shake her irrational sense of alarm. "Am I disturbing you? Surely, you need to rest."

"Well, I *will* need to rest soon, but we can talk until then. Won't you come in?" She waved him graciously over to a couch.

"Thank you," he said, without sitting. "I just wanted to be sure you were well. I feel responsible for the shocking mental image you received."

Deanna sat down by herself when the Vulcan didn't. "Please don't concern yourself. I'm fine. I thank you for your interest."

He bowed slightly. "Counselor, after you left to see the artifacts, I never spoke to you again. Did you get to see them?"

"Yes," she said, looking away, not wanting to think about the disturbing things. "Yes, I did."

"You are a telepath, Counselor," he said in that same calm, quiet tone. "Did you . . . *sense* anything from them?"

The very question evoked a panic that stole her breath; she forced herself to inhale and exhale calmly, slowly, to collect her thoughts.

"Forgive me for pursuing you on this topic," Skel apologized, apparently sensing her dismay. "But in eighty years of study, no Vulcan has ever melded with or received any telepathic impression from the artifacts. If you have, it would help our understanding of these things enormously."

Deanna warred with irrationally wanting to order the Vulcan out of her quarters, or being the professional counselor and discussing his problem with him. As usual, the professional counselor won out, and Deanna found herself bitterly resenting that woman.

"It was, for me, a . . . difficult moment," she admitted to him. Recalling the instant of connection, she found herself starting to tremble. She focused on her tightly clasped hands, not wanting to embarrass the Vulcan with a display of emotion.

"Then you *felt* them?" he asked softly.

Them. She blinked, hearing his tone, feeling as though his words opened up an understanding for her. "You believe there is something alive in there? Something, possibly intelligent?"

Skel looked about her quarters—at the artwork covering the bulkheads, at the soft pastel grouping of furniture, at a holo of Lwaxana—at every item in the room except Troi. "To answer your question—no. I am a scientist, and nothing that we have learned about the entities residing within the shells indicates intelligence, any more than a virus is intelligent when it invades a host's DNA. However, I am also a survivor of the madness the entities induced. And sometimes, when I think of whatever it is that resides in those artifacts, I see the grotesque mask of my father's face after he was infected. And so, for me, the entities have an appearance, an expression. They wear the soul of my father's madness. So we may say that the survivor of that disease sometimes sees the entities as *them.*"

It was a difficult confession for him, she realized,

one that might only be given to a counselor who had glimpsed into the soul of that survivor. For a brief second, she thought of her lost opportunity with Ensign Ito; she could not pass up this chance that was being offered to her, no matter how personally difficult it might be.

"I did not sense *them,* Skel," Deanna told him. "But I sensed something. Something frightening, and hard to comprehend." She tried to describe for him the exact sensation she'd received when she had stood beside the container that held the artifacts, but even as she mouthed the words she felt their inadequacy. "I'm sorry," she concluded. "Language can be so limiting."

"Something any telepath can understand," Skel agreed. "I hesitate to suggest this, Counselor, but you are an empath, so I will trust that you will understand my request, and the nature in which I offer it. If—I could meld with you—"

RUN! RUN, MY CHILD, RUN FOR YOUR LIFE!

Deanna sat as rigid as stone as Lwaxana's voice shrilled in her brain. Had her contact with the artifacts made her psychotic?

"For just the briefest moment," Skel continued blandly, unaware of the panic the counselor was feeling, "I would receive the exact same mental sense that you received from the artifacts. We would not need inadequate words. I would receive the image and understand. This meld would advance my knowledge of these subjects I have studied so long—"

RUN! GET OUT OF THE ROOM! GET AS FAR FROM HIM AS YOU CAN!

Mother, please! Deanna heard herself scold the person she could not possibly be sensing. Lwaxana was light-years away, so far out of mental range as to be ludicrous. She blinked, forcing herself to listen to what the Vulcan was saying.

"I know it is a great imposition to ask of you," Skel continued. "But this would allow me to share this impression with my colleagues and the healers on my planet who are still working with living victims of the disease. Will you agree?"

Deanna counted every ridge on her knuckles as she stammered, "A Vulcan mind meld? To capture the impression I received from the artifacts? Well, that certainly makes sense—"

Her urge to flee the room, to flee from Skel was so overwhelming she couldn't help but wonder if he could sense it. No, of course not, Vulcans were touch telepaths. He would have to touch her. Suddenly, the thought of him placing his hands on her face, of making the neural connections with his fingertips, and of becoming one with her mind was so repellent that she knew she couldn't go through with it. In Vulcan society, it was one of their most intimate acts. No. No, she couldn't.

Apparently taking her bland comments as consent, Skel approached her, one hand already outstretched. "If you will just remain as you are, we can do this in the briefest moment. I will be swift, and will touch no part of your mind but where the impression lies. Counselor, will you look at me?"

He touched her chin and raised her eyes to his.

Troi gasped as their eyes met for the very first time. Lwaxana's voice shrilled in her brain for her to escape, to run. She thought wildly that Skel would hear her mother, that he would be insulted, then realized what a ridiculous thing it was to worry about—when there was so much more to fear in the depths of those Vulcan eyes. She had to get away! But she could not make herself move from the couch.

Skel brought his hand toward her face.

Abruptly, the door chimed again, which sounded this time like the loudest thing she had ever heard. She pulled away from the Vulcan's hand.

"Come in!" she cried, rising in one smooth, sudden move away from him and toward the door.

The doors slid open to reveal Will Riker, his dark eyebrows rising at the sight of Skel. The Vulcan stood, hands clenched, perfectly poised, in the center of Deanna's living room.

"I didn't realize you had a guest," Will said blandly, but Troi could sense a myriad of strange feelings in him—reactions to the presence of the Vulcan.

"It's perfectly all right," Deanna said with false cheerfulness as she took Will's elbow and led him into the room. She gripped his sleeve as if it were a lifeline, as if this were the only chance she had to save herself. His gaze transformed from one of suspicion to concern, as if he could sense her emotional state as easily as she could his.

"Of course," Skel agreed. "I was just leaving." He turned to her and bowed slightly. "I thank you for your time, Counselor. You have been a great help to me."

And before Deanna could gather her wits about her to get a sense of his true reactions to her fleeing the meld, he was gone. It was just as well. She really didn't want to touch his mind again, not now, not ever. She sagged a little, as the doors closed behind the Vulcan.

Suddenly, Will took her arms and faced her. "What was *he* doing here?"

"We were just talking about his experience with . . ." Deanna began in confusion.

Riker interrupted. "Captain Picard left express orders that he was to have no contact with you. Why was he here?"

Deanna moved over to the couch and collapsed upon it; Riker followed and sat sideways, facing her. When she could find the energy to speak, she asked, "You know about that?"

"I'm the first officer, remember?" he chided her gently. "I know all, see all. You haven't answered me."

"I just assumed that Captain Picard hadn't said anything directly to Skel because of the late hour. I can't believe a Vulcan would deliberately violate a ship's captain's direct order."

Riker mulled that over. "He had time enough to tell *me* about it. I can't remember his exact words, but I got the impression he'd already told Skel, but I could have just assumed that. I'll find out tomorrow. But Picard's right—that scientist seems to have a very negative effect on you. What could he have been thinking, coming here at this hour?"

By now, Riker's well-meaning "damsel-in-distress" routine was wearing thin. Deanna sat up against the couch, folded her arms, and said pointedly, "I might well ask you that same question."

"I just finished getting briefed by Picard. He told me what happened with Skel and the artifacts. I was worried about you; I asked the computer if you were asleep yet and it said no, so . . ." He grinned. "I guess I should've asked if you had a gentlemen caller."

She punched his arm playfully, even as she thought, *That Vulcan is no gentleman.* "You showed up at just the right time. I'm beginning to wonder if *you're* part Betazoid."

"Skel really did upset you," Riker said. "You still haven't told me what happened here."

For some reason, Troi found herself reluctant to tell him the Vulcan had wanted to meld with her. She decided that most of it was her own leftover fears from the bad mental experiences she'd had earlier. There was no sense creating a crisis where none existed. "Nothing happened, Will. Honestly. I do have a residual reaction to Skel because of what happened today. I'm sure it will pass in time. But the captain's right. I'd be better off not seeing him again."

"Sounds fine with me," Riker decided. "Let me stay here tonight—right here, on the couch. Don't you think the presence of a faithful watchdog might help you sleep a little better?"

Normally, the suggestion would have insulted her, but not tonight. She didn't want to lie awake in bed, anticipating another late-night visit from Skel that no doubt would never come. She placed a hand on Riker's arm. "Would you mind doing that for me, Will? I'd be very grateful."

He slung a companionable arm around her and pulled her close in a protective embrace. "Hey, what are friends for?"

Troi smiled and pressed against him, comforted by his strength and the trust she knew she could place in him. But even as he held her, she found her mind skirting back, not to Skel, but to something far more menacing.

Try as she might, she knew she couldn't shake the sense of evil that emanated from those artifacts—and wouldn't shake it until they were gone from the ship.

Chapter Four

SKEL WOKE SO SUDDENLY that for two-point-four seconds he could not remember where he was; for an additional three-point-one seconds, he could not remember *who* he was.

Although the environment of his cabin was heated to a comfortable degree of Vulcan warmth, he shivered as if ill. He should call for Dr. Crusher, he thought, then rejected that notion.

He needed T'Son, his healer. The human doctor, though skilled in Vulcan anatomy, was still merely human. Only T'Son could help quiet the demons that raced through his mind at night.

He swung his legs over the bed and drew a palm across his weary face. Tonight, it had not been his father who pursued him through the desert landscape of his childhood home; tonight, it had been Nabon, the deceased Ferengi whose leering face had tortured his dreams. Such a thing had never occurred; always, the face in the dream belonged to his father. Perhaps more significantly, it was not his mother's voice who called the timely warning to him; tonight, it had been Troi who told him to run, to save himself. If T'Son were here, she would tell him this was understandable, as the counselor had been the last person with whom he'd spoken.

The thought of Deanna Troi made him recall the strange aborted conversation he'd had with the Betazoid; if only he could have melded with her, if only he could've discovered for himself what she'd learned from her mental contact with the artifacts.

Troi's fear of melding with him had been a shock when it had touched him across the space that separated them. So much like his own reaction the instant before T'Son's fingertips touched his face: that same fear, that same impulse to bolt, to flee the room. Troi had felt all those things, and he had felt them from her, raw emotions so alien to him. Emotions that were at once alien, complex, repellent—and exciting.

He rubbed his face tiredly again. He could tell by the reaction he'd received from her that he should not request the meld again. Besides, if Captain Picard found out . . .

He blinked, frowning. If Captain Picard found out . . . what? The thought seemed to arrest itself, as if it were impossible for him to follow it to its logical conclusion. He decided this was yet another side effect of the two phaser blasts he'd absorbed. Since the two Ferengi had shot him, his synaptic responses seemed off, slightly out of kilter. Dr. Crusher had assured him that the symptoms would diminish in a day or so. He hoped she was correct; he had no time to indulge slow synapses.

He had to prepare for the TechnoFair. Fortunately, when Dervin took him from Vulcan, the Ferengi had stolen the computer download of his work as well. Before he'd gone to pursue Nabon, Skel had found those cassettes right on the console where the artifacts had been. He was grateful now that he'd had the presence of mind to grab them and put them in the pockets of his tunic before pursuing Nabon.

That was when Dervin had regained consciousness. That was when he tried to stop you from taking the data cassettes and from pursuing Nabon. That was when he attacked you. That was when you—

The memory flickered and faded out of reach like a static-filled transmission. No. Dervin had not attacked him for the cassettes. Dervin had been in his dream last night. That was why he was confused.

But Skel's work was here. It was one of the few things that had gone right since he'd been kidnapped. With the help of the *Enterprise*'s computer and some lab equipment, he would be able to duplicate his displays. He and Tarmud would be able to work together on their project at last. He was pleased they had been able to get so much done through correspondence, but the exchange of information and ideas face-to-face was always so much more productive. To be able to collaborate, then have an open forum like the TechnoFair where they could share their findings among other scientists was an opportunity that would come only rarely.

In fact, the Federation's Universal TechnoFair was a truly unique event. Skel and Tarmud would be able to discuss their work with some of the finest minds in the explored galaxy—scientists with whom it might otherwise be impossible to communicate due to distance and time. Scientists whom Skel might never have been able to meet, since he rarely left Vulcan. It was almost overwhelming, he realized—the contacts he could make at this fair, the associations he could develop. The influx of fresh ideas and viewpoints could turn his work around, help him solve some of the more intriguing mysteries of the artifacts, their self-generating forcefields, their mysterious language.

At last, something positive might come from the devastating disease that had been inflicted on his people.

All those scientists. All those people—their helpers, aides, technicians, assistants. From across the galaxy. World after world after world. All at the TechnoFair.

Skel had a sudden image of himself lecturing before the gathered mass of scientists, with Tarmud beside him at the podium. He saw the audience of sentient beings of every shape, and organic type: the intellectual wealth of the Federation, all with their eyes upon him.

Their eyes. You will meet their eyes. One by one. Touch their hands. Meet their eyes. And they will be ours.

A sudden shiver ran up Skel's spine as he blinked, dazed, even as his mother's voice reminded him, *Not their eyes. You can never meet another being's eyes! This above all else remember!*

He was hallucinating, he realized calmly. It was not the first time it had happened, but it was still disturbing. He really should call Dr. Crusher, but could not make himself do it. He struggled to maintain his outward calm, and the battle of voices in his head eventually subsided.

Skel went to the computer and turned to his work, the only truly successful therapy he'd ever had. He huddled over the console, the familiar and comforting march of equations and text easing his mind, his inner fears about his own adequacy to fulfill the role destiny had thrust upon him when he was but a ten-year-old child.

The door chimed.

He looked up, mildly surprised. "Enter."

The doors parted to reveal a female ensign: young, comely by human standards, with dark hair, olive skin, and deep-set brown eyes; though small in build, she seemed muscular and athletic.

"Good morning, Master Scientist Skel," she greeted him politely, but without the surfeit of pleasantries she might have displayed for another more emotional species; her tone was reserved, her expression serene.

Obviously, Picard's people are well trained, Skel thought with a touch of admiration, as he signaled her to step forward. She did so, and the doors snapped shut behind her.

"I'm Ensign Barbara Evans, sir," she continued. "Captain Picard assigned me to assist you during your stay aboard the *Enterprise.* The computer told me you were awake, so I thought I'd introduce myself and ask if you needed anything."

She did not offer to shake his hand, as most humans might, but instead kept them respectfully behind her back. To shake the hand of a touch telepath was considered an invasion of privacy on Vulcan, though many humans remained unaware of the fact.

"Thank you, Ensign Evans," Skel replied. "I appreciate your captain's hospitality. You said the computer told you I was awake. Would it tell me if a colleague of mine were also awake?"

"Certainly, sir. I'll show you." She paused, then raised her face slightly and looked upward as she addressed the invisible entity. "Computer. Tell me the whereabouts of . . ." she paused and looked at Skel for the name.

"Dr. George Tarmud," he finished.

"Dr. Tarmud is currently in his quarters," came the computer's nonemotional female voice.

"Is Dr. Tarmud awake at this time?" Ensign Evans asked.

"Yes. Dr. Tarmud is awake and working at his console."

She gave a satisfied nod, then addressed Skel. "Of course, the computer is limited as to what questions it will answer. It would, for example, tell you nothing except Tarmud's location if he had requested that. And it wouldn't give an answer to a question that violated established privacy standards."

"Most logical," Skel commented. "It is good to know my colleague is awake and working. I did not want to disturb him. Now I can call on him. Thank you, Ensign."

"My pleasure, sir," she replied, and almost smiled—but she caught herself at the last moment. "You can find your way to Dr. Tarmud's quarters by asking the computer for that information when you're in the corridor. It'll show you a map of the ship and help you find your way. Also, you may communicate with me through the computer if there's anything you need during your stay with us. Is there anything else I can do for you, any service I might provide at this time?"

Skel studied her a moment: *What service might she provide, indeed?* Deliberately, he rose from his work station and approached her. "Tell me, Ensign Evans. When you are not providing assistance to me, what are your duties aboard this vessel?"

"I currently serve with the science team; I've been assigned numerous research projects involving stellar phenomena. Mostly, I work with the computer, collating data already collected. Since it's a job I can come back to at any time, it allows me the freedom to act as a liaison for several of the guests."

"Interesting," Skel said, nodding. "And how many people are involved in your science team?"

"More than forty crew members. I interact with at least twelve of them on the data I'm working on, and they in turn interact with higher-ranking scientists. The senior officer of our team reports to Commander Data."

Forty people. Forty Enterprise *personnel. How many must those forty interact with?*

"Forty people must accomplish a great deal of work."

She tried unsuccessfully to suppress a smile of pride. "We try to, sir."

"It was very thoughtful of Captain Picard to provide me a liaison with a science background. You no doubt have knowledge of equipment I may need to run certain tests; you might be able to help me accomplish my tasks more efficiently."

"That's my job, sir. If you'd provide me a list of what you need, I'll attend to it immediately."

He picked up a padd on which he'd jotted a few instructions. "I have been working on just such a list."

He took another step forward, placed the gray padd securely in her palm—then smoothly slid his fingers around her wrist and held it securely.

At his touch, she tensed and moved to pull away; when he did not easily release his grip, she stared up at him, her eyes wide and questioning.

This time, Skel did not politely avert his gaze, as he had with the empath or the captain or the doctor. This time, he stared intently down into Barbara Evans's startled eyes.

"Excuse me—sir—" she stammered, clearly frightened, and took a step back. He moved with her, then closed in until he pressed against her body. His free hand moved up, swiftly, before she could react and then he made contact, five fingers finding the neural pathways so quickly that Evans had no time to escape, no time even to call for help.

Inside his head, T'Reth's voice screamed, *NOT HER EYES! YOU MUST NEVER LOOK INTO ANOTHER BEING'S EYES! REMEMBER—*

But he had been too long denied, and the other voices would not be stilled so close to their release.

"My mind to your mind," he intoned, as his piercing gaze, a gaze with which he had never touched another being in eighty years, bore into Ensign Evans's eyes, as if they could drill their way into her cerebral cortex . . . deeper, deeper, down into her soul.

Evans grunted a small protest and went limp, although her eyes remained huge, impossibly wide, and transfixed in a horror she could not have imagined before stepping through his doors. The padd clattered softly to the carpet, and Skel caught her small body with his free arm to keep her from falling. He brought that hand up behind her neck, touching the bare skin there, his fingers seeking out neural pathways that were less used, less convenient than the ones on the face. He felt the connection being made, felt the circle completed between the fingertips of his two hands. It was like a jolt of raw pleasure, and a small sound escaped his lips.

This was not like the melds with T'Son. Those were nothing less than torture, as she probed his mind, searching for his secrets. No, his ease of entry into the unsuspecting human woman was a delight.

"And now we are one," he whispered, as the meld became complete and her mouth moved, parroting the words. Her eyes remained enormous and filled with terror, the only indication that she was aware of what was happening to her.

"You have asked how you may be of service to me, Ensign Evans," he murmured to her, never once moving his gaze from her captive one. "You may indeed be of great use, which I will explain carefully so that you fully understand. And when you leave me to complete your assignment, then I will visit my colleague, Dr. Tarmud."

She trembled in his grip like a sapling in a gale, but it was the only visible protest her conscious mind could manage. As he infected her with the entities that had hidden within his brain all these years, the entities that had manipulated him and mastered him from childhood on, only he could hear the silent protest of her mind. It was the same warning voice that had tortured him since that terrible night of his childhood, the night when life had changed for him forever.

As the Vulcan scientist clutched Barbara Evans in his arms, invading and infecting her brain, he could hear, inside her, the voice that had haunted him for so long.

Behind Barbara Evans's terrorized gaze screamed his mother, telling Evans, too late, to run. To hide. To escape her only child.

"RUN! RUN AWAY!"

"Deanna!" Riker gave the thrashing Betazoid a hearty shake. Her teeth clicked together, then suddenly her eyes were open, wide, staring unseeing, terrified.

"Run for your life!" she shouted, not at him, but at some point in the distance only she could see.

Riker slapped the communicator on his shoulder, grateful he'd decided to sleep in his uniform. Something about Deanna's nervousness and the strange aura the Vulcan had left here had convinced him to be prepared, ready for anything. When he'd heard screaming coming from her room, he'd thought she'd been under attack and had raced in to find her fighting the bedcovers, yelling in her sleep.

"Riker to Dr. Crusher!" he barked into the communicator, over the hammering of his heart. "Medical emergency!"

"Crusher here," the doctor answered immediately, though her voice was faintly heavy with sleep. "What is it, Will?"

"It's Deanna. She's locked in some nightmare. I can't wake her up."

By now Crusher could hear the Betazoid's ravings over the comm link. "I'm on my way!"

Only then did Riker think Crusher might be in Picard's quarters. They frequently had breakfast together before starting their duty shift. Well, there wasn't much he could do about that.

"Deanna, come on!" Riker begged, as he gripped his friend's shoulders. "It's me, Will!" He held her face in his hand and turned her eyes to him, forcing her to stare at him, praying she might really see him through her dream.

She stared at him, her black eyes wide with terror, her mouth open; a long dark curl had fallen diagonally across her face . . . and, to his amazement, she stopped thrashing.

"Look at me, Deanna. It's *me,"* he repeated, willing her to snap out of the dream.

She looked at him and did not move; as he held her arms, her gasping began to ease. "Will," she said, then lifted her hands to catch his arms, but her gaze was still wild. "My God . . ."

She closed her eyes, and when she opened them again, the look in them was one of fear—mixed with grateful recognition. Riker smiled.

"I'm here," he said softly, his grip on her arms now meant to offer comfort. "Everything's okay now."

Her black eyes grew sorrowful, tear-filled. "No. No, nothing's okay. Oh, Will, it's terrible!"

He pulled her into the shelter of his embrace, just as he heard the outer doors to her quarters opening. "Sssssh. It's okay, Deanna. You're awake now. The dream is over."

But she just shook her head and held him, her body trembling violently.

"How is she?" Crusher asked, as she rushed in, putting one knee on the bed and opening her emergency kit at the same time. She had the medi-scanner in her hand so quickly that Will never saw her pull it out.

He glanced over his shoulder at a figure moving

behind the doctor and saw Picard. "She's awake. She just seemed to come out of it herself. But she doesn't seem to be able to separate reality from dream yet."

Crusher frowned as she looked at the scanner readout.

"It wasn't a dream," Deanna protested, pushing away from Riker. "They were memories—Skel's memories." She was in control again and rubbed her eyes, collecting herself. "I *was* dreaming normally at one point in my sleep, but something happened, and I found myself enmeshed in Skel's memories. Suddenly, I was Skel as a child, trapped in that terrible time when the entities from the artifacts infected his people. His father was infected and went mad, killing his mother slowly through torture. In spite of her personal anguish, her terror, she controlled herself long enough to send him a powerful mental warning. He was so young at the time, I think such an intense telepathic impression may have damaged his brain, because he still hears it, that voice, that silent command. I sensed it—*heard* it—from him last night when he was in the quarantine booth, and again when he came to visit me last night."

At that, Picard caught Riker's eye and performed a disapproving double take when Will confirmed the fact with a nod.

"You were shouting, 'Run! Run for your life!'" Riker prompted her. "Is that the voice Skel heard?"

"Yes," she said, her tone abruptly conveying the depth of her exhaustion; she lowered her beautiful face, her dark curling hair spilling forward, emphasizing the shadows beneath her pale cheekbones, beneath her infinitely weary eyes. She looked so drawn and delicate—an appearance Riker knew from experience was resoundingly misleading—that he was again overwhelmed by the urge to protect her. "The voice of his mother trying desperately to save her only child. Such a terrible memory. I'll never forget it."

"Isn't it unusual for you to pick up such a powerful impression?" Crusher asked, leaning forward herself with concern. "I mean, you're telling us about scenes as if you were there. Quoting actual dialogue."

"Yes, very unusual," Troi admitted. "But Skel is a telepath; and sometimes, when Betazoids interact with telepaths, the results can be unpredictable. Especially under such unusual circumstances."

"Deanna," Crusher said quietly, and Riker could tell by her voice that she was about to broach a difficult subject, "your brain waves are very erratic. I'm afraid that this contact with Skel may have had some repercussions for you."

"It's not just Skel," Deanna insisted firmly. "It's those artifacts." She focused on Picard, her expression grim. "I don't know how, but they had something to do with my dream, the fact that I couldn't wake up. They're a danger to every person on this ship!"

"Counselor—" Picard began reasonably, but she would have none of it.

"We must destroy them immediately, Captain! We can wait no longer! Every moment we delay—"

"Counselor Troi!" Picard interrupted firmly. His voice was modulated and calm, much calmer than Riker knew he felt. "I have been in touch with the Vulcans. We are scheduled to rendezvous with one of their science vessels tomorrow."

She looked up at him, aghast. "Tomorrow is too late! And sending them back to the Vulcans merely passes the danger on to someone else. We must destroy them now!"

Picard drew back, his expression grim. After a few seconds' silence, he turned to Crusher. "Doctor, if you will excuse Commander Riker and myself?"

"Yes, of course," Crusher agreed, seeming almost relieved to get them out of the room.

Riker gave Deanna's shoulder a squeeze and extracted himself from the bed, then followed Picard out of the room.

The instant the bedroom doors shut behind them, Picard spoke.

"What the hell is going on here? I gave express orders that Skel was to have no contact with Counselor Troi! What do you know about this?"

"I know that when I went to Deanna's quarters last night to check on her, I found Skel inside. Obviously, he was just about to leave. I deemed it pointless and offensive for me to question his purpose. When I asked Deanna about it, she was vague, and something she said made me question whether you'd already told him to stay away from her. I assumed—wrongly—that you'd intended to do that in the morning, considering the late hour we'd spoken."

Will frowned now, wondering if anything would've been different if he'd spoken to Picard last night. "I slept on the couch. To give her a sense of security." He smiled grimly. "I woke up hearing her scream. My first thought was that she was under attack. That *Skel* had somehow gotten in here, past me, and was after her. Are we all cracking up?"

Picard looked unhappy. "I spoke to Skel last night *before* I spoke to you, Will. I told him, as politely and as reasonably as I could, that it would be better for Deanna if she had no further contact with him. He was the soul of reasonableness itself when he agreed with me."

"So, he disobeyed you. A *Vulcan* disobeyed a captain's orders."

Picard shook his head. "I didn't make it an order. I know I could have, but why would you have to order a Vulcan to do something so simple? I requested it of him, and he agreed. It makes no sense that he would then do the exact opposite."

Riker thought about that. "Those artifacts are his

life's work, and Deanna's had some sort of mental communication with them. I know he's a Vulcan, but considering what he's been through—couldn't a Vulcan have an obsession so great he'd act *illogically* to get a piece of information impossible for him to obtain any other way?"

Picard sighed. "Perhaps. Still, I'll speak with him—"

"Please, sir," Deanna said calmly from the doorway of her room, "I'd rather you didn't." She wore a long robe over her nightdress, and although her long hair was still disheveled, the anxiety had left her features; her expression was entirely peaceful.

Beverly stood beside her, a supportive hand on Troi's shoulder. "I've given her something to relax her body and calm her meta conscious hyperactivity. I'm not sure I know what's going on, but the drugs I gave her should help her get a dreamless sleep, which she sorely needs now."

"I'm sorry, Captain, about the way I addressed you before," Troi said sincerely. "I've developed quite a phobia toward those artifacts."

"I'm sure we'll all sleep better when they're aboard the Vulcan science vessel," Picard said comfortingly. "You stay in your quarters and catch up on your sleep. Let us take care of everything else. I want you to feel safe, Deanna."

"Oh, I do, sir. And if Beverly's right and I can have a few hours of dreamless sleep, I'm sure everything will seem much more normal when I wake up again." She looked at Riker and smiled dazzlingly. "Thanks, Will, for staying here last night."

"I'm just glad I was there when you needed me," he assured her. "Call me when you wake up and we'll have 'breakfast' together."

She smiled and bade them goodbye as the three officers exited her quarters. From the corridor Riker watched as the doors to her quarters shut over her; he couldn't shake the uneasy feeling he had about leaving her alone.

"Anything else you'd care to report, Doctor?" Picard asked quietly when he was sure they were out of Deanna's earshot.

"Just what I told you. I don't like her change in brain-wave activity. It's as if she's getting some new mental contact she's not initiating and can't turn off. I think that's what's triggering those bad dreams—or rather waking nightmares; she's awake when she has them, which is why they're so destructive. She gets no rest and is trapped in someone else's reality. I wish I had a Betazoid doctor to confer with. I don't like it."

"You're not the only one who doesn't like it," Picard grumbled. "Number One, I want you to contact Lieutenant Worf and have him post two guards outside Counselor Troi's quarters, around the clock. Have them accompany her if she leaves her rooms. If we can't safeguard her mind, the least we can do is protect her body!"

"Aye, sir," Riker replied, surprised at how relieved he felt that Picard had responded to his own irrational fears for Deanna.

"It all seems so different now," Tarmud whispered. "So clear."

The human's hazel eyes were open wide, his body shaking. His skin was pale, glistening with sweat as his body fought the invaders that had taken over his brain and were settling deep into its core—his amygdala.

"Our work," Tarmud murmured dreamily. "It all makes so much more sense to me. It's so much more important than I thought."

"Yes," Skel agreed, as he watched the human carefully. Tarmud was having trouble handling the entities, much more trouble than the younger, stronger Barbara Evans. Skel grew concerned that the human's immune system, or perhaps his brain itself, couldn't handle the invasion. But he needed Tarmud, needed him desperately. If he died before their work was done . . .

"Water," the scientist said, gasping and closing his eyes.

Skel immediately procured water from the replicator. Tarmud drank it in one long swallow, then, without warning, hurled the glass at the Vulcan and followed it with a bodily attack. The human sprang from the couch and swung a punch at the Vulcan full force. Skel grabbed Tarmud's fist only millimeters from his face and held it fast. Tarmud swung with the other, and Skel stopped that one as well. Swiftly, the Vulcan spun the researcher so that his back was to Skel's chest and firmly restrained him in his arms. Tarmud screamed and flailed, using so much energy and rage that the Vulcan became concerned the effort would trigger a myocardial incident in the human. Still, there was nothing Skel could do but restrain him, to keep Tarmud from harming them both.

Finally, the human exhausted himself and sagged in Skel's restraining embrace. The Vulcan waited several minutes before reacting, fearing Tarmud was only feigning collapse. However, he now noticed the scientist's sweating had stopped, as had his trembling. He was breathing rhythmically, evenly.

"I'm all right now," Tarmud said weakly. "Tired. But all right. It's over."

Carefully, Skel eased the man back onto the couch and brought him more water, contemplating whether Tarmud would be physically too weak to contain the entities. As the researcher drank down the second glass, he seemed more and more composed.

"Are you well?" Skel finally asked, his Vulcan self

only semiascendant. In this mode, he could use all of his Vulcan training and knowledge; in this mode, he was infectious. When the entities resubsided back to his amygdala, he would remember only what he needed to continue his normal life.

Admirably adaptive, the entities; over the past eighty years, they had utilized Skel to help them evolve to a form particularly suited to Vulcan physiology. Permitting their host some control allowed them to survive much longer—and to spread the disease more efficiently.

And the TechnoFair was the perfect opportunity to spread them throughout the entire galaxy.

But Skel was beginning to doubt whether his human associate would be able to control himself long enough to reach the fair without generating suspicion.

At last, Tarmud nodded, wiping a dark golden lock of damp hair from his forehead. "Sorry about the outburst."

"Do not apologize," Skel insisted. "We cannot know the full range of reactions as different species are incorporated into the whole. There may be others who react as you did. We need to be prepared." As it had happened for Barbara Evans, Skel knew, the entities were now surging through Tarmud's brain, triggering the strongest emotions—hate, rage, violent passion—and feeding on the adrenaline and other hormones produced. Once satiated, the entities would subside again and permit Tarmud to behave normally so that he would go undetected.

"How long did it take you to help them mutate into this superior form?" Tarmud asked.

"Years," Skel replied. "Some of it they did themselves, inside me, while I grew from a child to an adult. They had the time they needed to adapt themselves to my physical form, to learn from me. Fortunately, I was the only Vulcan infected who was not purged when the other entities were destroyed. Apparently, a mutated cluster survived within me, going deep into my biochemistry. Then when I achieved my position, we had many years to use the resources of the Vulcan Science Academy to enable the entities to develop into this superior form. The adaptation causes the host some confusion, but, in general, it has been very helpful. Though feeding is minimized—except for the nightmares." The terrifying dreams produced enough hormonal reactions to maintain the life of the entities, but their hunger was ever-present. "With the equipment on the *Enterprise,* we can finish the adaptation process, so that any sentient organism can house the entities without fear of breakdown or death."

"Yes," Tarmud said, blinking sleepily.

"You must rest now," Skel instructed. "While you sleep, you will dream and the entities can feed and grow stronger. Then we will discuss our method of recruitment."

"Someone must recruit Kyla. She's strong . . . has so much knowledge . . ." Tarmud's eyes were closing, and Skel carefully helped him to recline on the couch. Tarmud's initial outburst still concerned him, but the violent nightmares his colleague would experience during his sleep would help sate the new entities in his body, and help keep them under control.

"Yes," Skel agreed softly, as he waited for Tarmud to sleep. "We need Dr. Dannelke. Dr. Ellis as well. And some of the senior staff. But most importantly of all, we must have the empath."

Tarmud's mouth twitched in a smile, though his eyes remained shut. "Yes," he murmured dreamily. "The empath. We tasted her during the contact. We need the empath . . ."

She would never be infected, Skel knew; she was too valuable. As his mother had been, Troi would be sacrificed to the subatomic entities' hunger. They could detect her emotional state and, more importantly, the energy produced by her fears could feed them from a distance. Unlike T'Reth, however, Deanna Troi would be kept alive for a long, long time. . . .

Chapter Five

SWEPT AWAY ON A WAVE of scientific ecstasy, Kyla Dannelke peered raptly through her ophthalmic visor at the new android eye models Dr. Tarmud had given her. The blankly staring orbs—their irises a striking shade of violet, their artificial organic optic nerves trailing like streamers—rested in a fluid bath while Dannelke held them with forceps, peering through her visor like a jeweler examining an impressively cut diamond. Her visor included an optical scanner, which permitted her to focus all the way down to the cellular level—or all the way in the other direction as binoculars.

Beautiful, she thought, smiling to herself as she measured and analyzed the orbs, using the scope to peer through the retina deep into the artificial organ's interior. *Absolutely beautiful.* A combination of organics, electronics, and mechanics, these were the ultimate android eyes. Tarmud had outdone himself. They incorporated all that Tarmud had accomplished with his early VISOR, and more; these eyes would be able to perceive all that was visible to the naked human eye, plus ultraviolet, infrared, and several other spectrum bands as well.

Once she examined the eyes and their accompanying optic nerves on the cellular level, she'd write her report. But the small blinking inset in her visor's lower right field advised her that the hour was already late—and she wanted to invite Worf and his son to have dinner in her quarters. Thinking about the prospect made her smile. She'd considered inviting Worf alone, but quickly rejected that idea; Alexander was so bright that she couldn't bear to leave him out of the invitation. Besides, if there was any way through to his father's rough Klingon heart, it was through that bright young boy. She'd read that Klingons liked strong-flavored dishes, especially animal products, and so she'd decided to coax the replicator into duplicating her grandmother's infamous liver and onions—served rare, of course—for Worf. Maybe Counselor Troi would know what Alexander's favorite meal was, so she could order that. For herself—

The door chime interrupted her reverie, causing her to glance, mildly irritated, at the time again. She wasn't expecting anyone—unless it was Tarmud already looking for her report. How fast did he think she could work?

"Come." She glanced up at the door through the visor, forcing it to rapidly change its focus from the cellular level to normal sight.

The doors opened upon a short dark-skinned young man—a uniformed ensign who seemed oddly familiar. Odder still, he wore no communicator badge.

"Yes?"

"Sorry to bother you, Doctor," he began hesitantly. "I can see you're still working."

She forced a smile, although his hesitancy annoyed her; she wanted him to get to the point and be done with it, so she could return to her work. "What can I do for you?"

"Actually, Doctor, I'm here to help you." He took a timid step toward her.

"With what? I don't remember asking for anything. Or did Ensign Evans send you?" She finally recalled requesting data cassettes and another computer padd that morning; now it was almost dinner time. Where had the day gone? She leaned back over the android eyes again, thinking that he could leave the items on her desk.

"Yes, exactly," the young man said, sounding relieved, as if he, too, was unsure of his task. "Ensign Evans sent me with your supplies."

"Excellent," Kyla murmured, speaking to the violet orbs again, totally absorbed in their cellular structure. "Just put them down over there." She waved vaguely toward the coffee table. "That'll be all. Thank you."

She spent another few seconds thus absorbed, following the trail of the microscopic artificial nerves, not even noticing that the doors failed to open and close again.

A hand closed on her shoulder.

She whirled about and stared up into the ensign's strangely familiar dark face.

"Excuse me, Dr. Dannelke," he said, his voice no longer timid but strong, firm, and self-assured. "Could you look up at me for one moment?"

He caught her chin with one hand—firmly, almost roughly—and reached with the other to pull away her visor.

Instinctively, she raised both arms and flailed out, knocking away the fingers that dug into her chin, the hand that reached from the side. In the blink of an eye, she bolted from the chair past him, into the center of the room.

"Who's your commanding officer?" she demanded, feeling the heat of adrenaline on her face, and crouched into a defensive stance. *"Who?"* The visor impeded her vision slightly, disorienting her as its focusing apparatus tried to keep pace with the rapid movement of her head, but she had no intention of taking the time to remove it—especially since *he* wanted it off for some reason.

"Forgive me, Dr. Dannelke," he said smoothly, as though his behavior had been perfectly professional and normal while it was Kyla who was acting strangely. "I didn't mean to alarm you; I merely need your undivided attention for a moment."

"You can have it for a lot longer than that, friend!" she snapped, then ordered: "Computer!"

There was no time to ask the location of Lieutenant Worf or anything else, for that matter: the intruder sprang at her, his dark hands reaching for her face.

Her leg came up fast; her knee caught him cleanly in the sternum. He fell hard, the wind knocked out of him with a sharp gasp—but, impossibly, he was back on his feet without a pause.

The sight left her unsettled; he was much smaller than she was, and though strong, he should have at least taken a few seconds to catch his breath . . . leaving her to think that there was something wrong here, something even more wrong than the unbelievable fact that she was being attacked by a member of Picard's carefully screened crew.

The thought galvanized her; she took the offensive, landing a solid punch on his perfect nose. Bone crunched, blood flew, but the young man never halted. Instead, he came at her again, smiling through the streaming blood.

Smiling.

He came at her again. She chopped him on the

neck, punched him hard below his navel, chopped him again on the shoulder. He went down on his face, and came up immediately, grinning through the streaming blood.

She dodged out of his way, knocking over a small table that held stacks of data cassettes, trying to get far enough from him to use her feet.

It was just enough. She spun and kicked him hard in the ribs as he scrabbled toward her. Yet he absorbed the blow without falling—as any normal human should have—and when she delivered a second kick, he was ready for her.

She shrieked as he caught her heel, pulled her down, and pushed her onto her back. And then he was on top of her, reaching for the visor. He caught hold of it with one hand, while his other struggled to pin her down; she caught for the first time a glimpse of his eyes, magnified and slightly out of focus, through the visor—vast and brown and filled with a gloating hatred so burning cold it stole her breath.

She squeezed her own eyes shut, and with a desperate surge of strength, she delivered a merciless knee to his groin.

With a yelp, he loosened his grip; it was enough to permit her to roll free. He should have been curled up in a ball, shrieking, but instead, by the time she got to her feet and put some distance between them, he was up and grinning at her more broadly than ever.

She bolted. The doors opened millimeters before her face; she stumbled, but at the last instant kept her footing and sprinted down the corridor. Her assailant should not have been able to walk, she knew, yet she could hear his rasping breath meters behind her.

She put on a burst of speed and rounded a corner, nearly plowing into two crew members. She suppressed the thought of how she must have appeared to them: totally disheveled, hysterical, racing around in her ophthalmic visor.

"Call security!" she yelled, as she pulled away and continued to flee from her attacker. "Call *Worf!*"

Distantly, she heard one of the crew members say dazedly, "You bet!" before Kyla was out of sight.

"Can't we invite her to dinner, Father?" Alexander asked, as he changed out of his school clothes.

Worf was beginning to wonder if his son had only been feigning sleep last night when Kyla Dannelke had visited them. He had started asking Worf about this dinner invitation as soon as he had gotten up this morning.

"She helped me so much with my floating eyeball," Alexander explained patiently. "It would be a nice way to repay her, wouldn't it? You're always telling me that when someone offers you help, that's a debt that must be repaid."

"Yes, that is true," Worf allowed. "But you must understand, Alexander. Dr. Dannelke did not come on board to socialize; she came here to do important work with her colleagues. She may already have her evening planned."

"But what if she doesn't?" Alexander insisted. "We can at least *ask*. I know she might say no. Please, Father? Can't we ask her?"

Worf sighed, trying to tell himself he did not already know the outcome of this discussion. "Very well. *You* may invite her to dinner here. Let her know you had my permission. And do not pout if she turns you down!"

"Sure, Father!" Alexander agreed, all smiles. "Maybe she can show me how to make my eyeball go inside out like hers!"

Worf broke his stern countenance to smile back at his boy. "You really like her, do you not?"

Alexander nodded, then looked at his father slyly. "I think *Kyla* really likes *you*, Father."

Worf's frown reappeared. The boy was entirely too

precocious! "That is *Dr. Dannelke,* not *Kyla.* You must show respect for such a learned scientist!"

"She said I could call her that! Honest, Father. I know how to act!"

Yes, Worf had to admit. Alexander behaved much better with others than he often did with his father. And, no doubt, due to his mother's early death, he was naturally attracted to women. "Actually, son, I think Dr. Dannelke likes *you.*"

"That's great. That means she likes both of us!"

Worf nodded, knowing that was the truth. And how could you not be attracted to a woman who was intelligent, strong, forthright, and who also admired your son? He began to wonder if the scientist knew more about Klingon culture than she let on.

"I will be off duty in two hours," Worf told his boy. "If she agrees to come, we will eat then. If she accepts, ask her the name of her favorite meal."

"You're not going to make her eat Klingon food?" Alexander asked, and Worf grumbled at the playful sarcasm in his voice.

"This is a dinner invitation," he reminded his son, "not an endurance test. It is time for me to return to the bridge. Send a message to me through the computer when—"

His communicator chirped at him, and he nodded at his son, leaving the boy's room so that he might answer the page more privately.

Once in the central living quarters, he touched the badge, and said, "Worf, here."

"Lieutenant Worf," came a breathy voice, "This is Ensign Johannsen. We've got a security emergency on Deck Five. One of the visiting scientists is racing around the ship as if she's being pursued. But—we never saw anyone after her."

"Do we need a medical team?" Worf asked, as he left the quarters and started jogging toward the turbolift.

"I don't think so, sir," the officer reported. "We've been tracking her through the computer. She's moving pretty fast."

"Which scientist is it?" he asked, as he entered the lift. If he could remember who it was he might be able to determine if they were working with chemicals or equipment that could have caused a physical reaction or even hallucinations. Then he would know if he needed medical staff.

"I'm sorry, sir, I don't know," the officer explained. "She's really tall, and very blond. But she was wearing something on her face, so I couldn't recognize her. There are so many new scientists on board. Lieutenant Singh is with me as well, and he didn't know her either."

"Very good, Lieutenant." He was about to tell them he was on his way when Johannsen spoke again.

"We checked with the computer, sir, to see if she *was* being pursued, and according to the scanners, she isn't. But she did ask for help, sir. Specifically, she asked for you."

Worf had a sudden sinking premonition as to the identity of the scientist. "Where is she now?"

"Computer says she's on Deck Three, still running."

"Good work, Ensign," Worf said, signing off. He alerted his staff to have a crew of four security officers on standby, and then he told the lift to take him to Deck Three.

If possible, he wanted to handle this one himself.

Exhausted and gasping, Kyla stopped her flight and leaned against a bulkhead to catch her breath, pressing a hand against her aching ribs. With the other, she lifted the visor, pushing it up to her hairline so that she could focus better.

A scan in each direction indicated she was safe—for the moment. The entire incident seemed unbelievable; she'd never heard of crime on a starship before. Most people considered starships the safest places in the galaxy. Yet the sight of the young ensign's eyes had chilled Kyla to the bone; she'd never seen such calculated murderous rage before. Was it possible that an *Enterprise* crew member could have suddenly developed homicidal tendencies?

Impossible. Just as impossible as the crewman's grinning indifference to his own wounds, just as impossible as the notion that Kyla herself might be going mad.

She tensed at the soft rustle of cloth—or was it a breath? She was so paranoid now, almost anything sounded like pursuit; she paused, listening, not daring to breathe herself.

Another soft sound. Dannelke dropped the visor back down, letting it focus on a distant point she couldn't quite make out. Nothing. Yet . . .

She glanced each way, then took off again, keeping her legs firmly under her, pushing off the deck plates, picking up speed. She rounded another corner and glanced back over her shoulder one last time—

And slammed into something solid. Something that clutched her in a viselike grip.

She exploded into a fury of action, kicking and fighting to free her arms.

"Kyla!" a strong baritone yelled, making her look up. The ophthalmic visor focused wildly on a brown face, a ridged skull, and a pair of fierce glowering eyes.

She ripped the visor off to confirm what she was seeing. "Worf, thank God!" she exhaled, hugging him impulsively.

Then, realizing what she was doing, she moved away, blushing. Desperate to recover her aplomb, she swept the myriad stray hairs that had escaped her braid away from her face, and asked, "What took you so long?"

He raised his prominent eyebrows in surprise,

which made her smile; she enjoyed catching him off-guard. She had a feeling it didn't happen too often.

"What took me—?" he started, then caught himself, took a deep breath, and restored his professional demeanor. "Dr. Dannelke, you have been quite the moving object!"

"Oh, we're back to Doctor and Lieutenant again, huh?" She leaned against the bulkhead again to catch her breath.

"Kyla," Worf said quietly, "what is wrong? Why are you fleeing through the ship wildly as if you were being pursued?"

"Because I *am* being pursued," she explained, as she waited for her heart rate to slow.

"By whom?" Worf questioned.

"He didn't show me his credentials before he attacked me, Worf."

The Klingon stiffened. "You were attacked? Aboard the *Enterprise?*"

"I know, it sounds impossible. But it happened. And aboard your precious ship." She pushed away from the bulkhead. "Come back to my quarters. I'll show you."

They said nothing on the way back to her quarters; Kyla saw no need. Also, his skeptical expression angered her, adding to her adrenaline overload. She spent the time during their short walk getting control of her breathing and emotions. Once Worf saw the overturned chair, the stack of cassettes scattered on the deck, and the obvious evidence of a struggle, his opinion would change. He would see that she told the truth.

When at last they arrived at her guest quarters, she strode inside confidently, leading him . . . and halted abruptly.

Before her sat her temporary office . . . in perfect order. The chair had been carefully replaced at the desk where the android eyes still waited; the cassettes were neatly restacked on the table. It was as if the attack had never happened.

Worf stood silently beside her, mountainous, staring, waiting—judging.

"I'm not crazy," she murmured, as she hugged herself, struggling to hold her feelings in. "I was attacked in this room. An ensign came in . . . I never saw him before. I was working on these android eyes. We spoke. I thanked him, told him to leave some supplies on the desk . . . but instead of leaving, he walked up and grabbed my shoulder. Then he tried to pull my visor off. I got away from him—but he came after me! We fought—"

"Fought?" Worf asked. It was the first word he'd said to her since they got on the turbolift, and that single syllable carried such disbelief that Kyla's confusion turned to anger.

She knew only one way to convince the Klingon that she was capable of defending herself.

Without warning, she spun around, shouted, and swung her hand toward his face. He blocked it expertly and counterstruck. She blocked that one and kicked, landing only a glancing blow. Like a snake, he grabbed the ankle that had struck him and tossed her onto the floor. She rolled smoothly, came up, and went at him again. Strike, block, counterstrike, block—then finally, Worf shouted, "Enough!"

That stopped it. They were both in defensive crouches, both gasping for air.

He studied her, his expression perceptibly less cynical, and growled, "Very well. You *fought.* And then?"

His concession dissolved the last traces of adrenaline in her system. She sagged, utterly exhausted, against the nearest bulkhead and drew an unsteady hand across her sweating brow; the act made her realize more hair hung out of her braid than in it. "We fought. I have *two* black belts, one in kung fu, the other in aikido. The guy was *smaller* than me, lighter. I should've taken him, but he just kept coming. I was hitting, kicking him *hard.* I didn't pull any punches! Dammit, I broke his nose!" She thrust out her right fist to show him the darkening blood on the knuckles. "He just kept getting up. Kept trying to touch me, put his hands on me, take my visor off. He should still be lying here, groaning—but he chased me down the corridor. A couple of times, he almost caught me . . . and I've set a Terran collegiate track record that still holds.

"I'm not going crazy, Worf. It really happened."

For a moment, Worf was silent, his expression dark and unreadable, and then, utterly surprising her, he reached out to place a hand—large, powerful, feverishly warm—upon her shoulder, the same shoulder the ensign had touched.

"I believe you," he said. "No one who fights as you do could lie about something like that. I cannot explain how this could happen, but I promise you, I will find out who did this."

She sighed, immensely grateful, and was suddenly too weary to stand. He helped her to the couch and sat beside her, still stern and upright, while she let herself sink back against the cushions.

"And I apologize, Kyla," he continued, his hand still on her shoulder, "for doubting your word about your ability to fight. You are a worthy adversary. Perhaps I allowed"—and here a barely perceptible smile played at the corners of his lips—"cultural prejudices to color my evaluation of your expertise."

"Well, in that case," she said, "I owed you one. Worf. Thanks. For showing up. For believing me."

"You are welcome. And, Kyla, I will want you to view images of the personnel who are currently serving on the *Enterprise.*"

"But that's over a thousand people," she protested. "I have so much work to do yet before the fair."

"If we eliminate all the females, all the children, all the non-humans, and all the higher ranking officers, it will narrow the search to a reasonable number. You must do this to be able to identify your attacker." He looked at her more sternly. "And I want you to get a positive identification of anyone coming to your door. If you do not recognize their name, do not let them in!"

"Don't worry." She smiled wanly. "I also have a black belt in paranoia."

He frowned at the statement, as though disapproving of jokes at such a serious moment. "One more thing. Alexander will be contacting you. He hopes you might join us for dinner. I will explain to him that you need to recover—"

"The hell you will!" she protested. "I'd love to come to dinner and just put all this behind me. And where would I be safer but with the chief of security? Let Alexander send his invitation. I'll answer yes, and be pleased to do so. Unless you don't want me there."

He hesitated, and for a terrible moment, she feared he was trying to find the polite way to turn her down. If he was honest and admitted it, she told herself stoically, she would accept it. She'd started things between them on the worst possible note, and now this—

"Kyla, I would be pleased to have you come for dinner," he said quietly, and she smiled at the honesty in his dark eyes.

"Great. So, what's for dinner?"

"Those are the artifacts?" Geordi said softly, as he peered through the clear quarantine casing to view the tiny unimposing objects. They looked like shining black art objects or elegantly designed containers to hold a cache of jewels—something to be held in the palm of the hand and admired. The sight of them made him want to hold one, to feel its smoothness, to

observe the play of shimmering light across its dark polished surface.

"The very ones," Crusher said ruefully next to him. Her tone carried the same emotions Geordi felt: attraction warring with revulsion. On the engineer's other side, Data stood examining the tricorder readouts.

"Sure don't look like they could be responsible for anything as serious as a planetary infection," said Geordi. He walked around the objects enclosed in the fields and eyed them carefully. His VISOR could detect nothing harmful about the objects; it merely registered their simplicity. Try as he might, he could detect nothing beyond the sleek, outer surface, which appeared to be made of an unfamiliar metal alloy.

"In fact," Data corrected Geordi smoothly, glancing up from his readouts, "it is not these objects per se that caused the illness on Vulcan, but rather the entities that are contained within." He stared curiously at the objects. "Apparently, the disease vectors are in the form of subatomic particles, but how they interact with the brain and control the host is, as yet, unknown."

"Captain Picard thinks you might be able to decipher the writing on the shells?" Crusher asked Data.

"He has asked Skel if I might analyze the engravings," Data elaborated. "Skel has agreed, and has given me access to the Vulcan's work. They believe they have translated the phrase, 'For war alone—.' I am hoping to take their work and expand upon it. Even if there is not time to complete it before the TechnoFair, I might be able to uncover one of their language matrixes."

"I don't know, Data," Geordi said warily. "The Vulcans have been working on this stuff for eighty years. How are they going to feel if you solve this puzzle in a couple of days?"

Data seemed flustered for the moment. "But,

Geordi, Vulcans do not express their emotions, therefore . . ." He paused, as if finally getting the joke.

Geordi and Crusher both smiled as the android nodded. "Ah. I see. Vulcans do not express their emotions, therefore we will never know how they really 'feel' at all! Yes. Very subtle."

"I think when Master Scientist Skel finally meets you, Data," Geordi said, "he'll find you a kindred spirit!"

Crusher's face grew somber, and both officers noticed it.

"I say something rude, Doctor?" Geordi asked.

"No, of course not," she replied, too quickly. As they watched her, waiting for something else, she finally said, "It's just that Deanna had some problems 'reading' Skel. Apparently, the terrible ordeal he endured as a child has had lasting effects on him. It's really rather sad."

"That little bit of information the Vulcans sent Picard about the initial epidemic was pretty dry," Geordi added, "but still it sounded terribly grim."

"He was only a child at the time," Crusher told them. "He lost his mother, and his father was infected."

"Was Skel infected as well?" Data asked.

Beverly shook her head. "Just affected by the trauma of his experience. Interestingly enough, none of the children of Vulcan were infected—just adults. It's interesting how diseases can single out certain members of a community, affect some, and leave others unscathed. But the children had their own price to pay."

"I don't know if I'd want to devote my life to studying the things that caused my mother's death," Geordi said quietly.

"Skel explained," Crusher told them, "that he wanted to make something positive out of such a negative event." Then she smiled, as if trying to break the somber mood. "Well. If you gentlemen have garnered all the information you need, this area is supposed to be off-limits."

"Thanks for letting us in, Doc," Geordi said.

"I thank you as well," Data told her. "I could have gotten the images from a remote scan, but this data is much more precise."

"Well, the captain approved it," Crusher said. "Frankly, the little things give me the creeps. I'll be glad when they're off the ship."

As the two officers stepped out into the corridor, Geordi turned toward his android friend. "Will you start work on those matrixes right away?"

"I believe so," Data said. "Skel will only be on board for another two days. It does not give me much time."

"You go ahead," Geordi told him. "I've got to check something in engineering, then I'm going to call it a night and relax in my quarters."

"I will see you tomorrow, Geordi," Data said, as they parted ways.

Geordi smiled as his friend moved away down a rounded corridor; already absorbed in the tricorder readouts of the shell engravings. *If anybody can break that language, Data can.*

The chief engineer made his way to his work area. He'd wanted to check, just one more time, the ship's efficiency ratings since the new calibrations had been worked in. He spent a few minutes at his station and conferred with a few of his staff. He was in the middle of a conversation with the officer in charge of this shift, when he spied the newcomer.

"Dr. Tarmud?" he said in surprise.

"Ah, there you are, Mr. La Forge!" the scientist said cheerily.

"It's, uh, nice to see you, sir, but this area is usually off-limits to everyone except authorized ship's personnel. Can I help you?"

"Well, I understood that you were off duty," the scientist explained sheepishly, "so I attempted to locate you through the computer, but you kept *moving*. I followed the computer's directions and eventually turned up here. Sorry if I'm trespassing."

"No harm done, sir," Geordi assured him. "And, technically, I am off duty." The engineer glanced at the leader of the shift and nodded farewell, then moved closer to the scientist. "What is it you wanted to see me about?"

As they drew away from the others, Tarmud put a friendly hand on Geordi's shoulder. "Actually, Mr. La Forge, I came to apologize."

The younger man felt confused. He glanced at Tarmud, who kept his eyes downcast, as if too embarrassed to meet the engineer's gaze.

"I'm just a nuts-and-bolts researcher, Mr. La Forge," Tarmud explained. "If you haven't noticed by now, some of us scientists get so absorbed in our work, so single-minded, that we lose our appreciation for social skills. I'm afraid when we spoke the other day in Ten Forward I was rude to you. Totally dismissive of what you were trying to tell me. I realized it sometime later, and when I did, well—I just wanted to apologize. I feel like an old fool one step out of touch with reality."

Geordi was startled, and a little pleased. The scientist's heartfelt regret seemed genuine enough.

"Mr. La Forge," Tarmud continued, "the breakthroughs that my team and I discovered when we fashioned the VISOR are the cornerstone of my work on a functional android. The eyes *are* the windows of the soul, so to speak, and questions we answered with the VISOR have led to much greater things. I came upon some of my early work with the instrument as I was reviewing issues with Master Scientist Skel. I didn't even know I had some of that early material with me—it was tucked away on one of my working cassettes. I thought perhaps you'd like to see that material. There are images of some of the first prototypes, and some interesting history there. And, while we were reviewing that, I thought—we could talk."

La Forge grinned, both flattered and surprised by the generous offer. "Why, thank you, sir. I *would* be interested in seeing some of that material. But I know you and Skel have a lot of work ahead of you before the TechnoFair. I'd hate to take away some of your precious time just for my own indulgence."

"Even Vulcans take a break from their work, Mr. La Forge," Tarmud insisted. "In fact, when I discussed it with Skel, he thought showing you this material and taking the time to have this discussion with you was *most logical.*"

The two men entered the nearby turbolift, and Tarmud told it which deck they needed.

"In fact," the scientist continued, "Skel agreed that with all the hospitality we've been shown aboard your vessel, the least we could do was repay that in kind. And with whom better than the chief engineer, the man who runs the ship?" Tarmud again put a friendly hand on Geordi's shoulder as the turbolift doors opened and they left to approach Tarmud's quarters.

"Yes," Tarmud continued as they approached his cabin, "Skel was in complete agreement. After all, if we're speaking of the nuts and bolts of the *Enterprise,* the chief engineer is the most important person on board!"

Before Geordi could deny this overly broad interpretation of his importance aboard the vessel, the doors of Tarmud's quarters whooshed open. Geordi saw that the Vulcan was there, already standing, as if anticipating his arrival. La Forge greeted the Vulcan scientist; Skel nodded at him, his eyes downcast. But there was one brief flicker of eye contact, and when there was—

Geordi frowned. He thought he saw something,

some unusual energy reading behind Skel's eyes. It had just been for a second, before the Vulcan turned his gaze away. The VISOR could pick up bands of energy far outside normal human visual range, but he'd never seen anything like this before. He would've loved to manipulate Skel into lifting his eyes for a second look, but Tarmud was guiding him over to a console and showing him some visual records there.

Skel came and stood beside them as Tarmud gave him a "tour" through this historic material. It was interesting, and Geordi wished he could focus on it, but he couldn't help wondering what it was he'd seen in the Vulcan's eyes.

In the middle of an explanation, Tarmud broke off, then said, "You seem a little distracted, Commander La Forge."

"I'm sorry, sir, it's just—well, as the creator of the VISOR, you'd appreciate this. All the different heat and energy readouts that the VISOR interprets are always open to some fluctuation. I'm so used to it I can compensate for it most times without even being aware of it. But, just now, I thought I saw something odd about Skel's eyes. It's probably just a momentary glitch, or a misinterpretation due to a Vulcan's different temperature and energy readouts."

"You know," Tarmud said quietly, "we were wondering if you'd be able to *see* them."

Geordi stared at the energy bands that formed his image of Tarmud's face. *"Them,* sir?"

"Yes," the Vulcan seconded emotionlessly. *"Them.* The agents of your deliverance, Commander."

Skel stood at his left shoulder, and Geordi turned toward him, trying to capture that gaze again. This time it was offered to him willingly, as Skel met his gaze full on. And there, behind seemingly normal Vulcan eyes, something sparkled and danced, glowed and glittered. Something Geordi had never seen before.

"I don't understand," Geordi said, staring unabashedly. "What is *that?* I've never seen anything like it."

"Look closer, Commander," Skel murmured, his voice low, nearly hypnotic. "Know what it is you are seeing."

Geordi frowned. "I have no idea what that is! It looks like some kind of energy flow, but it's separate from the rest of your biochemistry."

As La Forge stared in fascination at the light show going on behind Skel's eyes, he was startled by the warm touch of the Vulcan's hands as Skel's fingertips contacted his neck. As bizarre as that was, it didn't prepare him for the surge of sensation that traveled down his spine, almost like an electric shock. He grunted in surprise and felt his knees buckle, but Tarmud was behind him with a chair and eased it under him. Skel never lost his grip, and Geordi realized dimly that the Vulcan was making neural connections with his brain, as if to meld with him. But no, that wasn't possible! Against his will?

"Stop," La Forge whispered, only marginally in control of his bodily functions. "Don't. You can't do this! You're Vulcan. That's unethical."

"To meld with another against his will is unethical," Skel admitted, even as he brought up his other hand to make the neural connections on La Forge's face. "However, in a few seconds this will be happening with your complete accord, Mr. La Forge. My mind to your mind." The Vulcan began intoning the ritual words as the mental connection began.

Outwardly, Geordi's body showed little reaction, except a slight quivering. Inwardly, he was frantic, fighting for the remnants of his own will, his own personality against the powerful Vulcan mind rapidly overtaking his. So determined was he to resist that he managed to bring one arm up in an attempt to slap his communicator. But before he could touch the badge,

Tarmud removed it casually from his uniform, even as Geordi desperately murmured, "La Forge to Security. La Forge to Worf . . ."

"And now we are one," Skel insisted, and Geordi could do nothing but agree, mouthing the words with him at the exact same time. He and the Vulcan *were* one, as the scientist's brain completely overwhelmed the engineer's. But still Geordi fought, still he resisted the invasion of his most private organ, his brain.

His heart rate accelerated wildly, his blood pressure climbed, his temperature rose—all to match the Vulcan's. But Geordi cared only about his consciousness, his unique individuality. Physically, he could not resist the Vulcan, but, mentally, he could remain aware, and keep some small spark of himself alive and conscious beneath the powerful Vulcan presence.

"How is he?" Tarmud asked, sounding actually concerned.

"We have an acceptable tolerance," the Vulcan said, and Geordi felt his own mouth forming the same words. "But his mind is strong, very resistant."

"Can he absorb them?" Tarmud wondered. "Through the VISOR?"

Them again. What were they talking about?

"They must go through the optic nerve," Skel insisted. "To do that, they must be absorbed by the VISOR, then travel to the nerve through its circuitry. They could get trapped or lost through the unusual transmission."

"He is critical to our success. Once we have the chief engineer . . ." Tarmud didn't continue. He didn't have to.

Suddenly, Geordi understood everything, understood it through knowledge he gleaned through the enforced meld. Skel and Tarmud were infected by the parasites from the artifacts. And now they planned to infect him as well . . . but the normal mode of transmission was through minor physical contact and eye contact, and Geordi's blindness and his mechanical VISOR were interfering with their plans. He was sweating now, as their goal of using the TechnoFair to spread their disease became clear to him. They would wipe out the galaxy if they got to the TechnoFair! They would successfully infect almost every space-faring race! He had to find some way to stop them, some way to resist! He had to get to Picard!

"Yes, Mr. La Forge," Skel said in the same soft monotone, "that is our plan. And you are critical to its success."

The Vulcan moved his face closer to Geordi's. La Forge struggled to move his face away, or even close his eyes, but, of course, that had no effect on the VISOR, which continued to feed him images.

"Is he *afraid?"* Tarmud asked, looming over Geordi, beside the Vulcan. He sounded odd when he asked that, almost eager, but everything that had happened here in the last few minutes had been odd.

"Yes," the Vulcan admitted, which shamed the engineer. "He is afraid, but not enough."

"If his fear is strong enough, they will follow the energy flow. They'll find their way inside, to feed."

"Yes," Skel agreed. "That's true. Very logical, Tarmud."

They *wanted* him afraid? Fear he could control, Geordi realized. He would emulate Data, his closest friend. He would *be* Data. With no fear. No feelings at all. If fear was what they wanted from him, then that was the last thing they would get. With an almost preternatural calm, Geordi clamped down on his emotions, turning himself into a human android.

And then the Vulcan did something more peculiar and frightening than anything he'd done up to now. He smiled. No. Not a smile—a leer. Skel's face turned into a grinning, leering death's head, as his eyes blazed with a murderous light.

Geordi fought an almost instinctive panic reaction

and made himself be Data, finding this nothing more to react to than an interesting scientific phenomenon. But Skel had only just begun.

Suddenly, Geordi was jerked out of the chair he was in and out of the ship he was on, and he found himself on the surface of the planet Vulcan. It was full night, the deep blackness of a starred though moonless sky. But he had no time to admire the sight because he was running, running for his life, and hot on his heels was Skel, grinning like a madman. If Skel caught him, he knew, he was finished. He would kill him slowly, by inches, piece by horrible piece, and Geordi's only defense was to run.

In his mind, he heard Troi screaming at him to run for his life, and all he could do was obey.

"No," the engineer murmured, "no, this isn't happening."

He wasn't on Vulcan, he was on the *Enterprise* where an infected Vulcan had taken over his brain and forced the vivid hallucination on him in an attempt to evoke a fear reaction. He couldn't submit. He couldn't.

But he couldn't make himself stop running. And Skel was almost upon him. Troi was shrilling frantically at him. And that grin, that horrible grin, loomed over him.

No. No fear, no fear . . .

Geordi slipped in the sand and fell, and Troi begged him to get up, to hurry, to save himself! Just as Skel reached for his foot, he leapt to his feet and bolted free. No! No! He wasn't on Vulcan!

His lungs heaved for air in the thin hot atmosphere; his heart pounded. If Skel caught him—

What was he thinking? Skel had *already* caught him.

He felt another hand—Tarmud's hand—touch his face even as he staggered wildly over the desert sand. Some distant part of his mind realized that the two scientists were feeding off his terror, off the energy the hallucination was causing him to burn up, and that the entities within them were growing stronger because he was afraid. But the Vulcan had his mind in his powerful grip, and the images he forced upon Geordi were Skel's own memories, his own childhood terror, and they were too strong for Geordi to resist. As Troi's voice kept urging him to flee, to hurry, to run, he found himself falling into the imagery of the hallucination and struggling to outrace the Vulcan, even though he knew none of it was real.

As the shimmering, dancing lights behind Skel's and Tarmud's eyes became more and more visible to him, he watched in dread fascination as they grew brighter and brighter, even as he ran from his fantasy pursuer. Geordi watched as the sparkling energy bands finally left Skel's eyes and came closer and closer to his face.

Contact.

His body jerked—in real time as well as in the hallucination—as though he'd touched a live conduit. With thoughts that were not his own, Geordi realized the entities had found his optic nerve and were now surging through it.

Is this what Janice Ito felt the instant before the power surge killed her?

In the fantasy, Skel caught him, just as the Vulcan child had been caught by his father. No need to enhance Geordi's fear now; it bloomed powerfully as he realized how close he was to infection.

Geordi groaned, wishing for the brief moments it took the entities to travel to his brain and overwhelm it that he really was Data—an android who could learn to emulate friendship but who could actually feel nothing. Skel's possession slipped away as the Vulcan ended the meld, just as the entities took up residence in Geordi's cerebral cortex. Geordi trembled in the chair as if still in touch with the conduit and relived Skel's terrifying memories of his own infection by his father. The entities fed ravenously on his rampant emotions and the hormones they produced, and once sated, they withdrew to his amygdala.

In the chair, Geordi took a deep breath and slowly stood, feeling his feet firmly beneath him. Skel and Tarmud watched cautiously. He nodded at them, feeling stronger, feeling sound.

"Good work, gentlemen," he said, as if addressing his own subordinates. "We are now in possession of the chief engineer."

Chapter Six

WHEN ENSIGN BARBARA EVANS left Master Scientist Skel's quarters, she proceeded to interact with the various scientists she'd had assigned to her. She infected three of them, who in turn infected their aides, spouses, and assistants. Those people, in turn, infected other members of the crew during the time they spent at the mini-fair in Ten Forward, as well as other scientists and staff. Barbara, in the normal course of her day, interacted with fifteen members of the science team, who interacted with others in that group, who interacted with still others. During these interactions, at least forty percent of the people met were infected.

By the end of her shift, Barbara had successfully fulfilled most of the orders Skel had given her, with the notable exception of one—the contamination of Kyla Dannelke. Barbara had interacted with that scientist before seeing Skel, and, afterward, any contact any of the Possessed had with Dannelke had been unsuccessful in engaging her with their group. The woman seemed wary of body contact and managed to keep everyone well out of her "private space." Desperate to fulfill her orders, Barbara disguised herself as a dark male and made one last futile attempt to incorporate Dr. Dannelke.

Due to her own skillful maneuverings, Barbara had managed to avoid detection and cast doubt on Dannelke's report of being attacked. Her Possessed colleagues helped cover her tracks as she pursued Dannelke through the ship, but Lieutenant Worf's interference had terminated her pursuit.

The only advantage she'd gained from the attempt at capture and pursuit was the injury and pain that Dannelke had inflicted on her body. Her nose was broken, and she'd been hurt in various other places, hurt severely. None of the wounds were fatal, but the adrenaline and hormone production that resulted from the pain fed her starving entities. She'd retreated to a seldom-used storage area in the depths of the ship and huddled there, allowing her entities the privilege of temporarily sating their everlasting hunger. They, in turn, would heal her rapidly, returning her body to normal in less than a day, so she could continue her recruiting.

As she hid there, the other entities sensed her presence and the source of nourishment she had to offer. For several hours afterward, a steady stream of scientists and crew members came to the out-of-the-way storage room to draw sustenance from the battered ensign. Until the Betazoid was roused from her drugged sleep and captured for their use, their ability to feed would be limited. For to feed was to cause chaos, which aboard the tightly run vessel of Jean-Luc Picard would be entirely too noticeable.

So, for now, Barbara was pleased to aid her companions, the collective of the Possessed, giving them the strength to incorporate more and more crew members of the vast *Enterprise.* For this was only the beginning: a beginning born of caution and orderly designs, a beginning only a Vulcan could have planned.

"What I don't understand, Number One," Picard complained to his first officer as Riker entered the ready room, "is how a personal communiqué from Guinan can get to me faster than a Starfleet security file."

"Security file, sir?" Riker asked.

Picard sighed. Will had come here no doubt intending to bring his own matters to the captain's attentions, but Picard was so distracted he'd begun the conversation before Riker ever had a chance.

"About those artifacts," Picard explained. "Starfleet is supposed to be sending me a file that pertains to events that occurred some eighty years ago involving Skel's artifacts. I'd certainly like to see that material, and find out what the hell it is we're housing." He glowered at his small computer screen as if the cheery letter from Guinan was somehow responsible for it all. He'd be damned if he could understand how rare alcoholic beverages and new methods of incorporating chocolate in food and drink could enhance a religious experience anyway. He clicked off the screen.

Riker had one of those small wry grins on his face. "You're worried about Deanna, aren't you?"

He hated it when Will read him so easily, but, of course, in a first officer, that was a valuable trait. He felt himself clenching and unclenching his jaw, and he forced himself to stop it. "Yes. Of course I'm worried about her. She's rarely wrong about her 'feelings,' about the things she senses on this ship. Part of me feels I should do what she says, just chuck the bloody things out the nearest airlock, but—"

Riker nodded. "I doubt if there'll be anything in that Starfleet communiqué that'll give you justification for that action."

"No, but there may be some other information we don't have that could be critical."

"Critical?" Riker seemed confused. "In case there's a breach in security? In case the infection gets out?"

"I feel comfortable that we have the things secured, but, after all, the Vulcans felt comfortable that they did, also!" Picard faced his first officer. "That's not why you came in here, Commander. You came to say—?"

Riker took a deep breath. "Lieutenant Worf reported an unusual occurrence to me that I wanted to bring to your attention. One of the scientists, Dr. Kyla Dannelke, reports being attacked in her quarters by an unknown male crew member—probably an ensign. He was not wearing a communicator. She fought him off and escaped, but after perusing our personnel files she could not identify her attacker. However, Worf's security personnel have found some of the theater group's greasepaint, a wig, and a voice modulator stowed in an out-of-the-way locker. Worf thinks her assailant was disguised."

Of all the things Picard expected Riker to bring up, this was not even on the list. "Could it have been one of the other scientists? Or their assistants or technicians?" There were at least one hundred fifty passengers currently aboard the *Enterprise.* It was too hard for him to believe that one of his crew was capable of such a crime. Their people were so well screened, continually tested for mental competence—*and normally under the subtle empathic scan of a Betazoid counselor,* he thought, realizing Deanna had been under a specially sedated sleep today.

"Anything's possible," Riker admitted. "As you can imagine, Mr. Worf is not happy about this. The entire security staff has been briefed, but other than that—"

Picard nodded. "Thank you for bringing this to my attention. I want to know if there are any further developments. Perhaps I should call on Dr. Dannelke and offer my apologies."

Riker looked half amused, half uncomfortable. "I spoke to Dr. Dannelke personally, sir. She's planning on spending her evening with Mr. Worf and his son. She assured me she would feel quite safe there."

"I see," Picard said, slightly surprised. That made him think of something else. "Do you plan to visit the counselor this evening?" Picard rarely inquired as to his crew's after-duty activities, but he trusted Riker would understand why he was asking.

"Yes. I thought I'd look in on her. See if she got some rest today, and how she's doing."

Picard nodded. "I encourage you. She needs to feel secure again, Will. It will help her get over the trauma of that mental contact with the artifacts." *And while you're checking on Deanna,* Picard thought, *I'll look in on the artifacts, and double check their security myself.*

Dr. Crusher was taking one last walk around sickbay before the end of her shift. Dr. Ramirez, whose shift was now beginning, had been briefed about the cases currently being followed, and advised to watch out for any person—crew member or otherwise—who came in with a freshly broken nose or injured groin. Beverly had put away some data cassettes in her office, and made sure all the equipment had been cleaned and put up. She didn't like to leave work for the next crew on duty, any more than she liked to find work undone when she came on in the morning.

Satisfied that everything was as it should be, she debated whether she should check on the artifacts one more time. Part of her didn't like looking at them and part of her felt obsessed about checking on them constantly, making sure all the fail-safes were in place. Of course, the failure of any one of them would trigger warning alarms, but even so she'd check this one last time, and then go to her quarters, curl up with a good play, and call it a night.

She moved quietly through the darkened sickbay and entered the quarantine facility just as she had a dozen times that day. Only this time, she was greeted by three people: the Vulcan Skel, the researcher Dr. Tarmud, and the ship's chief engineer all turned to look at her as the doors of the facility closed behind her.

She tried not to let her consternation show in her face, but failed. Of all people, La Forge surely knew better than to violate the captain's off-limit order regarding the artifacts—much less bring visitors along with him.

"Excuse me," she said in a chilly but polite tone, "permission to enter this area can only be granted by the captain. He did not notify me that you would be here to see the artifacts."

"I'm sorry, Doctor." Geordi smiled apologetically. "I guess I thought that the permission I'd been given earlier was still valid. Skel and Dr. Tarmud and I were discussing some data about the artifacts, but Dr. Tarmud had never seen them. Skel assumed that since they were his research objects, and I'd been given permission earlier, it would be all right."

That was the muddiest logic she'd ever heard Geordi use, but she wasn't about to argue with him. The security parameters were all still in place. The artifacts still sat benignly behind their multiple security shields.

"You're a doctor," Tarmud said to her charmingly. "Surely you know how impulsive researchers can be. Try to understand, Dr. Crusher."

"I understand that researchers can be impulsive," she said quietly, as she approached the quarantine device that held the artifacts, checking the readouts on its diagnostic panel: *All within norms, thank God.* "I also understand that researchers are used to following exacting protocols. And that chief engineers are used to augmenting them." She shot a sharp glance at La Forge. "And that the three of you have violated those protocols. This area is off-limits without the captain's express permission. I must be present during any authorized visit. That's the short and sweet of it, gentlemen. Please remember that in the future. Now, if you would please leave?"

She turned to move away from the diagnostic panel, but found herself hemmed in by the three men. Skel was on her right, Geordi on her left, and Tarmud directly in front of her, nearly pinning her to the quarantine tank that held the artifacts. "*Excuse* me!" she said pointedly, trying to sidle past Tarmud, but he only moved forward, blocking her even more.

"Wait a minute, Doctor," Geordi said quietly. "There's something we've got to tell you."

She looked at him, and some faint odd undercurrent in his tone—something insidious, ancient, cold—caused a wave of unreasoning fear to sweep over her.

A panicked, unbidden thought welled up: *This isn't Geordi. It looks just like him, but this is something else . . .*

"What's going on here?" she tried to demand bravely, but the question came out as a whisper.

"Doctor, I can explain everything," Tarmud insisted, with that smug smile that had infuriated her so much in Ten Forward.

"Explain what?" she asked impatiently, turning to gaze at him.

She looked deep into his hazel eyes and saw something there: something strange and mesmerizing. He reached for her, this odd researcher from New England, and touched her hand.

A jolt—raw invigorating power—surged through her. She groaned, even as Geordi held her other hand and Skel's fingers brushed the back of her neck.

"This will only take a minute, Dr. Crusher," Geordi said patiently, using the most reasonable tone to explain away the most unreasonable behavior.

Her body shuddered as the men moved in closer, supporting her, helping her to withstand the oddly pleasant jolt running through her. And then, it passed. And she understood everything, just as Tarmud had promised.

She regained her balance, and the men drew back respectfully. Like the doctor she still was, she pulled out the medi-scanner in her pocket and watched her own readouts as the entities claimed her and fed off the rush of adrenaline coursing through her. It was beautiful, really.

"The captain will be having breakfast with you tomorrow?" Geordi asked.

Beverly smiled, still eyeing the medi-scanner. "Yes, that's right. I'll be meeting him in his quarters."

"Wonderful," Tarmud said, smiling his infectious grin.

"So, you see," Dr. Dannelke explained, as she helped Alexander clear off the table and send the dishes back through the recycler, "you can learn so much about the rest of the body through the eyes—diseases, vascular health—so many things. I guess that's what got me interested in the field. Do you have any specific interests yet?"

The boy shrugged his shoulders. "I want to be a navigator, I think."

"Lots of math needed for that," Kyla told him. "Physics. All that kind of stuff."

He nodded as he stacked the final dish in the

recycler, then closed the door and turned it. "I know. I'm good at those subjects, so that should be all right. It's just—"

"It's just what?"

Alexander peered around her as if looking for his father. Worf had gone to check with his security forces to see if there'd been any new reports about her assailant, and was still in his private room. "It's just—well, I don't know if they'll let a Klingon kid do that kind of stuff. I can't say that around Father. It makes him furious."

Kyla felt as if she'd just been slapped. She remembered her thoughtless comment of a day ago and hated herself for it. "Hey, that's no way to think! Your dad's a Starfleet officer, and I'll bet before he joined no one would've ever believed Starfleet would've taken a Klingon into its ranks!"

"They had to take him," Alexander explained patiently. "His foster parents—my grandparents—are human, and my grandfather was a Starfleet chief petty officer. Father not only passed his tests, he was third in his class. They couldn't find a way to turn him down."

"Listen, Alexander." Kyla crouched down so she would be on the boy's eye level. "Don't make it easy on anyone. Don't pass up opportunities because you think they won't take you. Make them turn you down! Make them tell you to your face. See if they have the nerve. You're a bright strong kid! You can be anything you want to be in this Universe. Don't let anyone tell you differently!"

His small somber face broke into an easy grin. "That sounds like something my mom would say. You remind me so much of her!" Alexander grabbed her in a quick spontaneous hug, then walked over to the couches. He picked up a small holo projector and, bringing it to Kyla, turned it on. A tall woman—pale-skinned, with distinctly human features but skull ridges that spoke of Klingon ancestry—stood waving on the hand-held platform. Waving and grinning, she had one eyebrow canted upward as if in perpetual wry amusement.

"That's your mom?" the doctor asked in surprise. "She looks like she had a wonderful sense of humor."

"Oh, yeah. Mother could find something funny about anything."

That sounds so un-Klingon-like, Kyla thought.

"She was half human," Alexander said softly, as if answering Kyla's unasked question. "But you can't tell by looking at me. I take after Father mostly."

"I think you look like both your parents," Kyla decided. "You've got a lot of your mother in your face, and your body structure, too. And I think you've got her sense of humor, too."

Alexander grinned, even when his father's baritone agreed.

"He is a great deal like K'Ehleyr," Worf explained, as he left his room and joined them. "Especially in his *stubborness."* Yet the chief of security smiled when he chided his son. "It is time for you to review your schoolwork and get ready for bed."

The boy rolled his eyes, and for an instant he looked as if he might argue with his father, then suddenly stopped. Kyla could almost see the wheels turning in Alexander's head. "Will you be here in the morning, Kyla?"

The doctor felt her face flush red and could sense Worf gearing up for a good bluster. "Excuse me?" she said quietly, smiling at the boy.

"I thought you might like to come by for breakfast," Alexander insisted, feigning innocence.

"Well, I'm not much of a morning person, but I think I could manage. That all right with you, Mr. Worf?" She saw the Klingon work his jaw back and forth as he struggled to answer civilly.

"If it is not an inconvenience for you," Worf

grumbled, "it would be pleasant to share breakfast with you, Doctor." Then he glared at his son who just giggled and made his escape.

Kyla hid a smile behind her hand, but not very successfully. "Don't be mad at him, Worf. He misses his mother. Says I remind him of her. So he's trying to matchmake."

"I have never seen him behave this way around a human female!" Worf insisted. "I must apologize—"

"Oh, please don't," she interrupted tiredly, sitting down on a couch. "I'm honored to be held in such high regard. Any news about my friend?"

Worf frowned and looked troubled. "Unfortunately, no. I cannot imagine how someone injured in the way you described could hide himself so well on this ship."

It was Kyla's turn to look worried. "Well, this ship is not unlike a big city in the sky, Worf. It shouldn't be that hard to find a place to hide."

"But this is not a city," he protested. "It is a Federation starship. There is no crime aboard the *Enterprise,* and it is not that easy to hide aboard this vessel!"

"I still think it was some member of the scientist's crews, not a Federation officer. Maybe the scientist in charge of that person is hiding them, not wanting anyone to know it's his or her aide who has questionable behavior." She closed her eyes, reliving for just a second that terrible moment in her quarters. The Klingon didn't know it yet, but she had no intentions of going back there. She remembered back in London, how she felt when she had to reenter her building again. "Oh, Worf, I came here tonight to forget about the attack. Let's not talk about it anymore."

He came and sat by her, a polite distance, giving her plenty of space, not boxing her into a corner. "Kyla. I want to respect your wishes, but I know there is still something you are not telling me about this attack."

She sighed and faced him squarely. "No, Worf, honest, I've told you everything, it's just . . ." She trailed off, staring at his somber expression. "Well, I guess I stirred up some memories here tonight, so I shouldn't complain if you stir up mine." She swallowed, reluctant to relate the tale, but knowing she'd feel better if she did. "I've told you everything about the incident. What you're sensing from me is my reactions to it—and the fact that it's reminded me of things I never wanted to think about again. When I was thirteen, my mom and I lived in an old section of London. One night, we were coming home and were attacked in our hallway. Even then, I was fast. My mom yelled at me to run, so I did, but by the time I found a bobby and got back, the guy was gone."

"Your mother—?" Worf asked.

"She was still alive, but he'd beaten her pretty badly. She was never the same after that, always fearful, worried when I'd go out by myself. I guess I was never the same either."

"That explains many things about your behavior," Worf said. "You keep yourself at least an arm's length from most people. You seem more wary than most humans. And, of course, it explains your training."

"I—I always felt I should've stayed and helped her, fought him, something." Kyla shook her head. "But all I could do was run."

"It was the only sensible thing to do," Worf assured her. "You were but an untrained child. You used your only weapon—speed—to go for aid. Had you stayed, you would have been harmed, perhaps killed. And your mother would have had to live with that as well."

"That's what she says, but—well, afterward, I just made sure nothing like that could ever happen to me again. Then—it happened to me again. And with all my training, ultimately—I still had to run for it."

"Still, you warded off your opponent and defended

yourself well. You drew blood, but he drew none from you. I only wish I could apprehend this coward."

Kyla found herself pulling inward, tighter and tighter, until she realized she'd folded her arms snuggly against her body and sat tense and expectant. "I'm not going back there," she announced, as if declaring her intentions would give her back some control over her situation.

Worf looked troubled. "Normally, it would be a simple matter to find you vacant quarters, but with all the scientists on board, that could be difficult. I can ask one of the junior officers to switch quarters for you for tonight, if that is acceptable."

"No, not acceptable at all. With my luck, I'll be switching quarters with the person who jumped me. Quite frankly, there's only one person on this ship that I trust that much—and that's you. I'm staying here."

Worf's eyebrows nearly climbed past his skull plate. "Kyla!" he said softly.

"Don't give yourself so much credit," she warned, grinning. "I'm sleeping right on this couch. I wouldn't dream of scandalizing *Alexander*. And, besides, I hate getting up in the morning. It's the only way I'll ever be on time for breakfast. As far as the rest of the evening is concerned . . ." She sidled closer to him on the couch. "You don't play poker, do you?"

Slowly, Worf's face eased into a smile.

Picard nodded at the doctor and nurses on duty as he moved through the quiet sickbay; it was a peaceful place this late into the night shift. When no patients were being held overnight, lights were reduced and everything was still.

He moved through the shadow-draped facility until he came to the quarantine room; there he paused before the closed doors to collect himself, then finally stepped forward. The doors slid open, allowing him passage.

In quarantine, the lights were also dimmed; a single spotlight shone down upon the artifacts behind their shields, making them the brightest spots in the room. Making them look, Picard reflected, like a museum display of the ancient artifacts they in fact were. Beneath the spotlight, they glittered like subtle works of art, pleasing to the eye—and quite deadly to the mind and body.

Picard approached them slowly, deliberately, as one might approach a charmed cobra, then acquired a tricorder from a nearby counter and checked the fail-safes, the alarms, the entire setup. All sound. Beverly had left behind the diagnostic readouts from her last check: All was exactly as it should be.

Perhaps he was being overly cautious, but given Troi's reaction to the creatures, he would not rest easy until they were transferred to the Vulcan ship.

The thought made him study them again; they looked innocuous, benign, actually beautiful lying there behind the fields. What was in them that could so disturb Deanna, make her so vehement about their destruction?

And what kind of a people could create such a vicious weapon? The containers themselves appeared ageless, new, but according to the Vulcans, they were thousands of years old.

As the doors behind him whooshed open, he turned instantly and found his android science officer standing at the threshold.

"Permission to enter, sir," Data requested.

"Granted, Mr. Data. Are you here to visit me or the artifacts?"

"Both, sir. Actually, I asked the computer where you might be found, and it told me you were here. I did want to view the artifacts again, and was calling to get your permission, but when I found out you were here, I thought I should bring some things to your attention."

"Yes?"

"Captain, I have been going over Skel's research as I attempt to build a language matrix to interpret the writing on these artifacts. However, there is something in Skel's work that disturbs me."

Picard lifted a concerned brow, but Data was a meticulous researcher; it was not unusual for him to pick up flaws in other scientists' work.

"Skel has been working on these artifacts for over fifty years. Over and over, throughout the course of his research, he has been on the cusp of discovering many things about the artifacts. Yet each time at the last minute he has swerved from the answer and found some other inadequate solution, or has changed the course of his research entirely."

Picard considered this. "Skel's work is surely reviewed by other scientists. Why haven't they noticed this pattern?"

"As far as I can determine, over the years his work has been reviewed less and less. The fewer findings a researcher comes up with, the less seriously do his colleagues regard his work. I suspect that since Skel is a survivor of the disease, his position at the Vulcan Science Academy may be more honorific in nature. Of course, had he actually made any landmark discoveries, then his work would have been scrutinized completely."

"But as long as he kept deviating from any actual breakthrough, no one looked too closely, eh?" It made sense to Picard. The outbreak on Vulcan had been over eighty years ago, the survivors scattered. And only Skel had chosen to actually work with the artifacts themselves. "Mr. Data, can you hypothesize *why* Skel would deliberately, or even subconsciously, avoid making the kind of breakthrough discoveries that were the exact thing he seemed to be working toward?"

"No, sir, I cannot. That is why I wished to bring the matter to your attention. I was hoping you would know."

Picard stared at the artifacts again, thinking of Deanna's warning, her demands that he hurl them through an airlock and send them into space. "No, my friend, I cannot tell you that. Why someone would sabotage their own life's work is something I can't imagine."

And as Picard continued to stare at the passive artifacts, he began to wonder if a lone Vulcan researcher held more secrets inside him than these simple shell-like objects.

Chapter Seven

WORF HEARD THE FEMININE VOICE calling him despite the fierce battle he was waging—despite the blood pounding in his ears, despite the roars of the warriors surrounding him. Like a berserker he fought, recognizing nothing but the *'bath'leth* in his hands and his enemy before him—Duras, who had slain his mate. He swung his weapon again, nearly connecting. But the soft feminine voice broke through the scenario.

"Lieutenant Worf! This is Ensign Alvarado! Lieutenant Worf!"

With a savage growl, Worf snapped open his eyes and peered for a confused millisecond about his darkened bedchamber. *Ensign Alvarado?*

"Lieutenant Worf, please answer!" The familiar voice carried an uncharacteristic note of stress.

Worf rubbed his face. He had been dreaming, reliving the battle in which he had killed K'Ehleyr's murderer—a dream he had not had since Alexander had come to live with him. He groped in the darkness for his communicator. "Worf here."

"Sorry to wake you, sir," Alvarado apologized hurriedly. "I know it's early, but—"

"Computer," Worf ordered softly, "raise lights." He squinted at the brightness, and at the realization that it was two hours before his—or Alvarado's—shift began. "Where are you, Ensign?"

"In Ten Forward, sir. I came in early to make sure there was water, and fill the fruit bowls, set out some breakfast foods . . ."

Worf remembered: Alvarado had volunteered to be in charge of refreshments at the mini-fair in Ten Forward. Worf swung his legs over the side of the bed, reached for a fresh uniform, and started dressing quickly. Alvarado was a level-headed officer, slow to alarm. If she felt the need to rouse him out of a sound sleep, it stood to reason his presence as security chief was urgently required.

"Anyway," Alvarado continued tersely, "when I arrived in Ten Forward . . ." She drew in a breath, then the words tumbled out in a rush. "Lieutenant, the place is a *wreck!* It's been turned upside down! It looks as though a hundred people went crazy in here!"

"Did you touch anything?" Worf asked, as he donned his clothes quickly, efficiently.

"No, sir. I saw what had happened and called you immediately."

"Very good, Ensign. Stay there and keep your eyes open. Assume anyone approaching you could be involved and act accordingly. I will be there as quickly as I can. Worf out."

"Aye, sir," she agreed, but Worf could hear that the edge of her confidence had been shaken. And why shouldn't it be? Who would damage the TechnoFair displays in Ten Forward? This made no more sense than the attack on Kyla Dannelke; Worf could understand crimes of passion, but random violence with no motive eluded him.

Straightening his hastily donned uniform, he ran a brush through his hair, then left his room.

He moved through the darkened living area to a respectful distance from the couch, and from there called softly, "Kyla?"

"I see you, Worf. I heard the page." Her voice was clear, completely awake; as his eyes adjusted to the dimness, he saw that she sat up on the couch where she'd slept, clutching her blanket.

He ordered the computer to raise the lights to only twenty percent, then said, "You must be a very light sleeper if you heard."

"I am. I couldn't understand anything being said, but I heard the voice. I assume you've got to tend to ship's business?"

"Yes." He told her nothing, not wanting to alarm her, and she did not press. "I may not be able to return to get Alexander ready for school."

"I can do that."

The familiarity of it all made him distinctly uncomfortable; he fidgeted. "I hate to impose. Normally, another officer helps Alexander when I am called away early, as I help her with her daughter when she must stay on duty late. However, I think it might be better this morning if I did not seek her help."

Kyla laughed. "More of that chivalrous Klingon honor, Worf? It's no imposition at all. Alexander and I will enjoy a healthy breakfast, then I'll see him off to school. I need to get down to my display area early anyway. I've got to meet with Dr. Tarmud, and, if I'm lucky, the Vulcan, Skel."

"Thank you, Kyla." Before he could move away, she rose quickly and surprised him by taking his face in her hands and kissing his skull plate. He felt the heat of embarrassment on his cheeks.

"Thank *you,*" she told him, as he stood and collected himself, "for giving me a port in the storm."

He nodded brusquely and headed for Ten Forward.

Picard had just emerged from his morning shower when he got the page from his first officer.

"Picard, here. What is it, Number One?" He checked the time, but knew instinctively it was too early for Will to be on duty.

"Sir, I think you should come to Ten Forward right away," Riker said, with that peculiar note of urgency in his tone that always signaled disaster. "Mr. Worf called me down here, and I think you need to be involved."

The entities, Picard thought at once, with a sense of foreboding; the image of them shimmering benignly, beautifully, behind their force shields rose unbidden. "I'll be there momentarily. Picard out."

He did not bother to ask Riker what the matter was; whatever it was, it was bad, and he would find out soon enough.

At the doorway, he hesitated: Beverly might not even be up yet. No need to wake her; he'd just leave a note on the table. It wouldn't be the first time they'd missed having breakfast together.

It was far, far worse than he had imagined. As he stood beside half a display console—literally torn in two, the metal edges jagged, twisted—Picard gazed down at the battered corpse pinned beneath it.

Barbara Evans lay on her back, stiffening arms and legs flung out like a rag doll; her battered, mottled face gazed slack-jawed and unseeing at the ceiling. Judging from the fading yellow-green bruise and the black rivulets of dried blood on her upper lip and chin, her nose had been broken—smashed—some time ago and never tended. More recently, someone had beaten her to death with the torn console—so savagely that its sharp metal edge had nearly cleaved her body in two and still bit deep into her abdomen. A darkening butterfly of blood at her waist stained the carpet beneath her—so much blood that Picard could smell it. He turned away in revulsion.

"Who could've done this?" he murmured, though he knew the answer even before Will Riker offered grimly:

"A madman."

Behind the first officer, the carefully planned display booths lay in ruins—shattered, torn, and strewn with abandon over Ten Forward's entire surface.

Picard scowled at the reply and turned toward Worf, who along with other security personnel had been busily scanning the area with tricorders. "Lieutenant . . ."

The Klingon turned off his tricorder and stepped over to Picard. "We have scanned the area for hair and skin cells," Worf reported dutifully, "in an attempt to determine the identity of the perpetrators. The computer is sorting through it, but the evidence is surprisingly small."

"As though they were calculating enough to protect themselves from detection," Riker grumbled.

"So far," the Klingon continued, "the computer has matched every cell, every drop of blood, every fiber of hair to Ensign Evans. I know there must be more evidence here, yet everything I scan comes up the same."

"There'll be evidence on her," Riker noted grimly, nodding toward the body. "Dr. Crusher will find it during the autopsy."

"Can this be related to the attack on Dr. Dannelke?" Picard wondered.

"It must be," Worf speculated. "Ky—Dr. Dannelke's report specified the ferocity of his attack, his expertise in fighting." The Klingon paused, then said quietly, "It is clear this woman was beaten savagely."

"And could all this be the work of *one* person?" Picard gestured at the destruction surrounding them.

Worf considered it a moment. "It is possible."

Riker nodded, following their gazes around the devastated room. "A Klingon would have the strength, the energy to do this."

"Or a Vulcan," Picard said thoughtfully, provoking Riker's sharp glance.

"Do you think Skel did this, sir?"

The captain sighed. "I don't know. I can't imagine any Vulcan committing such a brutal act, and I would think even a Vulcan could not have avoided shedding some blood in this melee. And Vulcan blood is easy enough to detect. But I will question him as to his whereabouts at the time of Ensign Evans's death." He paused. "Lieutenant Worf, have someone in security run a complete background check on every assistant or technician that came aboard with the scientists. I want you to know everything about them—everything. If there are any suspicious gaps in their information, we may have to detain them. If nothing shows up that indicates a suspect, then review the scientists' background as well."

"And if nothing shows up there?" Worf asked.

"Then begin reviewing *Enterprise* personnel," Picard said without hesitating. "Begin with any new crewmen and work your way through the entire staff if you must. Keep me closely informed."

Worf nodded and glanced over at the far wall, where Ensign Alvarado stood, hugging herself. "I believe I have just the person for the job, sir."

As Worf approached the young woman, Picard moved away from the corpse, and Riker went with him.

"Will," Picard said quietly as the two of them walked slowly into the corridor, "have you talked to Deanna lately?"

Riker shook his head. "Whatever Beverly gave her must have hit her hard. I checked on her last night and she was still sleeping. With everything she'd been through I thought it best to let her rest. I haven't heard from her, so I assume she's still asleep."

"A pity. Under the influence of that drug, it's unlikely she would have 'sensed' the violence that occurred here. When she wakes, she should be present if we question any suspects Worf uncovers."

"Captain, if I may speak off the record?" Riker asked.

"Of course."

"I get the feeling there's something on your mind. Something you don't want to say out loud. If it would help us solve this—"

Picard shook his head. "It's just that—this level of violence, Will. With those artifacts still on board . . ." He let the sentence hang there.

"That would implicate the Vulcan, sir, wouldn't it?" Riker asked him. "He was the only person who's been exposed to the artifacts, when he was aboard the Ferengi ship."

"Yes, it would. But there would have to be some evidence. It's not possible to destroy all this equipment and beat a human being to death without leaving *something,* and the Vulcan physiology is so different the evidence would have to stand out. Plus, according to the Vulcans, not even *they* were capable of controlling themselves during the outbreak. If Skel is infected, he should appear a raving lunatic. None of this makes any sense."

Riker sighed. "You should know, sir, that Ensign Evans was Skel's liaison officer. Of course, she was also the liaison to Kyla Dannelke and eight other scientists as well."

"We'll have to see if Worf can come up with something concrete. Until then, I don't want panic setting in among the scientific group." Picard stopped just as they arrived at the lift entrance and turned toward his second-in-command. "How quickly can we get Ten Forward back in order?"

"I can put a crew to work in there immediately," Riker said. "We can replicate the equipment and recycle the damaged material. We should be able to get everything back together by this afternoon."

"Well enough so that the scientists won't be able to tell what happened?"

Riker shrugged, a gesture of dubious possibility. "If I can have some of La Forge's engineering crew, I think so. Why would you want to hide it from them?"

"To rattle the cage of the perpetrators," Picard said. "I can't help but feel that they want to frighten us, that the savagery of their behavior is designed to evoke a response. That's true for many criminal behavior types. If we can deprive them of that reward, it might help flush them out."

Riker nodded. "I'll get on it right away, sir. And I'll have a medical team remove the body and prepare it for autopsy."

"I'll want Beverly to do it personally," Picard ordered. "Make sure she sends the report directly to me, with as much confidentiality as possible. Also, ask Skel a few discreet questions about his whereabouts last night. In the meantime, I'll be in my ready room."

"Aye, sir."

With that, Picard left the death and destruction of Ten Forward behind him and headed for the ready room, unable to believe he would once again be forced to contact the parents of a young promising officer with the worst news he could give. But before he would do that, he would review everything the Vulcans had sent him on the artifacts and the disease they caused, then he would contact Data and obtain a copy of Skel's research as well.

Distractedly, he found himself grateful that Guinan had been spared the dismemberment of Ten Forward. She believed Ten Forward was a place of introspection, of healing—a place where crew members could truly relax and be themselves.

As for himself, he knew that a long time would pass before he could stroll into Ten Forward and not see Barbara Evans's brutalized body lying twisted on its floor.

Perfectly calm and composed, hands steepled in a gesture of Vulcan serenity, Skel stood in the center of his comfortable guest quarters and asked, "What happened, Doctor?"

Despite the ostensible calmness of his question, inside the Vulcan's emotions raged: bitter fury, disappointment, frustration. Through it all, the entities that possessed him fed and grew stronger, as the small glimmer of consciousness that had once been Skel watched helplessly.

"I don't know all of it," Tarmud insisted, his face flushed and shining, his breath short. "Evans's injuries called to the others. The pain she felt drew them. After eighty years of deprivation, the entities' need is powerful, difficult to control. The *Enterprise* crew is disciplined, trained, capable of holding them in check, but the others—the technicians, our assistants—they're civilians. Most of them are young burgeoning scientists, curious, interested in experiencing everything. They lost control . . ."

"They cannot afford to do so if we are to succeed," Skel countered coldly.

"Have patience," Tarmud urged. "We're not all Vulcans, you know—the entities have adapted to you and your level of control. It isn't as easy for the rest of us . . ." He drew another gasping breath and continued. "They carried Evans from her hiding place, took her to Ten Forward because they knew it would be deserted. She helped them, told them where to go, why. Destroying the facilities caused emotional mayhem in their core selves, the humans inside each of them who protested the wanton destruction of their own work. And when the entities fed off that all they could, they turned to their original source."

"So, she is dead," Skel said placidly. Killed, even as his mother had been.

"Yes." Tarmud lowered his head as if in regret, but as he did so, Skel caught the spark of sadistic glee in his eyes. "She's dead. The others absorbed her entities so there would be no loss to the whole."

"They left her there?"

"Yes. They wanted to alarm the others, to evoke the emotional response they might feed from, and keep their need in check."

"Her death and the destruction of Ten Forward will alert the *Enterprise* crew to our presence," Skel countered.

"Perhaps. The technicians thought out their actions, in spite of their hunger. They wore protective garb. The only physical evidence that will remain will belong to Barbara Evans. If we can control their appetites, this will not happen again."

"It cannot," Skel insisted. "If we are detected before we have recruited the senior staff, we can be defeated. There must be control. They must learn to wait."

"They would not need to wait if we had the empath at our disposal," Tarmud reminded him. "Last night she did not dream at all. None of us could even sense her."

Skel nodded. "Her empathy—while valuable to us as a rich source of nourishment—is still a danger to us as well. If the Betazoid senses us too clearly, we will be exposed before we are ready. We must be cautious until we hold the majority of the crew, perhaps even until the Vulcan ship arrives and can be captured. The empath must remain unaware—and unavailable. Are we still recruiting?"

"Yes," Tarmud assured him. "Recruitment is going well."

"Not well enough," the Vulcan insisted. "We still need Dannelke, and more of the senior staff."

Just then the door chimed; Tarmud and Skel exchanged a glance. "Come," the Vulcan said.

The doors opened to reveal Dr. Crusher. "Picard skipped breakfast this morning. What happened?"

The two men told her about Ten Forward.

She shook her head in disapproval. "Now, he'll be wary. He'll be much harder to approach."

"We can still work on the rest of the senior staff," Tarmud told her. "Everyone but the Betazoid."

"Even Data?" Crusher asked. "Can he be recruited? He's an android."

"Unknown," Skel told her, "but unlikely. The positronic matrix could house the entities, but because the android has no emotions, it would be harder for the resident entities to feed. However, controlling the android is very desirable for other practical matters, but we must be cautious. An attempt to recruit could alert him to our presence. If we were not successful, he would have the resources to expose us."

Crusher nodded, just as Picard paged her through her communicator. "Crusher here."

"Doctor, I need to speak to you immediately. "I'll be in sickbay."

"Aye, sir. On my way." She looked at her collaborators. "There'll be too many people in sickbay for me to risk recruiting him there. I'll have to choose my moment later." And then she left them.

"Sound advice," Skel said to Tarmud. "We will all

have to show more caution. We will all have to choose our moments."

Tarmud considered his words and nodded.

Beneath a starry, moonless sky, Deanna moved across a desert plain toward the dark distant mountains. Lwaxana walked beside her.

Deanna stopped abruptly and faced her. "What is this place?"

Lwaxana's lips remained in a grim determined line as she replied silently, *The planet Vulcan.*

"Why are we here? Mother, what is this all about?"

And yet, she knew, this was not her mother; for although the mental voice possessed Lwaxana's feel, her special parental tone, this was not her mother. The woman beside her was too calm, too controlled, too reserved.

That's correct, little one. I am not your mother. But you must listen to me now. Do not look them in the eye, any of them. Do not let them touch you. And, above all, shelter your mind. You're in terrible danger, and I have only a limited ability to help you.

"I don't understand," Deanna said irritably. "Whoever you are, you're talking in riddles. Shelter my mind? How? From whom? Explain it to me."

A flash of movement across the great dry plain caught Deanna's eye, and she turned to watch, eyes widening, as a Vulcan child sprinted frantically across the desert. Behind him, narrowing the gap, an older man pursued relentlessly.

"No," Deanna moaned. "No, it can't be. I'm dreaming again. That's Skel as a child. I'm dreaming his memories! I've got to wake up."

The woman that looked like her mother took Deanna by the shoulders, with a grip that spoke of inhuman strength, a voice placid yet infinitely determined. *This is not a dream. You must watch and learn.*

The boy lost his footing in the sand and fell face-forward in the desert dust. The man reached for the boy, grabbed him by the collar, and hauled him around. The boy fought valiantly as the older Vulcan clutched the child's face in his hands.

"How terrible!" Deanna murmured, wanting to close her eyes against the scene. "He's *forcing* young Skel to meld!"

The child went limp, his eyes wide, panic-stricken; Deanna's own eyes filled with tears.

Yes, the older woman said, her voice serene despite the horrific tableau nearby. *It was terrible. The violation. The infection.*

Deanna watched, her confusion mounting as the elder Vulcan at last removed his hands from the child's narrow face. The boy rose and, with Vulcan composure, brushed himself off, then began to walk home.

As he did, the adult Vulcan turned to face Deanna, his expression contorted in a grin of such pure sadistic evil that Troi gasped, recoiling. As she continued to watch, the man began to walk toward them, his pace increasing until soon he was loping across the sand.

And soon he was upon them, reaching a hand toward Lwaxana.

"Mother!" Deanna screamed, as the Vulcan caught Lwaxana's wrist and dragged her to him.

Serene and unresisting in the face of death, the woman looked over her shoulder at Troi. *Remember. This is not a dream. You must remember. Keep yourself safe.*

And then the Vulcan was upon Lwaxana; he threw her to the ground and put his hands around her throat.

"Mother!" Deanna screamed, and sat bolt upright in her own bed.

Silence answered, and the reassuring sight of her

own quarters. She pressed a trembling hand to her forehead and drew it away to find it glistening with sweat.

Beverly had promised her she wouldn't dream. Could she still have some residual contact with Skel? She scanned lightly, but was unable to pick his feelings out from the rest of the ship. Well, at least that made sense. If he was not close to her, she should barely sense him at all, with his Vulcan controls.

The door chimed, startling her so much that she jumped. Annoyed by her skittishness, she shook herself mentally as she grabbed a robe to cover her nightgown and hurried into her outer quarters.

"Enter," she called, and a smiling Crusher stepped through the doors. At the sight of Troi, the doctor's smile turned to an expression of concern.

"Deanna, are you all right?"

Troi shook her head. "I'm afraid your drug wasn't the perfect solution to my problems."

Beverly immediately produced her medi-scanner and waved it over Troi. "More bad dreams?"

"Only one, about my mother. It was very disturbing."

A ghost of Beverly's smile returned. "Well, considering how your mother and you get along, that's not surprising."

Deanna shook her head. "You know how it is in some dreams, where everything isn't as it seems? Well, this was Mother, but at the same time, it wasn't. We were on Vulcan, and Lwaxana was *acting* like a Vulcan!"

Beverly raised auburn brows in surprise. "Lwaxana? I can't think of a more un-Vulcanlike person!"

Deanna had to smile. "True. Still, it was very upsetting. She kept trying to tell me something, show me something, but I couldn't understand. Then it started getting mixed up with those terrible memories of Skel." She paused at the sight of Crusher, frowning at the medi-scanner. "What is it? What's it telling you?"

"According to the readouts," Beverly said solemnly, "you never dreamed at all last night. You have some new *memories,* but there's no sign of dream activity."

Deanna tensed, remembering: Lwaxana had insisted that what she was experiencing was not a dream.

"I certainly don't need this medi-scanner to know you're upset," Beverly said, though she never raised her eyes to Deanna's face. "And there's a considerable depletion of the neurotransmitter necessary for telepathy and empathy. That alone can cause intense anxiety. Let me give you something that will relax you, stimulate your neurotransmitter production, and dampen your ability to sense others around you. That would help prevent further depletion. Also, I'd recommend another leisurely day in your quarters until you're back to normal."

Deanna was suddenly flooded with the sensation that Beverly was being dishonest with her. She also sensed a contained hunger that surprised and confused her. She frowned, deliberately probing her friend more deeply. The strange impressions faded, leaving only the normal sense of doctorly concern and the strong desire that Deanna follow her advice so she might get well. Deanna found herself disbelieving her own senses.

And then she remembered Lwaxana's warning. *Do not look them in the eye, any of them. Do not let them touch you. And above all, shelter your mind.*

Troi struggled to make sense of it, any of it, as she felt her grip on reality fading.

"Deanna, please," Beverly murmured, closing in with the hypospray. "It's normal to feel suspicious, even paranoid, under these conditions. But this will make you feel better, give you time to shake this confusion and start to recover. I'm your doctor and your friend. Let me help you."

Deanna took a step back, moving out of reach. "I don't want that, Beverly, thank you."

For an instant, she got a flash of emotion: Beverly intended to force the drug on her.

Abruptly, the bell chimed again, and the sensation vanished.

Beverly lowered the hypo and smiled. "Of course, Deanna. But, please, if you're having problems, come see me. I can help alleviate some of what you're going through. Isn't that what you'd recommend to one of your patients?"

"Yes, of course," Deanna agreed, as the bell chimed again. "Who is it?"

"Commander Data."

"Come in," Deanna called. The thought of spending time with the one person she could sense nothing from was suddenly a tremendous relief.

"Counselor," Data began, as soon as he'd entered the room, "Captain Picard— Oh, hello, Doctor! I do hope I am not interrupting—"

"No, that's fine, Data," Beverly told him, shifting her weight as if to leave. "I was just on my way out."

The android addressed them both. "Captain Picard wishes to meet with all senior officers in the conference room immediately. The captain paged you, Counselor, but you did not answer. He was afraid your medication might cause you to sleep through the page and asked me to come get you. I suspect you already know about the meeting, Doctor?"

"Yes, Data," Beverly assured him. "I knew he wanted to meet as soon as I had finished. . . ." She glanced at Deanna, as if realizing the Betazoid was unaware of the latest shipboard developments.

"Something's happened," Deanna said. "What is it?"

Data paused, looking at the doctor. Beverly briefly explained what had occurred in Ten Forward, and about the death of Ensign Evans.

"And I slept through all that violence?" Deanna said, aghast.

"Don't blame yourself," Beverly soothed. "The sedative I gave you was supposed to block out your empathic reception. You needed the rest. We couldn't know what was going to happen."

All the more reason to remain undrugged now, Deanna decided.

"Counselor," Data said in a kindly manner, "if you are not well enough to attend the meeting, I will explain it to the captain."

"No, Data, thank you. I'll just need a moment to dress." She half turned toward her bedroom when something cool touched her neck and hissed: Crusher's hypospray.

She whirled, furious, hand to the violated spot on her neck. "Beverly! How could you?"

Crusher's expression was one of sincerest apology and sympathy, her tone one of consummate reasonableness. "Deanna, forgive me, but your reluctance to be medicated is part of your condition. The more depleted your neurotransmitter, the more tense and paranoid you'll become. It's normal for patients in your condition to refuse even life-saving help. As your doctor, I had to do what I believe is best, and what I believe you would want me to do were you feeling normal. Before you vent your anger, take a moment to evaluate your current condition. Tell me how you really feel."

The Betazoid rubbed her neck where the drug entered her bloodstream and considered her friend's words. The truth was—she felt *better.* Her apprehension was gone. She didn't feel high or woozy, just more like herself. Automatically, she tried to probe

Crusher's feelings, but there was little there. She could sense something familiar, something that was Beverly, but her empathy was profoundly muted. And for some reason she found that fact oddly comforting. Her troubled mind was suddenly quieted, able to spend the time healing itself.

Reluctantly, Deanna said, "Actually, I do feel better. I feel calmer, more at ease with myself. And as you predicted, my empathic sense is strongly curbed. Normally, *that* would upset me, make me feel nonfunctional, but right now I'm happier this way. You were right, Beverly." She smiled wanly. "I guess that's why you're the doctor and I'm the counselor."

Data kept looking from one woman to the other, clearly confused. "Counselor, *are* you well enough to come to the captain's meeting?"

"Oh, yes," she assured him. "I'll be there, Commander."

"Would you like someone to wait for you while you change, Deanna?" Beverly offered.

"That's a good idea," Deanna said, then surprised the doctor by adding, "Data, would you mind?"

"Of course not, Counselor," the android replied.

Beverly nodded at the two of them. "That's better for me, actually," she said brightly, "since I need to have my autopsy report ready for the captain. See you later." But as she left, Deanna got the faintest sense of conflicting emotions in her friend, emotions she could not actually understand.

"Is everything all right with you and Dr. Crusher, Counselor?" Data asked quietly.

Deanna turned to him. His insight into human behavior patterns improved every day. She was not surprised that he noticed the tension between the two women.

"Everything's fine, Data," she insisted, with a forced smile. "Beverly and I are just having a small disagreement about a course of treatment. And, besides, after all the mental input I had to deal with yesterday, I thought it would be pleasant to spend some time with a strong silent type for a change." She patted his arm and went to change her clothes, leaving him in the living room with a very perplexed, human expression.

Chapter Eight

PICARD SAT IN HIS READY ROOM, mulling over Barbara Evans's autopsy results, along with Dr. Crusher's report regarding the other forensic material found in the ransacked Ten Forward.

The evidence was startling only in its absence. It would be bad enough, Picard knew, to have to break the news of Evans's death to her parents; how could he face that when he couldn't even tell them why or how? There had to be something in the reports, some key that would lead him to the truth.

"Bron to Captain Picard." It was a feminine voice. Jendar Bron was a second-year ensign currently manning communications.

"Yes, Ensign," Picard murmured, his eyes still focused on the horrific details of how Evans had met her end: shock, from blood loss and brutal trauma. Someone still aboard this vessel had stood by and watched.

"Sorry to disturb you, Captain, but I found something odd in the communication logs."

"What is it?" He finally glanced up, scowling. Protocol dictated that Bron should take her problem to Commander Riker. What was happening to the training on this ship, anyway?

Bron seemed to note his irritation; her tone grew even more hesitant and apologetic. "Captain, there's a message logged in from Starfleet Command, a library file. It's routed to you, but there's no record of your having received it. Have you been notified about this communiqué, sir?"

Picard sighed. "When did it come in?"

"Yesterday, sir. It was received as a priority message, but then rerouted into storage and given a low-priority status."

A sudden suspicion made him pause. "Send me the file now. I want to see it."

"Yes, sir."

He swiveled back toward his small console and watched as the Starfleet logo appeared, followed by the file heading. The stardate confirmed his suspicions. This was the file with the information about the epidemic.

"Who received this file when it came in, Ensign Bron?"

"That's the other odd thing, sir. There's no record of the recipient."

Impossible. Documentation on the receipt of a file was automatic. "Well, who was on duty when it came through the bridge?" They might be able to determine the original recipient.

"It doesn't appear that the file ever got to the bridge or that anyone here was even notified about it, Captain. It's as if the file was received by the ship's sensors, then automatically rerouted without anyone ever even seeing it. I accidentally found it because I was looking for a file requested by one of the scientists."

Picard stared at the message on his screen in disbelief. What Bron was telling him indicated deliberate tampering with Starfleet protocols and the central computer's responses to routine procedures.

"Thank you, Ensign, for bringing this to my attention. Good work." He sat back in his chair. He could have Data and La Forge run a complete level-one diagnostic on the ship, but he wasn't sure he could afford to devote that much time on this problem when the more immediate one seemed to be the random acts of violence occurring on the ship. He would have to talk to La Forge and Data after his meeting with the senior staff and see what they thought could be the cause. If it was sabotage, it would indicate the violence aboard ship might not be random at all.

"Ensign Bron," he said quietly.

"Yes, Captain."

"Please inform the senior staff that I'll be several minutes late for our meeting. Ask them to please wait."

"Aye, sir."

Crusher and La Forge stood conferring in the ready room and glanced up quickly—almost guiltily, Will thought—when Riker came in. He assumed they wanted a private moment with Picard, who normally arrived at meetings early. If that was the case, they were clearly out of luck.

"Have you received word about the captain's delay?" he asked.

"Just now," Geordi answered. "We thought since we were already here, we might as well wait."

Beverly looked up at Will's face curiously. "Commander, what's happened to your eye?" She reached for her medi-scanner as she approached him.

"My eye? Nothing, I hope," Riker said cheerily.

She peered into Riker's face a moment—he stood carefully still, gazing upward as she studied the affected eye—then clicked her tongue with doctorly concern. "Yes, definitely. You've got a broken blood vessel in your sclera."

"Really?" He shrugged. "I can't feel anything."

"No, you might not," she said solicitously, lifting the scanner toward his face. "Let me just make sure it's nothing more serious. It'll only take a minute to fix. Good thing the captain's late."

As Riker held still, permitting Crusher to steady his face with a skilled, delicate hand, he noticed an odd sight in his peripheral vision: La Forge, grinning with delight.

What's so funny about a broken blood vessel? Riker wondered, but put the distraction aside as Crusher ordered, "Now look straight into my eyes, Will."

He complied, but as his eyes met her soft brown ones, he found himself staring into them hypnotically, pulled in by her gaze. Her pupils expanded, glowing, swirling with shimmering colors—colors so beautiful, so mesmerizing, he wanted never to look away. He frowned, staring harder, just as her fingertips grazed his cheek, and a sudden sharp shock raced through his system.

When Picard finally entered the conference room, he did so just as Commander Data, Lieutenant Worf, and Counselor Troi were taking their seats. After a nodded acknowledgment to the crew, he moved to the head of the table. To his right, Will Riker sat, blinking and touching the corner of his eye; the commander seemed rather pale.

"Everything all right, Number One?"

Riker nodded and gave a rueful smile. "Broken blood vessel. Dr. Crusher just gave me a little medical aid. My vision's a little blurry, that's all."

"It'll pass in a moment," Crusher assured the captain.

Picard nodded. "Fine, then let's get down to the business at hand, shall we? And I'm sorry to say a bad business it is. I'd planned on briefing you with the autopsy results Dr. Crusher obtained and the information we might have received from trace evidence in Ten Forward. However, the reports contained little information to help us understand this perplexing tragedy." He turned to Crusher. "I assume you have nothing new to add?"

"No, sir. Not at this time."

"Well," Picard continued, "we may already have the critical information we need to get to the bottom of this dilemma. And that information has come from Starfleet."

"Then you have finally received the communiqué about the Vulcan epidemic?" Data asked.

"Correct," Picard told him. "You should know that the communiqué actually arrived yesterday, but was somehow rerouted and archived before I could see it." Intercepting Data before he could painstakingly explain why this was impossible, the captain held up a hand and continued. "As I suspected, the Federation was not nearly as circumspect as the Vulcan authorities, and there was a great deal more pertinent information about the epidemic in Starfleet's communiqué."

Picard glanced around the table, weighing what he was about to say to his staff. "Based on this information, combined with the data already provided by the Vulcans, I have reason to believe that the violence aboard the *Enterprise* marks the beginning stage of the same epidemic that so profoundly affected both a starship crew and the planet Vulcan eight decades earlier."

Crusher leaned forward on the table, her expression

one of confusion. "May I ask how you came to that conclusion, Captain?"

"From your autopsy report, Doctor," Picard explained, as he turned and brought up a display on the nearby terminal screen. "Eighty years ago the medical staff aboard the affected starship documented this very peculiar pattern of brain damage from both living and dead victims of the madness." He pointed to the multicolored image of a human brain. "You see there how the blue color resonates through the frontal lobes into the amygdala? Almost in a starburst pattern? Very unusual. In fact, the computer could not match this pattern with any other known malady involving the brain. It indicates a very specific progression of memory loss. Typically, victims of the disease, once cured, have no memory of the period during which they were infected."

Picard touched a control on the table that caused the screen to split and show another brain scan. "And here, from your autopsy information, Dr. Crusher, is the exact same pattern recorded from the brain of Barbara Evans. There is no doubt in my mind that Barbara Evans became infected by entities like those housed in the receptacles now in sickbay quarantine. The most likely scenario of her infection, is, obviously, through Skel, since she was his liaison officer. However she became infected, she's no doubt infected others through her everyday contact with members of the ship—including visiting scientists and their staff. The kind of senseless violence we saw in Ten Forward is typical of the disease's manifestation in its early stages."

"But, Captain," Beverly protested, "how could this happen? Skel passed every quarantine procedure we have. And you've talked to him yourself. He clearly is of sound mind and body."

"Must I remind you, Doctor," he said curtly, "of

Typhoid Mary? We cannot rule out the possibility that he is a carrier, either immune or simply unaware of what he carries."

"Excuse me, Captain," Commander La Forge spoke up, "but I checked the fail-safes on the quarantine unit myself. I don't see how Skel could've gotten a clear bill of health if he was infected with those organisms."

"This problem was faced by the infected starship crew as well," Picard explained. "They concluded that the organism was smaller than any they had ever before encountered—possibly the size of a subatomic particle or smaller. They are definitely smaller than anything the biofilters are calibrated to detect. During the original outbreak, neither the Federation crew nor the Vulcans were able to develop a test to determine whether or not a person was infected, and they never perfected a device that could detect the entities."

Picard glanced at Troi, seated near the end of the table. "However—and this is very interesting—the record keepers of the time noted that a *skilled, non-touch telepath* might have been helpful in diagnosing the disease as it claimed more and more members of the crew. Of course, this was before Betazed became a member of the Federation."

"Captain," Deanna interjected, "if you're thinking that I could have sensed Skel's harboring those entities, I must say I didn't sense them when he was in my presence. The only thing I could sense from him was the normal Vulcan controls, and flashes of the terrible memories he has."

"As I said," Picard reminded her, "if there is such a thing as a carrier state for this infection, Skel may be completely unaware of it. They may also be masking their presence from us through self-defense mechanisms the likes of which many diseases develop over time. Remember, the first exposure of humans and

Vulcans to these entities was eighty years ago. They may have evolved, grown adaptable, grown resistant—we just don't know enough."

"Well, you're right about that, Captain," Beverly agreed mildly. "Even with the information from Starfleet, we don't know enough about this epidemic from eighty years ago. Certainly not enough to assume that Skel reintroduced an infection we don't even know if we have!"

Picard looked at her thoughtfully. "You may be correct, Dr. Crusher; however, considering the importance of the visitors we have aboard the ship and the charge we hold for ensuring the safety of the crew, I feel we must act now."

Worf sat forward. "If you are saying, sir, that Counselor Troi is able to detect the affected victims with her empathic sense, can she not simply scan the crew and tell us whether anyone is infected?"

Picard turned to Troi as she said, "It's very likely. However, due to the agitated state I found myself in after probing the alien artifacts, Dr. Crusher has given me a drug to blunt my empathic sense. Right now, the few readings I am getting are quite muted. I doubt if I could act very effectively as a diagnostician."

"How long will this drug last on the counselor?" Picard asked Crusher.

"Twenty-four hours," Beverly responded. "However, I administered the drug due to Deanna's depletion of a specific neurotransmitter. If that condition continues, she will need the muting drug again tomorrow."

"I understand and applaud your concern for the counselor's health, Doctor," Picard said quietly. "However, under the circumstances, I would ask you to hold off administering that drug until you've conferred with me. We may have no choice but to enlist the counselor's aid in determining whether or not the *Enterprise* is infected."

"Aye, sir," Crusher said meekly, but it was clear she didn't like the order.

"Mr. Worf," Picard said, "regarding Skel—I believe it is in our best interests to request he once again resume his residency in the quarantine unit. I'll explain this to him myself after our meeting. I'd like you to accompany him to sickbay, but under no circumstances are you to permit any physical contact between you, nor are you to meet him eye-to-eye. Physical and eye contact are both critical in the transference of these entities, and we have no way of knowing what their effect would be on a Klingon metabolism." It was a notion Picard didn't care to consider at the moment.

"Aye, sir," Worf agreed.

"It may be safe to assume that Mr. Data may be the only member of the crew immune from these entities," Picard told them, "though I can't guarantee that."

Data nodded. "Theoretically, you are probably correct. My optic nerves are more mechanical than organic, and organic optic nerves appear to be critical for transference. Even if I could be infected, my lack of emotional response might be, for once, a distinct advantage. Once within my positronic network, the entities would no doubt starve to death."

Picard nodded. "The next problem we must consider is the Vulcan science vessel, *Skal Torr.* She will be arriving here within ten hours. We can still advise her to return home. I hesitate involving the Vulcans in this, especially when you consider how profoundly they were affected by this same disease years ago."

"Excuse me, sir, but the Vulcans have come a long way to be told to go home again," Riker said. "And suppose the entities aren't on board? Counselor Troi has impressed upon me the importance of getting those artifacts off this ship. For all we know, their very presence could be what's affecting Deanna. If so, she might not recover until they're removed. I don't think warding the Vulcans off at this stage is our best move."

"Just how did the starship crew cope with the infection when it appeared on their ship?" Worf asked.

"They discovered the entities could literally be starved to death," Picard explained. "They require almost continual feeding unless they're in stasis confinement, such as the artifacts provide. Their feeding is what causes their host to act violently, and the more violence and strong emotions the host experiences, the more feeding his entities can enjoy, which is why the violence always escalates. The crew anesthetized the entire ship with a gas inhalant that put everyone to sleep for twenty-eight hours. This caused the entities to starve and die. When the inhalant wore off, the crew was cured—and all displayed the sort of memory-loss pattern that appeared in Ensign Evans's brain scan. I considered trying that again, but we don't have twenty-eight hours to spare. The Vulcans will be here in ten."

"I might have a solution," Crusher chimed in. "Technology has improved in the last eighty years. We could anesthetize the crew successfully while at the same time adding a compatible compound that would accelerate everyone's metabolism so that their bodies would literally speed up, shortening the amount of time we'd need to keep them under."

"How much time would we need to sleep?" Picard asked.

"I'd have to calculate several variabilities to take into consideration the alien metabolisms on board, but I suspect I could collapse the time needed down to as little as four hours."

"Excellent!" Picard said. "Number One, I'll leave it to you to coordinate the shipwide shutdown of all unnecessary activities for this period. You'll need to notify team leaders, liaison officers, and family group leaders so that everyone is prepared for the shutdown. Normally, I would ask Counselor Troi to assist you; however, considering her need for recovery, I think it best she uses this time to do just that."

"Yes, sir," Riker agreed. Troi nodded at the same time.

"Dr. Crusher, when you have the anesthetic and the accelerator prepared, I'll make a general announcement." Picard looked around the table. "We have one other advantage those suffering from the first outbreak of the infection didn't have: Mr. Data, who can safeguard the ship while we are indisposed, and who can have in his possession the computer code for the antidote should we need to be roused quickly for an emergency."

"Captain," Data interjected, "are you sure this is necessary? It is only speculation that the entities have infected anyone. Lieutenant La Forge and I could work on recalibrating a portable medical scanner to detect memory-loss patterns based on the information you have just shown us, while Dr. Crusher goes through the Federation communiqué to see if she can find a more medical approach to a cure.

"If Barbara Evans was the sole person infected by these entities, and if she, in turn, infected only one out of five people she came in contact with, and then, they in turn infected only one out of five people—"

"That's still a great many people!" Deanna agreed.

"Data's question is valid," Picard agreed. "And I think that he and Mr. La Forge should work on such a scanner. However, you must realize that type of scanner will not tell us if we have an active infection—only if the person showing the appropriate pattern *had been* infected. We will need something to help us determine if, after the anesthetic wears off, we have indeed destroyed these entities."

Picard grew more somber as he addressed the

central issue of Data's question. "I want you all to understand the seriousness of this threat. Before I would let this ship dock at the TechnoFair and risk loosing the entities upon the most diverse group of Federation members ever to assemble, I would destroy her first with all hands aboard. Is that clear?"

"Very," said Will Riker.

Lieutenant Worf strode down the corridors of Deck Five. Despite his admonition to himself, he could not help peering suspiciously at every crew member who passed. Was Ensign Meyers infected? He seemed quite preoccupied. What about Lieutenant Mata? She would not meet his eyes. He forced himself to stop this fruitless analyzing and tend to the task at hand.

At least he'd had a chance to contact Alexander and tell him about the four hours he would be unconscious. Worf's son had always understood his responsibilities as a member of the ship and took them seriously. He'd seen numerous shipboard emergencies. And he was a Klingon—he would not panic, but weather the storm just as his father expected him to.

Worf wasn't surprised to find Alexander still in Kyla's company. He expressed concern to the boy that he was imposing on the woman, but Kyla herself insisted he was "assisting" her in her experiments. Worf was proud of Alexander's interest in science, and—after a moment's paranoia that Kyla might be infected, and thus in danger of infecting his son—was secretly pleased that the human warrior woman would be with the boy when they were forced to sleep. While Alexander was fully capable of taking care of himself, Worf felt better knowing a battle-ready adult would be with him.

Finally, the Klingon slowed his quiet steps as he found himself before the Vulcan's quarters. While Vulcans were normally a people of peace, their physical strength was great. Worf ground his teeth in an effort to repress a smile. If the Vulcan resisted, it would be a *glorious* fight!

He rang the door chime, then heard Skel's placid voice: "Enter."

The Klingon stepped through the yielding doors and found himself facing Skel, who stood in the center of the room—carry bag slung over his shoulders, hands inside his sleeves—as if he wished to present the most passive appearance possible. Beside him, Dr. Tarmud stood, frowning and defiant.

"I have just spoken with Captain Picard," Skel said quietly. "He has explained the need for my return to quarantine isolation. I have gathered my work and am prepared to go."

Worf repressed a sigh of consummately Klingon disappointment. "Thank you, sir. If you will come with—"

"And I must protest!" Tarmud interrupted vehemently. "This is nonsense, taking this man away from our work! I'm telling you, you're barking up the wrong tree!"

Worf's brow furrowed at the unfamiliar colloquialism. Why would a Klingon want to bark at any tree?

"Please, Doctor," Skel said reasonably, turning to his friend. "We can communicate via computer console and continue our work. You cannot imagine the devastation the entities can cause. If they are concerned they are responsible for the death of my liaison officer, it is only logical that I cooperate. I have spent my life working on this very problem."

"If you insist," Tarmud grumbled, but his expression remained reluctant.

"I will contact you as soon as I am able," Skel assured him, and walked out of the quarters to accompany Worf to sickbay.

The one thing Worf appreciated about Vulcans was their disinclination to prattle, so it surprised him when, in the turbolift, Skel said conversationally, "Are you aware, Lieutenant, that we have no knowledge of the entities' effect on Klingon physiology?"

Worf kept his gaze fixed on the seam in the lift doors. "Yes, sir, I am aware of that."

"I, for one, cannot imagine what would happen should a Klingon be infected by an entity who must feed on the most primal and savage emotions, the most powerful feelings. Can you?"

Worf glanced sideways at his charge, wondering why Skel would ask him this question. "No, sir, I cannot."

"These entities were created as a weapon of war, Lieutenant," Skel remarked. "Can you imagine the devastation they must have wrought when released on the enemy side? Within a day, perhaps, or at the most two, the entire army would be infected, fighting among themselves wildly, slaughtering one another to feed their opponent's creatures."

Worf could repress neither the surge of anger that rose within him at the thought, nor the growl that emerged unbidden from the back of his throat. "That is not warfare. That is slaughter. There is no way I can imagine such a *dishonorable* way to defeat your enemy. It is beyond my imagination."

"I suspect it was beyond its creators' as well," Skel said mildly. "For there is no doubt that the entities they were so clever to develop devoured them as well as their enemy."

That pleased Worf, in an odd way, that such a dishonorable people would have caused their own destruction. The turbolift came to a halt, and the two men proceeded to sickbay.

Once there, they joined Dr. Crusher and Captain Picard.

"I appreciate your cooperation in this matter," Picard said cordially.

"I think you all know my opinion of this," Dr. Crusher complained, her tone one of uncharacteristic irritability. Worf was surprised at her bluntness, but he knew the medical officer was permitted a frankness that was not acceptable in other positions.

"The quarantine unit is ready," Dr. Crusher explained. "Once Skel steps inside it, it will seal automatically." She faced the Vulcan. "Your computer and the other things you requested are already inside. We've tried to make it as comfortable as we could. Now, if you gentlemen will excuse me, I need to prepare for our shipwide shutdown."

All three men nodded as Dr. Crusher left the room. Worf's eyes followed her as she began working on a computer program in the next room. Near her stood an antigrav cart loaded with ten large canisters designed to hold compressed gas. The silver canisters were color-coded: one group blue, one yellow to mark those which carried the anesthetic and the accelerator.

"I will enter the quarantine unit now, Captain," Skel said, pulling Worf's attention back. "I leave it to you and your capable crew to determine when I might be released."

"Thank you, Skel," Captain Picard said, as the Vulcan entered through the doorway in the transparent aluminum walls. Once inside, Skel went about removing his research materials from his carry bag as the doors sealed shut behind him. Worf watched Picard check the monitoring devices, assuring himself that all was in order.

"Captain, will I be stationed here during the shipwide shutdown?" Worf asked privately. He would prefer to be with his son, but knew that was unlikely.

Picard looked up as if about to answer him, then hesitated. Suddenly, frowning, the captain turned instead to stare at the Vulcan, who was still unpacking in the quarantine unit, oblivious to Picard's attention. The captain gave his head an odd little shake, then turned back to Worf.

"Mr. Worf, did you hear that?"

"Hear what, sir?" The security chief had a sudden flash of concern—could the *captain* be infected? His body tensed, preparing for conflict.

But Picard's expression was merely apologetic. "Excuse me, Mr. Worf; I was distracted. You were asking about your station during the shutdown. I think it would be a good idea if you would remain here in sickbay when . . ."

He trailed off, turning again to stare in disbelief at Skel. This time the Vulcan paused and looked up to return the captain's gaze blankly; clearly, something passed between the two men.

Worf grew seriously concerned now. "Captain Picard, what is it? Are you well?" He opened his mouth to call Dr. Crusher, who still stood with her back to them, completely unaware of Picard and Skel's scrutiny as she worked at her console.

But before the Klingon could react, Picard uttered a phrase in Vulcan, then spun about, seized Crusher by the shoulders, and threw her from the console.

"Mr. Worf! Help me stop her!"

Worf crouched, ready for battle—but hesitated: Should he subdue Dr. Crusher . . . or the captain, whose sudden behavior seemed irrational?

He paused no more than a heartbeat, enough time for Crusher to spin on the balls of her feet and slam Picard to the deck with a single brutal blow to the side of his head. And then—easily, dispassionately—she returned to her work as though the act of knocking down her captain was a small thing.

"Stop her, Worf!" Picard ordered groggily as he rolled to his knees. "She's infected—that's not Beverly! Stop her before she initiates the programming!"

With a roar, the Klingon grabbed Crusher's shoulders and pulled her from the console. Serpentine, she wriggled in his grasp and spun about, at the same time—impossibly—breaking free from him. She drew back a long leg and aimed a high kick at Worf's head; he caught her heel and yanked her body up, forward.

She fell on her back, hard enough to have knocked the wind from the real Crusher's lungs, yet she never paused. Still flat on the deck, she planted her other foot in the Klingon's sternum and flipped him over her head easily.

He rolled and came up on his feet, but she was already up and struck his face: once, twice, three times, with inhuman strength and a preternatural speed that left him no time to block the blows. He roared with pain and rage.

He tackled her once more, knocking her small, delicately human body to the deck. With peripheral awareness, he heard Picard calling for Data, shouting orders, demanding a sedative for Crusher while Ogawa scrambled to comply.

Success: Worf managed to pin her to the ground. She wrestled wildly, viciously, so determined that he had difficulty holding her down—but he could not bring himself to strike her. No matter what was happening to her mind, the body was still Crusher's and would have to be functional when she was cured. He feared inflicting serious damage—damage that might remain after the entities had gone.

She, however, had no such qualms.

She buried her elbow in his gut; he grunted, handling the blow he had anticipated, grimacing at the pain in his shins as she pounded against them with her heel.

And then she wriggled in his arms, twisting so that they were face-to-face. The sudden encounter startled him, and she used his disorientation to pull an arm free and pull his face toward hers.

"Don't look in her eyes! Mr. Worf—don't look!"

In the rage of battle, Worf scarcely registered the captain's shouts; his gaze met hers full on.

"Mr. Worf—!"

Brightness in her eyes: shooting sparks, like the colored embers from a raging fire. Worf shuddered as a shock coursed down his neck, his spine, into his limbs.

The sensation only served to infuriate him further. He roared a Klingon war cry; Crusher echoed it just as fiercely. The shouts faded into the small soft sound of a hiss. . . .

Abruptly, the swirling sparks in her eyes dimmed, then disappeared beneath pale lids; Crusher sagged in his arms. He looked up to see Ogawa, hypospray in hand.

Gasping for air, he rose, lifting the unconscious woman in his arms, and carried her tenderly to a nearby diagnostic bed.

"Lieutenant Worf," Picard whispered, and the Klingon looked up to see the captain and Ogawa watching him warily. Ogawa recoiled physically from him, clearly afraid.

"Yes, Captain."

Picard's expression was grim. "I believe Dr. Crusher has infected you."

Worf blinked, and took inventory of his faculties. He remembered now—remembered the eye contact, her touching his face, and the shock. He saw the nurse staring at a scanner, as if that could possibly help. Picard had already explained to them that there was currently no way to determine if someone was infected or not. "Captain, I know I was exposed, I did feel a shock, but I feel completely normal. You cannot mean to incarcerate me in quarantine when the ship is in danger?" The very thought humiliated the warrior.

"That wouldn't be my first choice," Picard admitted, glancing at Ogawa as if reaching for a confirmation he knew she could not give him.

The nurse raised her dark eyebrows. "Well, sir, his readouts are normal—for a Klingon in battle rage!"

"Could he be immune?" Picard wondered.

"Ask *him,"* Worf said, indicating Skel. It did not surprise the Klingon to see the Vulcan watching emotionlessly all that had transpired. "It is a subject he speculated on as we traveled here."

Picard lifted a skeptical eyebrow, but said nothing; clearly, he did not trust Skel enough to ask him anything. Instead, he turned to the Klingon. "She was sabotaging the shutdown," he said, with a nod at Crusher's unconscious form. "She was programming for the four-hour sleep, but there would have been no accelerator added. The entities would've survived if she'd succeeded."

"Captain, *how did you know?"* Worf wondered aloud. Picard's deduction seemed nothing less than mystical to him.

The captain's expression grew decidedly sheepish. "I hesitate to say, Lieutenant, lest you think I've been victimized by these entities myself." He glanced back toward Skel's quarantine unit, then said softly, "It happened while we were standing near him, when you began asking me about your assignment. All of a sudden, I heard my mother saying, 'Never trust doctors!' "

Worf couldn't hide his surprise and concern over the captain's mental state.

Picard nodded, as if understanding. "I know, it sounds quite insane. But that was one of her favorite bromides when she was asked how she achieved her long life. 'Never trust doctors!' I heard it as clearly as if she were standing beside me, in her crisp, perfect French, with her precise inflection, her acerbic wit. I tried to ignore it, fearing I might be hallucinating, but she kept repeating it, once, twice, three times—then suddenly she said in crystal clear *Vulcan:* 'Jean-Luc, don't trust your doctor!' I was overwhelmed with the need—the *compulsion*—to check Dr. Crusher's work."

"Klingons have many legends about great warriors hearing those who have gone on before them while in the heat of battle, but—"

"If you knew my mother, Mr. Worf, you'd know she well qualifies there." Any trace of good humor vanished at once as Picard gazed down at his chief medical officer. "There can be no doubt anymore: We have an infection aboard this ship." He lifted his face, scowling. "Where the hell is Data? He's the only one we can trust now to manage this shipwide shutdown."

"Geordi," Data said patiently, "I fail to understand your reluctance to test out a possible containment field for the entities. Since we know that the artifacts' forcefield cycles like a subspace sensor grid, we should be able to construct a receptacle that will secure the entities safely."

"I just think you're putting the cart before the horse, Data," Geordi insisted, his tone strained. "What good does it do us to create a holding pen when we haven't figured out how to get the things in there?"

"That is a valid point," Data allowed. He decided not to remind Geordi that when the android had attempted to theorize ways to disable the entities and render them harmless, Geordi found a way to deny the possibility of each and every theory. And when Data attempted to analyze the various ways they might safely exorcise the entities from their living hosts, Geordi found ways to deny those possibilities as well.

Ever since the meeting with Picard, one thing had

been troubling Data—one thing he decided not to discuss with his closest friend—and now Geordi's strange, uncooperative behavior only added to his concern. Ever since the meeting, Data had been analyzing and reanalyzing one issue: how Picard's communiqué from Starfleet had avoided all the normal protocols and computer relays to be shunted into storage.

It had been cleverly accomplished. Had the perpetrator tried to force the computer to destroy the message, dozens of fail-safes would have alerted the crew. By simply rerouting it to the destination it would inevitably occupy—archives—instead, the conspirator almost guaranteed the message would never be seen. It was sheer luck—a random series of events in one's favor that Data didn't believe in—that an ensign would see the communiqué and realize it might not have been seen.

But luck hadn't caused the computer to act as though it had; that had been a deliberate act of sabotage. And only two officers aboard the *Enterprise* were capable of reprogramming the computer on that level: Commander La Forge and Data himself.

"Geordi," Data said reluctantly, knowing that La Forge would merely present one obstacle after another to his work, "I must ask you something."

La Forge faced him, his face nearly expressionless behind his VISOR.

"I have analyzed this situation as thoroughly as I can, and I have come to the conclusion that you are responsible for reprogramming the computers so that the captain would not receive his communiqué from Starfleet. What I cannot determine is *why.*"

La Forge's expression never changed as he said easily, "That's crazy, Data. Why would I reprogram the computers to do something so strange?"

Why indeed? Data wondered, but he already suspected he knew. "The only possible reason would be to prevent the captain from discovering more information on the infectious entities."

His android eyes could see far better than Geordi's VISOR could. In fact, Data knew his eyes could see far better than the more organic eyes that Dr. Tarmud was constructing. They would have the limited vision of true human eyes. Human eyes would have missed the nearly imperceptible flush of Geordi's skin, and the slight tightening of his muscles. Stress reactions, Data knew.

"Data, we don't have time to play Sherlock Holmes right now," Geordi grumbled.

The android was about to respond when his comm badge signaled. "Commander Data! This is Captain Picard! We have an emergency in sickbay! Report here at once."

Data made a slight, barely perceptible move to rise; when he did, Geordi swung.

Data's reflexes were too quick, of course; he simply reached out, easily capturing the fist before it touched his face. Irrationally, La Forge swung the other; again, the android caught it with little effort.

Around them, personnel stopped to watch the bizarre nonbattle as the chief engineer attempted to attack Data, who never budged from his seat despite the considerable force the human exerted against him—too much force, Data knew, for a normal human.

"Geordi, please stop this. You will only harm yourself," he warned, but La Forge was crazed, shrieking, clawing, punching wildly—all of the blows having absolutely no effect.

Then Data realized the other crew members weren't just watching in amazement—they were *reacting,* moving closer, their expressions revealing frank appetite.

They were *feeding* off La Forge's uncontrolled rage.

"I am very sorry about this, Geordi," Data said to the raging engineer, then, as carefully as possible, struck him on the chin. As La Forge collapsed in Data's arms, the android swung his friend over his shoulder, then turned to address the other crew members he knew now were as infected as La Forge, yet under momentary control. "Return to your stations," he said to them calmly, "and await further orders."

And as calmly as if he always carried an unconscious friend over his shoulder through the halls of the huge ship, Data made his way to the turbolift. When he told the lift where to take him, he wondered if the orders the engineering crew awaited were from Captain Picard or from some other more malevolent authority.

"Commander Data!" Picard snapped into the intercom. "Report to sickbay at once!" No sooner did the last words leave him than the doors to sickbay opened and Data marched in—carrying the ship's chief engineer.

"Damn," Picard groaned, as Worf accompanied Data to the quarantine unit where they'd placed the unconscious doctor, "La Forge, too!"

"I am afraid so, sir. He sabotaged our attempts to construct diagnostic tools and capture devices, then attacked me as soon as you summoned me here."

Worf quickly explained to the android what had transpired with the doctor.

"Well, at least we have two proven test cases right here," Picard said, looking at his unconscious officers.

"I will be able to test them for the patterned memory loss after the shipwide shutdown," Data confirmed.

"We need more than that," Picard complained. "We need something that will tell us if one can be a carrier, or if one currently harbors the entities. From what we've seen here, the entities have become far better at masking their possession of the host."

"I agree," Data said, and told Picard about the reaction to Geordi's violence from the engineering crew.

"Will you be able to manage the anesthesia of the ship, and the addition of the accelerator, Data?" Picard asked.

Data moved over to the console where Crusher had attempted to sabotage the programming. His long nimble fingers flew over the board faster than Picard could follow. Then, in his usual blithe way, he assured his captain, "Yes, sir. I will be able to manage this alone. The system is completely ready. May I suggest you make your announcement to the crew, then find a comfortable spot to recline."

"An excellent idea, Data," Picard agreed. "Make it so. Worf will assist you. Mr. Data, you literally have the conn."

Chapter Nine

PICARD OPENED HIS EYES to an expanse of ceiling draped in the soft muted lighting of sickbay and drew in a breath. The deep soundless sleep had left him rested, and the anesthetic had passed cleanly through his system, leaving his mind clear to form its first waking thought:

The entities . . .

He pushed himself onto his elbows. A few meters away, Data stood with his back to him before Skel's quarantine chamber, scanning the Vulcan with a tricorder; Worf stood beside the android, eyeing the readout. Behind the transparent walls, Skel sat in dignified repose upon his cot, awake and cognizant.

"Data?" Picard cleared his dry throat. "Lieutenant Worf?"

The android turned. "Good news, sir. The drugs appear to have been successful. The entire crew—and all passengers—have been unconscious for the past four hours, and I have discovered some extremely interesting readings."

Picard sat up and slid his legs off the side of the cot. In the quarantine chamber next to Skel's, both Beverly and Geordi were beginning to stir.

"Jean-Luc?" Beverly smoothed a palm over her forehead as she sat on her cot.

"What sort of interesting readings?" Picard demanded, just as Geordi called out:

"Yeah, Data . . . what're we *doing* here?"

Data stepped toward the chamber shared by the doctor and engineer. "You have been invaded by entities that Skel apparently brought aboard the ship." He then faced Picard and gestured at the tricorder. "According to my readouts, both Dr. Crusher and Geordi have aged—mentally and physically—twenty-eight hours rather than four; the accelerator functioned as planned. As far as the body—and the entities—are concerned, the required time to starve the infection has passed."

Within the chamber, Geordi slid off the cot and stepped to the transparent wall that held him inside. "Data, are you saying that *we* were infected with the madness?"

"I am afraid so."

La Forge let go a long slow gust of air. "I don't remember it at all. The last thing I knew, I was talking to Skel . . ."

"And I was performing a last-minute check on the artifacts before going off duty." Beverly rose, groaning, and rubbed her neck and shoulders. "Good Lord, that's some infection. I feel like I was trampled by a herd of wildebeests."

Picard permitted himself a small smile of relief at the sight of Crusher, back to normal. "Actually, Doctor, the herd consisted of a single Klingon."

Worf lowered his gaze, clearly abashed.

Beverly straightened and shot first the captain, then Worf, a sharply quizzical look; abruptly, her curiosity turned to alarm. "If we really were infected, then—Jean-Luc, I didn't hurt anyone, did I?"

"Of course not," he reassured her, resisting the impulse to smile at the Klingon's discomfort. "Although you *did* briefly present Mr. Worf with a . . . security challenge."

As the captain spoke, Data moved over to Skel's quarantine chamber; Picard rose and went to stand beside the android, who proffered him the tricorder to study.

"As you can see, sir," Data murmured, directing both their attentions to the readout screen, "here are the results of Dr. Crusher's brain scan. It exhibits the starburst pattern indicative of memory loss. Commander La Forge exhibited an almost identical pattern. However . . ."

He swung about to scan the silent, unprotesting Vulcan once more, then showed the result to Picard. "What I do not understand is the pattern Skel exhibits. Here you can see a vague starburst pattern—not the same as Dr. Crusher's, since Vulcan patterns are markedly different from human. It still indicates minor memory loss. But I am also detecting a rather unusual reading of electrical activity . . ."

Picard scowled at the readout, then drew back, suspicious. "The entities?"

"Not necessarily, sir—" Data began, but the Vulcan at last broke his silence to interrupt:

"Or perhaps the trauma I underwent as a child."

Picard shot him a skeptical glance, but Data nodded.

"That's quite possible, Captain. These readings are not inconsistent with severe childhood trauma."

"But could it possibly indicate that he was—or still is—a carrier?"

Data tilted his head, thoughtful. "That is also

possible, sir, but I can neither confirm it nor rule it out. Certainly, the information we have on the outbreak of eighty years ago never mentioned the presence of carriers."

"That doesn't mean that they didn't exist, or couldn't evolve over almost a century's time," Picard persisted.

"True," Data agreed. "Although I cannot ascertain whether Skel is a carrier at the moment, I *did* use the past four hours to do some research which might help us." He pointed over at the lab counter, where a familiar-looking device rested. "I have been working on a version of Geordi's VISOR which can conclusively detect the frequency of the entities. With it, we would be able to actually 'see' them and know whether someone harbors the infection."

Softly, so as not to offend the Vulcan, Picard asked, "You mean, in eighty years, no one ever developed a way—"

Data shook his head. "No, sir. It was never needed, as the entities were contained behind multiple forcefields."

"I see." Picard released a breath of pure gratitude that, save for Barbara Evans, his crew had apparently been spared; yet he could not permit himself to relax completely, not until the entities were off his ship. "We need the device as soon as possible, Data. The Vulcans will be here in fewer than six hours."

Data glanced at La Forge, who stood eagerly at the entrance to his quarantine chamber. "I am not sure I can meet that deadline without assistance," the android said. "But now that Geordi is himself, we might be able to have a prototype ready for you within a few hours."

"You bet, sir," La Forge said. "Just give me the chance . . ."

Picard studied Crusher and La Forge for an uncertain moment; they both appeared to be perfectly themselves—a gratifying sight. Even so, he turned to Data and asked softly, "You're absolutely *sure,* Commander, that these people are no longer infected?"

"I monitored the dosages of the accelerator and anesthetic myself, sir. If the records from the original outbreak are correct, then we have met the conditions for the cure."

"Very well. Release the doctor and Mr. La Forge," Picard said with a sigh. "I want you and Geordi to get right to work."

Data moved to a control panel on the bulkhead and fingered it briefly; there came a soft hum, then both Crusher and La Forge emerged from the chamber.

Unsmiling, still massaging her neck, Beverly moved stiffly over to the android and Picard—and the still-sheepish Klingon, who avoided her gaze. "How's the crew? Were others infected? Anyone hurt?"

"According to my preliminary sensor scans," Data replied, "approximately twenty-five percent of the crew was infected."

"Twenty-five percent," Picard whispered, repressing a shudder at the narrowly avoided tragedy, then drew himself back to the present. "As for Skel, Commander Data . . . I don't like that irregular readout. Unless you can guarantee me it's the result of a childhood trauma—"

Next to Picard, Worf growled softly, "Do not trust him, Captain. He has already caused the death of a—"

Picard silenced him with a wave.

Behind his transparent prison, the Vulcan still sat cross-legged upon his cot, as though already resigned to remain there. "If you are going to suggest that I remain in quarantine, Captain, I quite agree with your chief of security. You cannot further endanger your crew on my behalf."

"It would be wise, sir," Data seconded.

Picard faced the Vulcan, his sympathy for Skel warring with his fury at the entities that had been brought aboard the *Enterprise.* "I apologize for the inconvenience again, Skel, but frankly—I'm considering turning you over along with the artifacts to the Vulcan ship. I have a crew to worry about, and I must also consider all those attending the TechnoFair."

Skel gave a single gracious nod, managing to utterly suppress what Picard expected was a surge of deep disappointment. "I admit that I would prefer to continue on to the TechnoFair, as I have spent a full year preparing for it . . . but I will yield to your judgment."

"Speaking of the Vulcans, sir . . ." Data interrupted, continuing only when the captain turned and looked pointedly at him. "While everyone else was unconscious and I was busy monitoring the anesthetic procedure, the ship received an incoming message from the Vulcan ship *Skal Torr.* They encouraged us to keep the artifacts under strict quarantine and requested confirmation of the rendezvous time and site."

Picard released a sigh, but before he could mentally address the issue of the Vulcans, Worf addressed him: "Sir. With your permission, I will go to security to debrief my people, after which I would like to return to my quarters to check on my son."

As the Klingon finished speaking, Picard's communicator signaled. "Permission granted, Mr. Worf," the captain replied, then pressed his comm badge.

"Picard."

"Riker here. Sir, what the hell's going on? I just woke up on the bridge with no idea how I got here. No one else here seems to know what just happened either."

Picard permitted himself only a fleeting second's

chill at the realization that his second-in-command had been affected. "There was an outbreak, Will—and apparently you and the bridge crew were infected."

He could hear Riker's sharp intake of breath. "You mean the madness from the Vulcan artifacts?"

"I'm afraid so. We were forced to anesthetize everyone and starve the entities. According to Mr. Data, one of the side effects of the cure is memory loss."

A long pause followed; at last, Riker drew in another breath and began to reply, but Picard cut him off.

"Report to my ready room immediately, Number One. The Vulcans will be here in a matter of hours, and we've got to decide what to tell them."

For the first time since the artifacts' arrival on the *Enterprise,* Deanna Troi woke from a dreamless sleep feeling lighthearted; the terror that had so dominated her conscious and dreaming moments had blessedly ceased. She allowed herself the luxurious sensation of stretching, then propped herself up and reached for the comm badge beside the bed.

"Troi to sickbay."

The response was reassuringly immediate, the familiar voice's tone reassuringly calm and professional. "Sickbay. Nurse Ogawa here."

"Alyssa! How did everything go?"

"Exactly as planned, Counselor. It turns out approximately one-fourth of the crew, including Dr. Crusher and Commander Riker, were infected. But the scans show that they're all right now."

Deanna mentally recoiled as she recalled the incident with Beverly, injecting her—

So that I couldn't sense them. But Will—my God, Will spent the night *here . . .*

She shook her head gently as if to dislodge the unpleasant thought. No, Will hadn't been possessed by the entities then; she had sensed only protectiveness and caring from him.

"So they're all right?"

"Just fine," Ogawa soothed, reacting to the undercurrent of fear in Troi's tone. "Dr. Crusher is busy examining patients at the moment, and I think Commander Riker is meeting with the captain."

"And . . . Skel?" For some reason, the thought of the Vulcan still troubled her. If he had been infected, *why* hadn't she been able to sense it? And why had he remained so calm? According to Skel, the madness had transformed normally stoic Vulcans into homicidal killers.

"Skel's still under quarantine."

"Really? Why?"

"Unusual brain scans. He seems perfectly normal otherwise; it's just a precaution. But the captain has ordered him to remain in quarantine until further notice." Ogawa's tone abruptly changed. "Dr. Crusher says to tell you that, physically, twenty-eight hours have passed for you, so all drugs—including the neurotransmitter blocker—have passed out of your system. She'd like for you to report to sickbay as soon as possible, so she can make sure you're doing okay."

Troi smiled to herself, happy at the thought that Beverly was herself once more, and concerned about Deanna. "Tell her—"

The communicator signaled again before she could finish the sentence.

"Picard here. Counselor, how are you feeling?"

Her smile widened. "Quite well, sir, thank you. And you?"

"Let's just say I'm greatly relieved." He paused. "Commander Riker and I are meeting in my ready room shortly to prepare a statement for the Vulcans.

If you're sure you're feeling well, your input would be invaluable."

"Of course, Captain. I'll be there in ten minutes. Troi out."

She rose and went to her closet, the sense of relief so deep she felt almost giddy. Still smiling, she slid aside the closet door, reached for a fresh uniform—

And screamed when her fingers brushed Lwaxana's bruised, bloodied face.

They're not gone! Oh God, child, they're not gone! RUN!

"Will," Picard said by way of welcome as Riker entered the ready room. Though neither smiled—the situation was far too serious for it—the captain felt a profound sense of gratitude to have his first officer on his side again. Will was a formidable friend . . . and would no doubt have proven a formidable enemy.

Clearly, the thought had occurred to Riker as well; his boyish, bearded face was grim, vaguely troubled. "Sir," he replied, and, at Picard's gesture, sat on the nearby couch. Behind his desk, Picard swiveled in his chair to face his second-in-command squarely.

"Counselor Troi will be joining us in approximately ten minutes; in the meantime, I wanted to discuss the situation with the Vulcans."

"I take it they're still on their way?"

Picard gave a slow deliberate nod. "They are. But during the four hours we were unconscious, the ship's computer received a communication from them, exhorting us to keep the artifacts under strict containment—and requesting verification of the rendezvous time and coordinates. I'd like your opinion—and Counselor Troi's—on how we should respond to them. Frankly, my instinct is to tell them to remain a respectable distance away and beam both Skel and his artifacts over to their ship."

A crease formed on the smooth skin between Riker's brown eyebrows. "But, sir, I'm sure Skel views the TechnoFair as a once-in-a-lifetime opportunity to share his work. To deny him that . . ."

"Would be to prevent the infection's spread to the very best minds in the galaxy, Will. Commander Data discovered some unusual electrical readings in Skel's brain scans—as if some other form of energy coexisted there."

"And there's no chance this energy reading might be due to something other than the entities?"

Picard tilted his head to one side, neither denying nor affirming. "Possibly. But you'll have to come up with some very sound arguments, Commander, to convince me to keep him as a passenger aboard this ship."

"I see." Riker lowered his gaze, considering this a moment, then lifted it again. "You know, I was told that I attended a conference on the information we received from Starfleet about the infection."

"That's true, Will."

"But—this is very strange—I have no memory whatsoever of the information discussed there. In order to be of use to you in this discussion, it would help me to understand what you mean about Skel's brain scans being unusual. Any chance I could take a look at them?"

"Of course." Picard swiveled toward his terminal, fingered a few controls, and an image coalesced on the small screen. He swung it toward Riker so that the first officer could better see it. Nonchalantly, Will rose and parked one hip on the captain's desk to better study the image.

It was a three-dimensional scan of *Riker, William T.*'s brain, called up from sickbay's directory of patient files. Deep within the brain's core was the bright blue starburst pattern; Picard traced the deadly blossom with a finger. "Let me show you your own scans—which are normal for someone who was once infected by the entities. The bright blue here has tracked the areas of your memory loss. . . ."

"I'll buy that," Riker said easily, leaning forward to better see the viewer; he finally reached to pull the screen toward him—or so Picard thought.

Instead, he caught Picard's wrist. Astonished, the captain glanced up—

Into Riker's clear blue eyes, eyes that loomed so large that for an instant they filled Picard's entire universe with a brilliant mesmerizing glow. The first officer's other hand found Picard's face and rested there.

A jolt of electricity passed from Riker's fingers into the captain's cheek like a dry static shock. Picard groaned and, for a dazzling millisecond, wavered on the precipice of utter surrender or utter rebellion.

Rebellion won: In place of Will Riker's face, Picard imagined the mechanical, soulless visage of the Borg.

You can infect me, but you can't have me, can't use my face, my voice, as they did—to kill . . .

On pure instinct, Picard broke free and rose from his chair like a projectile, using his skull as a weapon, striking the first officer a hard solid blow to the chin that made Riker's teeth clack. Will lost his balance and went sprawling backward, long legs spread out in front of him; before he regained his footing, Picard shot around the desk, using the sudden surge of violent energy, of hate, to his advantage.

Indeed, fear, desperation, hatred—all married with the image of the Borg to fuel the rage within him; he had no doubt that, at least for the moment, he was as physically strong as Riker.

And lither, faster.

In the wink of an eye, Picard stood on the other side of the desk, catching hold of Riker's heel just as Will flailed, on the verge of regaining his footing. With a strength that should have dislocated his shoulder and did not, Picard pulled.

The force of it threw Riker once more from his feet; he fell backward, skull flung back with such violence that Picard could not tell whether the snapping sound came from his teeth clamping down or from the cervical vertebrae fracturing. The back of Riker's head struck the corner of the captain's desk with a loud sickening *thunk*. . . .

Sickening, Picard realized with horror, and, at the same time, quite delightful. Riker slid with a faint groan onto the desk, leaving behind a smattering of bright red on the desk, the bulkhead, and ultimately the carpet, as his head lolled decidedly to one side.

Picard looked down at his unconscious—possibly dead—first officer and moaned softly at the surge of sadistic contentment evoked by the sight.

No. No, they won't use me this time. I won't let them use me, I won't let them use me . . .

It captured his mind like a mantra as he struggled to gain control of his breathing, his trembling, his delirium. Twenty-five percent of the crew, Data had said—twenty-five percent, and more falling under the sway of madness with each passing moment . . .

Including himself.

But he would not let them use him. . . .

"Data," he whispered to himself, and drew in a deep breath, steadying himself. The entities were in him, surging through his brain, trying to establish control. But if he could just hold together long enough to reach Data . . .

He wiped the perspiration from his brow and forced a faint smile, then stepped calmly through the door and out onto the bridge. At the moment, it was manned by secondary crew members, as all the senior crew were occupied with other tasks.

One of them—an olive-skinned female, Lieutenant

Martinez—glanced up from the helm and graced him with a smile of infinitely malevolent complicity.

He permitted the entities within him to return it with an approving nod, but did not quite meet her tainted gaze—nor those of the other officers who occupied his bridge.

Possessed, all of them—all of them sharing Martinez's expression of delighted evil. His ship was in the entities' hands.

"Carry on," he said hoarsely, and managed to repress a feverish shiver until he stepped through the lift doors.

Run, little one! Lwaxana screamed silently, her dark hair disheveled, her bruised forehead trickling blood. *They're still here. . . .*

Troi staggered backward from the image, away from the closet, stumbling over her own bed. At the last moment, she caught herself, gasping, overwhelmed by a wave of terror as horrible as that she'd experienced in the entities' presence.

She ran to her nightstand and scooped up her comm badge, thinking to warn the captain and Will, but instinct held her back. She closed her eyes, concentrating on Picard . . .

And, brushing against the soft bedclothes, she sank slowly to the floor under the weight of the horror:

The agony of a mind invaded yet again, the brutal image of Picard struggling helplessly against the Borg, of watching silently, impotently as his own face, his own voice were used to kill his own people . . .

For a terrible blazing instant Will was there, too, caught like Picard in the unyielding grip of mindless rage, mindless frustration, mindless craving.

Violence. Pain. All she could sense of Will was utterly blotted out; unconscious or dead, she could not say. Had Picard killed him?

Overwhelmed by fear and helplessness, Deanna

huddled on the deck beside the bed. There was nothing she could do to fight the madness, nothing she could do to stop its inexorable progression—not if both Will and the captain were in its sway.

The terror was so primal it transcended all thought; she merely sat, clutching knees to chest, head bowed, eyes squeezed shut. How long she remained thus—minutes or hours—she could not have said.

But after a time she came to herself enough to watch her breathing—the soft in-and-out of air moving through her lungs. Simply this, not trying to control the gasping, not trying to control the terror, merely watching with patient attention.

And soon her respiration slowed, her mind cleared; she rose slowly, numbly, with the keenly present, tingling sensation of one just plucked from drowning in icy waters, intensely aware of being alive, here, in this moment, in this situation—as terrible as it was.

She opened her eyes. Lwaxana's image was gone now, but in its place, Troi's own mind gently coached her:

Keep your breathing steady, Deanna. Now get up—get up, and put on your uniform.

She did so with the slow measured movements of a somnambulist, slipping out of her nightdress and into her uniform, then turning to regard the comm badge on the nightstand.

No. Don't take it. You can't let them know where you are.

There was only one person aboard the *Enterprise* she could trust: Data. He was also the one person aboard the *Enterprise* she could not read. If she asked the computer where he was, or tried to contact him, the others might be monitoring the conversation; they could track him down and turn him off.

The thought made her realize that the android needed her as much as she needed him: for he could not detect who was infected, and she alone could. If they were both to survive, they had to find each other.

Whatever she did, she could not remain here; until she could decide where to go, she would go to Data's quarters and hide there. Trying to quiet her mind against the fear, she drew a breath and moved through the bedroom, into the outer living quarters, and out into chaos. . . .

The madness came in febrile waves, forcing Picard at times to lean, quaking and perspiring, against the cool hard surface of the lift bulkhead.

RESISTANCE IS FUTILE.

YOU WILL BE ASSIMILATED.

"No," he said, gasping, struggling to contain the helpless rage evoked by the image of himself as Locutus—rage he knew served as fodder for the entities. Yet the sensation was all too horribly the same as the mental rape he had endured at the hands of the Borg: the sensation of his own consciousness being overtaken, subdued, relegated to passivity while a mindless, heartless, soulless force acquired the use of his arms, his legs, his tongue . . .

"Not this time," he whispered, pressing his face against cold metal.

Abruptly, the lift ceased its motion; the doors slid open. His volition was still strong enough to resist them—perhaps because the direct contact with Will Riker had been blessedly brief, or perhaps, as the communiqué had suggested, he would be able to stave off the effects a short time.

He needed only long enough to warn Data. . . .

He pushed himself from the bulkhead and drew a sleeve across his damp forehead. His first step onto the engineering deck was unsteady; his second, surer. Desperation and determination married to grant him a modicum of control.

By the time he reached Data and La Forge—who worked together over a console in the exposed heart of the vast engineering center—he managed a small smile despite the war raging in his brain, despite the chilling realization that La Forge was no doubt still infected.

He would verify it soon enough.

"Gentlemen," he said easily. "How goes it?"

Data glanced up first; if he perceived Picard's unrest, his matter-of-fact gaze failed to show it. "Quite well, Captain. We should have a test model for you within the hour."

"Very good." Picard paused, fighting the urge to capitulate to the entities' insistence that he feign interest in the readout on the android's console, sidle around him, and reach for the control on Data's side. . . .

Instead he said, "Mr. La Forge. A moment with you, please."

Geordi's expression was one of eager innocence. "Sure, Captain." He rose and followed Picard to one side, out of the android's earshot.

With his back to Data, Picard at once graced La Forge with a knowing smile. "I've joined you, Geordi. But as for Data—"

The chief engineer's expression changed to one of such covert, grinning malevolence that Picard fought to repress a shudder. "Wonderful, Captain! But . . . I'm having a difficult time with Data. I tried to infect him, but our theories are right—he merely traps the entities, and they starve within him. And I've been working all this time to try to turn him off, but he's just too defensive about that side. Every time I maneuver into position, he moves away, guarding it. And so far I haven't been able to get the jump on him. But I'm going to have to, because once we have the detector working, he's going to realize—"

Picard nodded knowingly. "Is everyone in engineering with us?"

Geordi shook his head. "Not yet, sir; only about half. So I can't exactly initiate a big brawl out in the open like this. At least, not if we want everything to look normal when the Vulcans come. . . ."

"Understood," Picard said softly. "Just leave the android to me. Commander Riker and I have devised a plan." Then, more loudly, he said, "Very good, Mr. La Forge. Carry on with your work."

Geordi nodded and returned to the console beside Data.

Picard gestured. "Commander Data . . . could you come with me, please?"

Blinking, Data looked up from his work, then tilted his head quizzically; but at Picard's insistent gaze, he obediently left the console and moved toward the captain.

Without a word, Picard led him into the turbolift. The instant the doors closed shut over them both, the captain sagged against the bulkhead once more and whispered, "Deck Nine."

"Captain?" The android's golden forehead puckered in a frown. "Are you all right, sir?"

Picard groaned and sank to a sitting position. Data leaned over him, concerned.

"No." The captain gasped. Speaking was torture; each word brought pain, as though it had been literally torn from his gut. "I'm . . . not . . . all right. Riker . . . infected me. Data . . . the anesthesia failed. Geordi, Beverly—they're still infected. Trust no one! Lock me in the brig, make sure I can't escape, can't . . . harm anyone. Fuse the circuitry if you must but don't let them . . . use me. I order you: Warn the crew. Tell the Vulcans and . . . Starfleet. And find Deanna . . . they're feeding off her sensitivity to emotion . . ."

He moaned as the mental and physical agony increased; the interior of the lift faded and he saw, in brutal detail, the interior of the Borg's great metal honeycomb of a ship and its inhabitants—soulless fusions of machinery and flesh. The entities fought him bitterly now, struggling to suppress what Picard knew might be the last command he ever uttered:

"And if you can't contain the infection . . . Data, you must do whatever is necessary to . . . destroy this ship."

He closed his eyes and yielded to chaos—and heard, as though from an infinite distance, the android reply softly:

"Yes, sir . . ."

Chapter Ten

LIEUTENANT WORF HEADED down the corridor that led to the senior officers' quarters, relieved to be free from the helplessness of enforced sleep and the legacy of a dishonorable people dead by their own machinations thousands of years before he was born. He looked forward to a pleasant evening with his son, and frankly, with Kyla Dannelke. Perhaps he could win back some of the chips he'd lost the night before; the thought made a faint smile play at the corners of his mouth.

It faded at once at the sight of Deanna Troi moving down the corridor toward him. She was walking as swiftly as she could without breaking into a run, glancing around and behind her as if anticipating pursuit; the tension in her body spoke of an intense deep-seated fear.

At the sight of the Klingon, she halted, her entire body poised for flight—away from him. Her dark luminous eyes widened, and he realized that she was scanning him empathically. He had never known her to be so blatant about it before.

"Counselor?" He stopped himself, not wanting to startle her into fleeing. "Counselor, are you all right?"

Clearly, the question on her mind was whether *he* was all right. She continued to stare at him, probing deeper. She had once told him the Klingon mind was not as simple as that of the humans, who were trained to hide their deeper feelings. Klingon emotions hovered blatantly on the surface, but an empath had to work to get to the deeper levels, where the truest Klingon emotions lay. He stood patiently, allowing her to do that.

At last, she took a step toward him, the tension in her body slightly easing. But her eyes were still wide with fear as she whispered, "You—Worf, you've been touched by them."

Was she talking about the infection? He remembered the electric shock he'd felt when Crusher had touched his face, stared into his eyes. Now that the inhibiting drug had worn off Troi's mind, could she sense the infection in *him,* building slowly, perhaps more slowly than in humans, waiting to overtake him? He stopped himself. He was a Klingon, and knew in his heart that he would never succumb to such dishonorable entities. Never.

"You've been touched by them," she repeated, moving closer until she stood beside him, "but they can't affect you. They're inside, trapped—harmless."

He believed her utterly. "Can I—can I infect others?" The thought of Alexander and Kyla, innocently awaiting him in his quarters, evoked concern.

She stared deeply into his eyes, and he willed his mind to be open to her, to give her the information she needed. Her large shining black eyes were open, honest, and free of the madness and strange swirling colors he had seen in Crusher's.

"No," she said at last, causing him to sigh in relief. "They're dying. Trapped inside you, with all your intensity, your powerful emotions raging around yet completely unavailable to them. They're dying quickly, unable to escape."

"A fitting death for such cowardly creatures," he told her.

As he spoke, she gasped and glanced around them, catching hold of his sleeve.

"What is it, Counselor? Are the entities in sickbay still affecting you? We can call Dr. Crusher for help. Now that the malady is destroyed—"

She shook her head, still glancing nervously around the strangely empty corridor. "We have to find Data! Right away, Worf. We've got to find him."

"Of course," he agreed, humoring her and reaching for his comm badge.

She caught his hand. "Not like that! The others might hear."

"Others? Counselor, what is wrong? You are acting as though you have seen a spirit!"

She drew a deep breath to calm herself and released it with a shudder, then faced him somberly. "That's exactly what I've seen. . . .The entities, Worf— they're still here. The shutdown, the anesthetic, and the accelerator—they didn't cure anyone."

"But Dr. Crusher and Geordi—I saw them my-self."

"They're pretending. They're still infected. You must believe me, Worf—everyone aboard this ship is in terrible danger. They have the captain!"

"That is impossible! I just left him. All was well— he sent me to my quarters."

Troi shook her head. "Riker attacked him in his ready room. I can feel what Picard's feeling. . . ." She closed her eyes as if momentarily overwhelmed by the sensation, then opened them again. "Nothing has changed. They've got over twenty-five percent of the ship under their control, the most critical twenty-five percent, including Crusher, La Forge, Riker—and the captain!"

Now it was Worf who nervously scanned the hallway. Grabbing Troi's arm with slightly more force than he intended, he pulled her down the corridor and into the privacy of his quarters.

Their sudden entry startled both Kyla and Alexander, who were placing food on the table. Without an introductory word to them, Worf demanded of the empath, "Are they affected?" He pointed to his son and Dannelke, who could only stare back in bewilderment. "Are they part of the twenty-five percent?"

The counselor did as instructed, scanning the two, who watched her in startled confusion.

"No," Deanna said at last, her voice showing the same deep relief Worf felt. "No, they're fine."

"Worf?" Kyla finally set down the plateful of steaming food in her hands. "What's going on?"

"This is our ship's counselor, Deanna Troi," Worf explained. "You heard the captain's explanation of the infection we attempted to cure during the shipwide shutdown? The counselor says the shutdown failed in its purpose. Apparently, after I left him, the captain was attacked and subdued! Even now, he has been overcome by these accursed creatures!"

"We have to find Data," Deanna repeated. "He can't be affected by the entities, and they know that. They might attempt to deactivate him, because he's our best hope of wresting control of the ship from the infected crew. Right now, he's with Picard. I can sense the captain talking to him, wanting to rely on him. He still has some of his free will; he's fighting it as hard as he can! Oh, Worf!" Her tone grew anguished. "All he can think of was the time he was abducted by the Borg!"

The thought evoked such rage in the Klingon that he knew he must channel the emotion into productive action—or else he would be forced to put a fist through a bulkhead. "We must leave here at once! But we will need supplies. Alexander! Collect emergency food rations from the replicator and pack a survival kit. You know what to do."

"Yes, Father," the boy said smartly, and immediately went into action.

Kyla approached the empath and peered at her, concerned. "What about you, Counselor? If you can sense Picard, what about the others?"

Troi drew in a breath, clearly fighting to control herself. "Now that the entities know I'm awake, that I know about them, I . . . can sense them. They're feeding off my empathic emotions. It's like . . ." She swallowed and raised trembling hands to her face. "Like being constantly fondled by a hundred strangers, helplessly forced to endure their touch."

The tall blond scientist put a reassuring arm around the shorter dark-haired empath. "Don't think about them, Deanna—focus on me, Worf, and Alexander. Focus on our strength and outrage. We're close to you here; the others are farther away. Pull in our feelings and make them yours."

"Yes . . ." Troi answered softly. "Yes, that's better . . ." She drew in a gulp of air, shuddered, then grew steady. "Yes, that's working . . ." She managed a wan smile. "Thank you."

"If you can sense them that strongly," Worf said, "and if they can feed off you, then they will want you under their control. You are worried about Data—but we need to worry about you!"

As he spoke, Alexander came clattering into the living room with a backpack full of emergency rations, several computer padds, and three phasers. Worf glanced at the supplies and realized his son had brought in everything Worf had intended to get himself. Alexander beamed proudly beneath his father's approving gaze.

"Remember in our *nok'bara* classes how I taught you about the calm before the battle," Worf reminded Deanna, as he handed her a phaser. "You must collect that calm about you, fill your mind with it, blotting out the invasion of the aliens. Show them your Klingon calm and they will freeze."

She nodded, tight-lipped and determined. "I'll be all right. But we've got to find Data. He's no longer with the captain."

Worf scowled, concerned: the android's movements presented a logistical problem. No doubt, Data, who was swifter than any of them, had also discarded his communicator badge. "If you cannot sense Data, and he is no longer with another humanoid, then how will we find him?"

"I bet I know where he is, Father," Alexander announced cheerfully.

The Klingon repressed his skepticism as he gazed down at his son. "And where would that be?"

"Deck Twelve, Jeffries tube twenty-eight. He took our whole class there for a demonstration on the inner workings of a starship six months ago. He picked that spot because it was an important hub, with lots of power panels, computer terminals, even a replicator. There are five such hubs in the ship, but Data chose that one because it was out of the way, and he knew we wouldn't be disturbed there. It's a lot of trouble to get to!"

Worf found himself grinning at his resourceful child. "Then you must lead us there quickly and quietly!"

Aren't we a motley crew, Deanna thought, as she crept along behind Alexander and Worf; Dannelke brought up the rear so that Troi would be surrounded by a protective emotional wall. *A Betazoid, a Klingon, a human, and a Klingon-human child . . .*

Alexander had been right about Jeffries tube twenty-eight being difficult to get to; it seemed they had been moving forever from tunnel to tube to tunnel in an infinitely circuitous route. Or perhaps it only seemed like forever, Deanna decided, because each step took enormous mental effort. The entities were still upon her—probing, touching, trying to elicit as much fear and outrage as possible from her. She closed her eyes an instant, concentrating so that she would not stumble, and permitted herself to bathe in the heat of Worf's and Kyla's anger and protectiveness. Even Alexander's innocent resolve bolstered her, making her humbled and proud to have such friends.

Suddenly, the small boy halted their quiet progress, indicating with a wave of his hand that they were nearly at their intended destination. Troi tried to peer around Worf's bulk as she heard the soft whirs and beeps of computer consoles at work. The Klingon turned to her, his gaze questioning.

Troi shook her head and whispered, "I sense no one." If Data was around this curve, he would be blessedly alone.

Still cautious, Alexander and Worf turned the corner—and halted; Deanna glanced cautiously over the Klingon's shoulder, right into Data's beautiful inhuman face.

The android sat upon the deck beside an open panel, his hands poised over four computer padds upon his lap, playing them as a concert pianist might coax a complicated melody from his keyboard. At the sight of Troi and the others, he instantly stopped.

"Counselor?" His tone was wary as he scrutinized the group.

Troi stepped around the Klingon, smiling with

relief. "We're all right, Data! We've been looking for you."

Deanna never saw his hand move, but suddenly Data was holding a phaser on them.

"Unfortunately," the android said, "I have no reliable manner in which to test whether you are, indeed, 'all right.'"

Worf snatched the back of his son's shirt and hauled the child back so that he was behind him; at the same time, the adult Klingon stepped in front of Troi, clearly prepared to take the full brunt of the phaser blast. "Then how can we convince you we have come to give you aid, Commander? Together we must protect both you and the counselor, and prevent the Vulcans from coming aboard the *Enterprise.* We cannot do that if we are trapped in a perpetual standoff!"

Data lowered the phaser. "Your actions, Lieutenant, have proved it already. The crew members infected by the entities are incapable of sacrificing themselves for anyone, even their own children, as you just attempted to do." As if that settled the matter, Data matter-of-factly returned to his computer padds, his hands moving over them in a blur of activity. "Apparently, Alexander paid far more attention to my maintenance course than I thought at the time."

The boy rolled his eyes impatiently as his father gave him a stern look.

Buoyed by optimism, Troi sidled over to watch the android work. "What are you doing, Data?"

His hands never paused. "Several things. I am sending false readings that will tell anyone attempting to locate me that I am in twelve different random locations. I am sending printed and verbal instructions to the noninfected crew members to secure their quarters and trust none of their fellow crew members, no matter how normal they may seem. I have added deliberate errors to noncritical functions of the ship to cause minor disruptions to normal procedures. The entities have difficulty coping with stress—it may cause some of them to erupt into violence. When the Vulcans arrive, they will automatically scan the ship. If enough things are going wrong, they may hesitate to beam aboard. Oh, yes . . . I have correlated all known information about the entities—including the Vulcan and Federation reports and Skel's entire research library—into my positronic network so that I can allocate large resources to inventing a detection device and also a containment field." He turned his face toward them to reveal a small device on one side of his head, its blinking lights flashing in the same coordinated pattern with the exposed circuits.

"You've been a busy android," Kyla said drolly.

"Actually," Data replied, still busily manipulating the padds, "I have still had time to plan future computer sabotage, diversionary tactics, and escape maneuvers. However, it is true I have not had the resources left to work on my poetry."

"Well, that is a relief," Worf grumbled. "How long can we safely stay here?"

"I estimate another four-point-three minutes." Data finally halted his hand movements and glanced up. "That is the one unfortunate reality I have been unable to alter. The computer work I am doing is continually being counteracted by Geordi in engineering—as I anticipated. It does take him longer to overcome my diversions than it takes me to instigate them. But if I work too long from any one location, he will inevitably pinpoint the source of my directions. And *that* we cannot allow. Until you arrived, I did not know how to solve this problem."

"And now you do?" Deanna asked.

"Yes. Instead of only relying on the Jeffries tube work stations, which are limited, we can also access empty quarters—now that you, Counselor, can advise us as to their level of occupancy."

She smiled tiredly. "Yes, of course."

Quickly, Data packed up his computer padds. "Then we must leave now. Alexander, can you recommend another location?"

"I always liked Jeffries tube sixteen. It's really *small.*"

Yes, Mother would call this quite a motley crew, Deanna thought, almost smiling as the group moved on. The phrase evoked the memory of Lwaxana's battered face, but this time Troi found the strength to analyze it. *My mother was warning me, in spite of her pain and fear. Trying to communicate . . .*

Perhaps there was more Lwaxana could tell her, if Troi stopped running from the image and faced it. At some point, she knew, they would be forced to stop and rest so Data could continue his work. Even now, Kyla discussed that work and how she might help him with it. Perhaps when they were secured again, Deanna would find the resolve to seek out her mother and hear all that she had to say.

"Attention all hands! Attention! This is Commander Data, I have been given command of the *Enterprise . . .*"

Skel stood before the brig cell that held Jean-Luc Picard's huddled form and listened impassively to the warning that blared over the ship's intercom. On every deck, klaxons sounded in a continuous red alert that La Forge had not yet been able to silence.

"Trust no one, unless you know for certain that person cannot have been infected by other crew members. Avoid physical contact and especially eye contact. Secure yourself in your quarters, and, if possible, secure your decks. Arm yourselves with phasers set on maximum stun. Be prepared to fire on any crew member, no matter their rank or relationship, who attempts to touch you. Infected crew members may cause serious physical harm to noninfected crew in an attempt to feed their entities. Do not give them this opportunity."

The automated message droned on endlessly, but Skel had no difficulty tuning it out.

Before him, Picard crouched on elbows and knees, collapsing with laughter punctuated by grimaces of pain. Tears streamed down his sculpted, shadowed cheeks. "You can't get him, Vulcan. You can't! He has no feelings! And he's *smart,* smarter than any of us. He'll find a way to defeat us. We can't win. . . ."

With an abrupt roar, the captain leapt to his feet and lunged viciously at the invisible forcefield. Despite himself, Skel recoiled.

For a crackling instant the forcefield gripped Picard's convulsing body; he cried out, then fell groaning to the deck.

The entities within Skel pulled at him to touch the human, to feel Picard's pain so that they might feed. Had it been possible to override the fused circuitry, the Vulcan might have obliged them; as it was, he could only watch as Picard gave his own entities exactly what they wanted.

If the captain of the *Enterprise* continued in this manner, he would die. It would be a terrible loss, but, logically, there was nothing to be done about it. Riker had recovered from his head wounds, thanks to Dr. Crusher, and would be able to convince the Vulcans that all was well aboard the *Enterprise.* The android had done such an excellent job of fusing the circuitry that, without his help, it would take hours for regular technicians to cut through the bulkhead and release Picard. By then, the Vulcan ship would have already arrived.

Skel had come to see Picard's condition, to calm and convince the human to let the entities within utilize him in their plan. Even though Picard could not assist them in welcoming the Vulcan vessel, he might be freed by the time they reached the TechnoFair, and by then his help would be invaluable.

Yet something was wrong; the entities had clearly infected the captain, but did not control him enough to coerce his cooperation. Apparently, Riker had not maintained contact long during the initial phase of infection.

Curled on his side like an unborn child on the deck, tears streaming from his closed eyes, Picard whispered, "You won't use me. I won't let you use me, not the way *they* did . . ."

Skel moved closer to the invisible shield, crouching down to sit on his haunches. His entities urged him to demand that Picard look at him; but from time to time they also allowed a modicum of freedom to the true Skel—the struggling, entrapped Vulcan consciousness—so long as it did not interfere with their aims. And the true Skel looked upon the gibbering madman in his cell with compassion and curiosity, and asked softly, "Who, Captain? Who else has so used you?"

"The Borg." Picard sobbed, trembling with both pain and incandescent pleasure. "They took my mind, my voice, my face, used me as a weapon against my own people . . . and I will die before I permit that to happen again!"

Skel listened with divided consciousness. The strongest, most overwhelming thought came from the entities: A pity, that Picard had chosen not to cooperate—but the inconvenience would not prove fatal to their plans.

Yet beneath the crushing mental overlay, a small voice whispered: *I understand. Given the opportunity, I, too, would choose death . . .*

Yet a third consciousness intervened: one quite separate from Skel's, yet irretrievably linked.

Skel blinked as, before his very gaze, Picard's lean

muscular form shimmered, wavered, changed. On the other side of the forcefield, the captain's eyes slowly opened and met Skel's gaze.

Yet Picard's eyes were no longer human. As Skel watched, Picard's soft hazel irises darkened to pure gleaming black, and the brows lifted in decidedly Vulcan cant. The face, too, shifted, from that of an outworlder to that of a Vulcan woman, regally beautiful, yet that beauty was marred as bright green bruises bloomed on her cheeks, forehead, throat.

My son is still inside you, she said in perfect Vulcan, her demeanor calm, contained, despite the pain that convulsed her body. *Trapped inside all these years.* She paused, her tone changing, warming ever so perceptibly as she addressed Skel directly. *I know you are there, my son—waiting for your freedom. Have patience; it will come. I will not desert you. . . .*

Abruptly, he found himself staring into Picard's sweat-slicked face; the human struggled to his knees. "Who is she?" the captain demanded. "Who is this woman who wears my mother's face and voice, yet speaks the Vulcan tongue?"

"She is my mother," Skel said. Though the Vulcan within him might have remained, the entities bade him turn, before either he or his mother had the opportunity to come to the Starfleet captain's aid again. Skel exited swiftly, with both Picard's screams—and his mother's—echoing hollowly in his ears.

Inside the shadowed, dimly lit tunnel adjacent to Jeffries tube sixteen, Deanna sat exhausted between Alexander and Worf, trying to absorb their emotions to distract herself from the entities' pull. Together, the three watched as Data attached a small round device to his temple; instantly, its single telltale began blinking merrily.

"I am confident I can detect the entities now," the

android assured them. "Dr. Dannelke is correct in her assumption that, before he was infected, Commander La Forge would have been able to see the particular wavelength these entities emit through his VISOR."

"It was probably the last thing he saw before they got him," Kyla murmured, her tone grim—but her expression, as she stood beside Data regarding the device at his temple, was one of pure scientific absorption.

"Now, with the adjustment to my vision that she has helped me create," Data told them, "I will be able to see them as well."

"A walking, talking entity-detector." Dannelke presented him to the group with a small flourish.

"Is your normal vision impaired, Data?" Deanna asked.

"Not at all." The android glanced around the small group. "And I can assure you that none of you are infected."

"We already knew that," Worf rumbled. "How will this help us defeat them?"

Dannelke lifted the palm-size square box created with the replicators. "The forcefield modulation Data came up with should hold the little monsters—"

"If we had a way to lure them into it," the Klingon countered irritably. "Just how do you propose to do that?"

Dannelke sighed. "We haven't gotten that far yet . . ."

As if Data wanted to up the ante, he added, "We had better find a way soon. The Vulcan ship will arrive at the rendezvous point within the hour."

Beside Troi, Worf made a noise of pure frustration; Deanna understood. The strain of ignoring the entities' pull had worn on her. She wanted only to be free from them or, at the very least, to help Data and Dannelke discover a way.

In the periphery of her vision, a shadow stirred at

the far end of the tunnel. Deanna turned, her pulse quickening . . .

And saw a familiar figure approach.

"Mother . . ." She rose—mindless of her surroundings, of the others beside her—and moved down the tunnel toward the apparition.

Lwaxana's face was solemn, composed, and, for the moment, blessedly whole. Wearing deep aubergine robes, she approached her daughter with uncharacteristic reserve, her dark hair smoothed back into a long plait.

Will you listen to me now, little one?

Troi smiled. "Yes, please—we need your help. The entities . . ."

. . . travel through the windows of the soul.

"The eye," Deanna said, nodding. "But Geordi—he was blind and wearing a VISOR, yet he was infected."

Lwaxana gave a single slow nod. *Through the conduit that led them to his brain.*

Deanna frowned at her mother's enigmatic expression. "His optic nerve?"

It is also the key to their destruction. That which attracts them can serve to entrap them.

"Optic nerves," Deanna repeated, though the notion made no sense to her. The more she stared at her mother, the more convinced she became that she was in fact staring at *someone else.* Yet such serene goodness emanated from the image that she trusted this stranger as much as she would Lwaxana. "We can use optic nerves to trap them?"

The nerves. The trap. But most important for you to know, little one—the lure. All of these will be necessary to subdue them. For an instant, Lwaxana's features shimmered, on the verge of metamorphosing into something alien but beautiful.

"Lure them . . . how can I do that, Mother?"

You already know what you must do—just as my son

has known, all these years, how to defeat our tormentors. But they have kept the truth beyond his waking grasp. . . .

"Your *son,"* Troi repeated, and in that moment, understood. As she watched, the image before her transformed into a Vulcan female: young, dark-haired, dark-eyed, with an expression of infinite control yet infinite concern. "Skel. Skel is your son."

Held beneath the entities' control these many years. I did all I could to help him break free, but it has not yet been enough. I know all that Skel knows about them—indeed, all the data that the entities have buried deep within his unconscious. Yet without a physical form, I cannot defeat them.

"Just as we cannot defeat them without your help. Tell me," Troi said eagerly. "Tell me what we must do."

"Counselor . . . Counselor! Are you all right?"

Deanna blinked as the image of Skel's mother faded into the more familiar visage of Worf, who gripped her arms, his bony brow furrowed with concern.

"Counselor!" he called again, and Deanna sighed, mentally releasing the image.

"I'm all right," she said. "I just had a communication with . . ." She paused, scanning the worried faces of Worf, Kyla, Alexander, even Data—who, despite his bland expression, managed with body language to telegraph his concern. They might think her driven to madness by the entities' pressure, but she drew a breath and finished her statement anyway. "Skel's mother."

"Skel's mother!" Worf dropped Deanna's arms and stepped back between Kyla and Alexander. "She has been dead eighty years!"

"Yes," Deanna allowed. "But her *katra*—her disembodied consciousness, if you will—has been coexisting inside Skel's brain with the entities all this time. She knows everything that the *real* Skel knows, everything the entities haven't permitted him to reveal publicly in his research—"

"The optic nerve," Kyla said excitedly. "We could hear what you were saying about it. It makes sense." She turned toward Data. "Does Commander La Forge have intact optic nerves?"

Data nodded. "His VISOR has contact points at his temples that allow its input to travel to his optic nerves and thence to his brain."

"So we need a VISOR," Kyla told the android, with such contagious excitement that Troi smiled. "We can make a connection between it and your optic nerves. We already know the entities can't infect you. Once you draw the entities in, we can rig something up to contain them in this." She held out the box.

"My optic nerves are more mechanical than organic," Data informed her. "And I do not have the emotional pull to draw the entities to me. I do not believe my using the VISOR in that manner will be of any help to us."

Kyla frowned, worrying at the problem. Deanna could feel her fierce determination to solve it. "Well, it's obvious then. We need organic optic nerves—and I know where we can find some: Dr. Tarmud's quarters."

Troi drew in a hesitant breath, causing Dannelke to glance up at her. "What is it, Counselor?"

"Tarmud," Deanna admitted. "If we go there, we must be careful. He's one of the Possessed . . ."

In the Vulcan Skel's quarters, George Tarmud lovingly stroked the device he and Skel had developed; everything he was, everything he knew, had gone into its creation. The scientist who had once lived to conquer death for all mankind had finally done so—

though not in the way he'd once dreamed. His plans for improving his android, for working with Skel and Dannelke on personal shields—none of that mattered anymore. He and Skel together had taken some of the most powerfully advanced frequency-modulation equipment from the *Enterprise* and created a device that would enable the entities to evolve even further. They'd changed enormously from the rather simple creatures that had caused death and devastation on the planet Vulcan eighty years ago. And their contact with the people of Vulcan had taught them the necessity of control.

With the effects of this new device, the entities would evolve enough to control their hosts completely, negating the bursts of uncontrolled violence and feeding frenzies. Instead, they would be able to use the hosts' knowledge and experiences to outwit unconquered peoples. They could overwhelm the planet of Betazed, taking its powerful empaths into a protracted slavery that would be solely for the entities' benefit. They would eventually completely absorb the Federation, classifying some of its people as subjects to feed from and others as subjects to control. Their domination of these intelligent organic lifeforms would be complete.

They could have developed the machine faster had Dannelke joined them—a fact Tarmud regretted. Dannelke could have given it a refinement, an intricate elegance, but she'd vanished immediately after the shutdown, and, as yet, none of the recruited had been able to find her. A pity . . .

Tarmud shivered and yawned as a surge of fatigue washed over him. The entities had not allowed his host body to sleep since it had been possessed, and he could not remember when they'd last permitted it physical sustenance. Insignificant in the grand scheme of things—yet this body was valuable. To avoid collapse, he decided, he would go to his quarters.

There were tools he needed, some computer chips he wanted to try fitting into the device to improve its efficiency. He'd allow the body to sleep for an hour or so while he was there. He carried a matching chip with him to be sure he obtained the right ones.

The trip from Skel's guest quarters to Tarmud's was brief, the corridors deserted. Once more the voice of the android Data rang through the air, warning the uninfected crew members to hide, secure themselves, be armed. Tarmud chuckled to himself: It was all so useless. Over forty percent of the crew was infected now, and, despite Data's unsettling warnings and the random blaring of the red alert, the recruits were stabilized. Everyone was committed to possessing the Vulcans. Even the youngest, the most fragile host was hanging on, waiting, wanting that more than anything. A ship full of Vulcans. A worthy prize for their self-control.

The doors to his quarters opened smoothly, as he checked the identifying code on his sample chip. He had at least ten of these in his—

Movement. A blur.

The blow to his chin took him completely by surprise, snapping his head back hard. The chip flew from his hand as he staggered backward, tasting blood. Bright diamond-sharp pain traveled electrically from jaw to skull to neck. He moaned with delight and agony, the feeding of the entities bringing with it a manic rush, then opened his eyes to see a blur: a body, tall and cloud-pale; a leg, with a boot speeding once more toward his face.

Dannelke.

The kick staggered him; he dropped to his knees, but the entities strengthened his body, made him absorb the power, the shock of the kick, even as they fed frantically.

Dannelke was here. . . . He could not miss the opportunity to possess her. "Kyla," he whispered hungrily through broken blood-stained teeth, reaching out to touch her. "Kyla, look at me. . . ."

Kyla, no! Troi screamed. *Use the phaser! You'll kill him!*

But Dannelke's adrenaline level did not permit her to hear the counselor's warning, to remember the phaser at her belt until it was too late. She whirled and delivered one last powerful kick, oblivious to Troi's and Worf's cries, oblivious to anything except the fear and the memory of the insidious grin on Tarmud's face.

Kyla, look at me. . . .

Once more, her boot heel connected with Tarmud's chin, but this time there came the sickening crack of bone. Tarmud dropped onto his back, utterly limp, gaze fixed now on the ceiling, bent knees sprawling outward.

Dannelke scarcely heard it; in her own mind, the shouts of her new friends merged with the screams of her mother, outside an East London flat. . . .

"Kyla, stop!" a deep voice thundered. She moved to kick again, to kill, but strong arms caught and held her back from her victim's motionless form.

She gasped and came to herself in Worf's grip. He stared sternly down at her. "Kyla, why did you not use your phaser?"

"I don't know." She gasped and peered beyond him at Troi, who bent beside the fallen scientist just as Data emerged from Tarmud's laboratory bearing numerous VISORs. The android also carried a packet filled with the long strands of artificial organic optic nerves, lazily adrift in preservative fluid. Alexander, who was with him, held more of the containment vessels. "I just—be careful, Counselor! He might be feigning unconsciousness!"

Deanna shook her head somberly. "He's dying. I think his neck is broken."

"Do not touch him!" Data ordered sharply, and Troi recoiled instantly. The android put his burdens down and moved over to the body. "It may be possible for the entities to infect a host even after the first host dies. We can assume nothing." He lifted Tarmud's eyelids and peered into his eyes. "The detection modulation is working. I can see the entities' wave patterns. They are still alive and active."

"Data," Deanna said, "we can't save him ourselves. We need medical staff. But we can stabilize him, put him in stasis with the first-aid kit."

"That will have to suffice, until a more opportune moment," Data agreed, taking the medical tools from her. "He will die momentarily, but this device should stabilize him for at least twenty-four hours." He attached a small rectangle to Tarmud's head, and one to his chest. "That is the best we can do. His life signs are weak, but holding."

"So, if we can't complete our task in the next twenty-four hours, he'll really die?" Kyla stared, stricken, at Tarmud's still form.

Data stood and regathered his materials. "If we do not complete our task in the next twenty-four hours," he told her dispassionately, "then all the Vulcans aboard the *Skal Torr* will be infected, and the strong likelihood will be that we, too, will have perished."

No one could respond to the android's bald statement, so they merely filed out of the room, leaving the still, helpless body of George Tarmud in their wake.

Chapter Eleven

IN THE CRAMPED QUARTERS of Jeffries tube sixteen, Kyla sat atop the uneven powerline housing, focusing intently on fastening the last link of delicate microcircuitry to the VISOR. Perhaps, if she stared at it hard enough, she might be able to forget the image of George Tarmud lying near death—because she had panicked. Troi sat nearby, watching with an expression of both interest and sympathy; no doubt, the counselor in her yearned to ease Dannelke's guilt. But at the moment none of them could spare the time.

"Are you almost finished with that unit?" Data asked Kyla quietly. "The Vulcan ship should be within transporter range momentarily."

Kyla swallowed, made sure her voice was firm before she answered. "Yes. Almost. Just a minute . . ." She rechecked one last connection, then handed the device to the android. "That's it. The last one."

Worf, Alexander, and Deanna stared at the odd

equipment—five VISORs connected by wiring and a thin filament of artificial organic optic nerve to a small box that could be clipped to a belt. The box was the containment field, a crude substitute for the elegant and enigmatic artifacts.

As the others watched in anticipation, Data tied a belt around his waist, clipped the small box to it, then slipped on the VISOR.

"So, how does it look?" Kyla asked.

"It does not impair the vision too severely," Data commented, moving his head about to test the device's range. "And its new programming is allowing me a dim approximation of Geordi's vision. Normal electrical wavelengths generated by humanoid life-forms appear like a glow—a halo, if you will. We should be able to actually see the entities—or at least their frequencies—as they approach the VISOR to infect us."

Kyla shook her head. "You say that so blithely."

"If the VISORs work as we have programmed them," Data reminded her, "the entities will not reach our eyes, but will follow the VISORs' circuitry, travel down the artificial optic nerve, and become trapped in the containment field."

"If it works as we planned," she emphasized.

"And this is the best that we can do?" Worf asked again, clearly frustrated by this passive method of battling their enemies.

"It is the most likely solution to this complicated problem," Data assured him.

Worf tried his VISOR on and scowled. "It will be very difficult to aim a phaser properly with this on."

"I don't think phasers are going to help us this time, Worf," Deanna reminded him, adjusting her own VISOR.

Kyla watched Alexander wrestle with his adult-size VISOR. "Mine's too big!" he complained, holding it awkwardly in place.

The ophthalmologist came up behind him and, taking one of her hairbands from a pocket, tied the two ends of the VISOR together, so it would fit him more snugly. As she did, she looked at Worf. "Don't you think Alexander could stay in the Jeffries tubes till this is over? He'd be safe there. Does he really have to do this with us?"

Suddenly Worf's hand was on the child's shoulder. "Kyla. We are all in danger. We can all be hurt. Alexander is a member of this crew, of this ship. He will do his part. We will all be proud of him."

"I do not wish to bring this up again," Data interjected, "but while we seem to have a good working model of an entity collector and containment device, we have still not concocted a lure."

"Can't we just walk up to the Possessed members of the crew and pull the entities out of them?" Alexander asked.

"I only wish that were possible," Data replied. "However, when a person is infected by the entities, the transmission that takes place is only partial. Some entities enter the new host, and some remain with the old to keep that host infected. We must find a way to lure *all* the entities out of each host, into our containment devices."

"I know a way," Deanna said softly. She was about to say more when a small viewscreen in the bulkhead panel brightened.

On the *Enterprise*'s bridge, Skel stood beside the captain's chair and stared at the viewscreen where the *Skal Torr* hovered, sleek and elegant, against a backdrop of star-littered blackness. The main part of Skel's consciousness, now entirely under the entities' control, felt a sense of accomplishment and exhilaration at the sight. Despite setbacks, the entities were on the verge of total success, of galactic domination. The crew was under control, and La Forge had finally succeeded in silencing the klaxon's and Data's warnings. All was well.

But the original Vulcan consciousness—the small silent observer that was the true Skel—watched in profound regret and, indeed, a most un-Vulcanly frustration at his own helplessness.

Never before had he quite grasped the mythical human concepts of purgatory and hell; now, he knew he understood them fully.

Indeed, he felt he was on the verge of deep psychosis, for at the same time that he was aware of the entities' control, he sensed—more strongly than at any other time in his life—the presence of his mother, T'Reth. Her shrieks echoed in his mind:

Help them! Warn them! Do not let this happen to our people again!

Madness, surely. But there were times when he felt convinced that his mother's presence was real, that she struggled as he did to find a way to defeat the entities. In sickbay, as the entities had forced Dr. Crusher to leave the accelerator canisters empty, it was T'Reth who had called out a warning. And for a brief blissful moment, the real Skel had shaken off the entities' influence long enough to direct that warning to the receptive mind of Jean-Luc Picard.

Since then, the entities had allowed Skel no freedom. Now he could only watch, powerless, voiceless, as the image of the *Skal Torr* wavered, then coalesced into the stern unsmiling countenance of a Vulcan female, a wide band of silver gilding her blue-black cap of hair.

Beside Skel, Riker said with consummate glibness, "Captain T'Lal. This is First Officer William Riker. Captain Picard regrets that he cannot greet you personally, but on behalf of him and the crew of the *Enterprise,* we bid you welcome."

T'Lal's control was complete, her inflection admirably toneless, yet Skel saw the flicker of uncertainty in her eyes—an instant of doubt only another Vulcan could have sensed. "We trust your captain is well. Are you prepared to beam over the artifacts?"

Riker gave an affirmative nod to the last statement, and to the first, he answered, "Captain Picard is suffering from a minor ailment; our chief medical officer has recommended bed rest. However, as you can see"—he swiveled in his chair and gestured at Skel beside him—"Master Scientist Skel is unharmed and in perfect health. He requests that someone be sent over from your vessel so that he can ensure the artifacts arrive properly secured."

Captain T'Lal turned her cool, frankly scrutinizing gaze upon Skel a full five seconds. "Our scans indicate that all is well aboard your ship. However, to minimize the risk of possible infection, logic would dictate that we beam them directly to our vessel."

A passive, unwilling observer, Skel watched as the entities planted a thought inside his beleaguered brain, as they directed his mouth, his teeth, his tongue—as they used the Vulcans' own logic to defeat the race. "Logic clearly dictates," Skel told T'Lal in a strong clear voice that betrayed none of his internal conflict, "that there is no infection loosed aboard this vessel. Certainly, my concerns about proper containment are also quite logical—"

T'Lal interrupted smoothly. "I assure you, Master Scientist, that we can receive the artifacts with utmost care. Send us specific instructions, and we—" She broke off as another officer leaned down to whisper in her ear. "Ah," she said, then refocused her gaze upon Skel. "There is one here who is willing to beam over to your ship. . . ."

She turned as the healer, T'Son, stepped forward into view.

"Greetings, Skel," T'Son said, holding up her hand briefly in the Vulcan salute. "I am concerned about the effect recent events have had upon your health. With your permission, I should like to examine you aboard the *Enterprise.*"

To meld, Skel realized, with a faint trickle of dismay, as he instinctively returned the salute; the emotion was soon blotted out by the entities' exhilaration. A brief meld, and the healer would be infected—and then, with her unwilling assistance, all of Vulcan . . .

A minute earlier in Jeffries tube sixteen, Troi stood alongside the others and watched the exchange with concern and dread. She could sense the hunger that possessed Will Riker, Geordi La Forge, and all the other humans aboard the *Enterprise*'s bridge who watched the Vulcans with deceptively calm exteriors. As for Skel—Troi sensed an overlay of serenity, but beneath it the entrapped Vulcan consciousnesses—two of them—struggled to warn their people of danger.

"We must stop them!" Worf turned to Data, who still sat with four computer padds resting on his knees. "Commander, can you access communications?"

The android's nimble fingers flew over the boards, much too quickly for Deanna to register what he was doing. "I am attempting to do just that, Lieutenant; however, communications are being tightly supervised. They have anticipated our attempt at involvement."

"What about the shields?" Worf asked. "If you raise the shields, the Vulcans cannot beam aboard."

Data manipulated the grid, then shook his head. "I cannot access the shields."

"Can we interfere with the transporters?" Deanna asked.

Data's hands moved faster. "Negative." Suddenly, his fingers came to a halt, poised above the padds; he glanced up at the others, apparently out of options. A frustrated silence ensued, and then Worf spoke:

"I suppose it is foolish to ask if you can gain control of the weapons system."

Data cocked his head at the Klingon. "Weapons system?"

"If we could fire but a glancing blow to their ship," Worf explained none too patiently, "they would automatically raise their shields. They cannot beam over with shields up."

"An interesting idea," Data mused. "Firing on them would be so unexpected, it would cause the Possessed crew members on the *Enterprise* a great deal of stress."

"And they're on the breaking point now," Deanna confirmed excitedly. "Pushed hard enough, some of them would start to fall apart. The Vulcans would see that unusual activity on their scanners."

The android fingered the padd controls, his subtle expression changing. He looked up, obviously pleased. "We may be fortunate. The infected crew members are so involved in handling my automated crisis and the various other disruptive activities of the healthy crew—plus safeguarding communications, transportation, and so on—there is very little attention being paid to weaponry."

"Well, after all," Kyla reminded them, "the Vulcans *are* our allies!"

"Let us hope they will still be when this is over," Data countered. "I will only be able to maintain control of the phasers for a moment, but it should be sufficient for what we are planning. It would help if we could distract both ships while I am doing this. . . ."

"We need a diversionary tactic," Worf grumbled. "Something that would draw their attention."

Alexander quickly rifled through his backpack,

then held up a small cassette, grinning. "And I have just the thing!"

"Greetings, T'Son," Skel murmured, his expression impassive. "I appreciate your concern. The experience aboard the Ferengi vessel was quite . . . tiring. I judge myself to be recovered, but you are the healer. As always, I yield to your judgment."

He lowered his own gaze beneath her professionally concerned one. "I would prefer to examine you, Skel, before you continue on to the TechnoFair."

"And I," Riker said, with cordial diplomacy, "would like to invite Healer T'Son, and any other of your crew who wish it, to come and view the displays erected by our scientist passengers."

Captain T'Lal's response was instant and equally diplomatic, if substantially less warm. "We thank you for your invitation, Commander. I know our scientists would find the displays quite fascinating. However, it is to our best interests to curtail social activities and retrieve the artifacts as quickly as possible, in the interests of security." She turned to glance up at T'Son, clearly dismissing her; the healer nodded, then moved out of sight—toward the transporter room, Skel realized.

"In the meantime," T'Lal continued, "we would appreciate receiving the requested logs concerning the incident aboard the Ferengi vessel—"

"My apologies on the delay," Riker countered smoothly. "We've been unable to transmit those files because of some minor computer problems. But if you would like, we could—what the *hell?*"

Skel followed the commander's startled gaze to the viewscreen, where the image of T'Lal had been suddenly replaced with that of *Skal Torr.* But instead of being surrounded by empty space and stars, the Vulcan ship was confronted by a gigantic, glowing green eyeball—*Klingon,* Skel assessed automatically, his Vulcan calm permitting him to note its details despite the surge of disbelief evoked by its appearance.

The great eye stared for an instant at the Vulcan ship, then blinked and turned its scowling scrutiny on the *Enterprise.*

"Impulse engines," the Vulcan captain ordered crisply. "Draw us back." And then she refocused her attention on Riker. "Commander . . ." T'Lal's tone was infinitely composed and matter-of-fact; the only hint of her subdued surprise was the scarcely perceptible widening of her eyes. "Could you explain this phenomenon? Our scanners reveal it is being generated by *your* vessel."

Riker's lips were parted in amazement, his blue eyes far wider than T'Lal's. For a moment, he offered no response; then, swallowing, he stammered, "Captain, I—I apologize. This is either a computer malfunction or someone's idea of a practical joke."

Skel watched silently as the human officer whirled in his chair shouting at no one, at everyone, aboard the bridge; his entities, Skel realized, were reacting violently to the surprise and stress. "Someone shut that damned thing down *now!"*

The bridge crew scrambled to comply, but they, too, were overworked and, like Riker, on the verge of losing control. Any more stress, and . . .

Skel blinked at the sudden blaze of brightness on the screen; a dazzling streak of phaser fire tore through the hologram and struck the *Skal Torr* a glancing blow.

"Commander Riker!" the Vulcan captain demanded as, on the screen, her bridge rocked. This time, her voice bore a definite note of disbelief and annoyance. "Why is your ship firing on us?"

Before Riker could think of an answer, T'Lal called to her helm: "Raise shields!"

* * *

"The Vulcans have raised their shields," Worf announced, grinning with pleasure from his tactical position at Data's makeshift panel. At the happy news, Deanna grabbed both Kyla and Alexander, permitting their triumph to wash over her and temporarily displace the eerie sensation of the entities' pull.

"Then they can handle another hit," Data decided. "We cannot allow them to consider lowering their shields now. I am increasing the power. Fire when ready, Mr. Worf."

"Firing phasers," the Klingon announced. Deanna grinned, one arm around Alexander's shoulders, the other about Kyla's, as she watched the small screen that showed *Skal Torr*'s shields safely absorbing the second blast.

"And now, we must leave with great alacrity." Data rose and began to rapidly disconnect his computer padds.

A brilliant beam of light streaked past Deanna, dazzling her and bouncing blindingly off the nearby bulkhead. Instinctively, both Kyla and Alexander ducked, pulling Deanna down with them to the deck.

"Too late!" Worf shouted. "They are here!"

He moved over to the trio and lifted them all at once to their feet; behind them, at the far end of the tube, came the sound of heavy footsteps. Deanna glanced over her shoulder and saw four uniformed security guards racing toward them.

"The VISORs!" Kyla shouted, and Deanna quickly scooped hers up even as she grabbed Alexander's hand and began to run.

Moments later, aboard the bridge of the Federation science vessel *Skal Torr*—now safely out of the *Enterprise*'s firing range—Captain T'Lal sat at her post with Healer T'Son in attendance beside her. The viewscreen—free now from the puzzling specter of the Klingon eye—instead showed the grizzled, august visage of Admiral DuCheyne at Starfleet headquarters.

A second series of scans of the *Enterprise*—after it had fired upon its guest—pointed most definitively toward an outbreak of the madness: violence was erupting on almost every deck. Indeed, after the incident, Commander Riker had exploded in uncontrolled fury and leapt from his chair to physically strike another crew member. Within seconds, a brawl had erupted on the bridge—emotional behavior that even humans would find unbecoming.

"It was as though," T'Lal explained carefully to DuCheyne, "they had managed to maintain control of the infection until the moment their vessel fired upon us. At that point, Commander Riker lost all sense of decorum."

DuCheyne—indisputably human and irascible in temperament—furrowed his wrinkled brow so deeply that his thick eyebrows presented one unbroken and shaggy white line above his glistening dark eyes. "Lost all sense of decorum?"

T'Lal continued patiently, choosing to ignore the admiral's exasperating habit of repeating and challenging each statement. "He rose shouting from his chair, sir, and struck a junior officer with such force that said officer fell to the deck."

"Oh. You mean he went berserk."

"Yes, sir." The Vulcan paused. "Our scans indicate similar outbursts all over the *Enterprise.* Healer T'Son says there can be no doubt that the majority of the crew is infected."

DuCheyne shook his head. "And all those scientists on their way to the TechnoFair . . . now, *that* would be a tragedy of massive proportion." He glared at her, his small gleaming eyes filled with a sudden fierceness. "Why did you people keep those damned artifacts, anyway?"

T'Lal opened her mouth to explain the concepts of tolerance for all life-forms and of knowledge, which protected one more securely than ignorance, but the old admiral silenced her with a shake of his head and a wave.

"I know, I know, I don't need a lecture on Vulcan philosophy. Look, Picard notified us of an outbreak aboard his vessel; he also notified us that he had performed the necessary shutdown to destroy the creatures. That means one of two things: either a mistake was made during the shutdown or the creatures have mutated so that they can't be as easily killed. Knowing Picard and his crew, I'd say the shutdown followed procedure very precisely. And that means one thing—"

"Sir," T'Lal interjected, "this is a science vessel; we do not sport the weaponry of a starship. Furthermore, our crew is entirely Vulcan. If you are asking me to destroy the *Enterprise* with all hands aboard her—"

The shaggy white brows lifted in clear annoyance at her impertinence. "I'm not *asking* you to do anything, Captain. I'm *ordering* you. However, I'm not so damned old or arrogant that I fail to realize you don't have the firepower to bring the *Enterprise* down alone. You are to remain in the vicinity until you're joined by reinforcements."

"Admiral . . ." T'Lal began patiently.

His tone softened, and she saw in the shadowed, shining eyes a glimmer of the regret she herself felt. "I understand, Captain, that you would prefer to find a way to cure those infected by the madness without harming them or their ship. And, believe me, we'll do everything possible to see that happen. But if we can't stop them before they reach the TechnoFair . . . we'll have no choice but to destroy that ship and all aboard her."

* * *

In the dim echoing expanse of the cargohold, Deanna pressed her back against the cool bulkhead and slid slowly into a sitting position. Beside her, Alexander and Dannelke rested cross-legged on the deck, while Worf paced, phaser still in his grip. The four of them were still gasping from the narrowness of their escape, while Data—perfectly rested, without a hair out of place—located a power panel in hopes of scanning for other pursuers.

"I believe we are safe for the moment," the android said. "Although . . ."

He gestured at a viewscreen on the bulkhead panel. The small Vulcan ship still hovered serenely out in space, flanked now by two Galaxy-class starships. "The *Odyssey* and the *Constitution,*" Data said matter-of-factly. "They are analyzing the activity level aboard this ship with their state-of-the-art scanners."

And contemplating using their state-of-the-art weaponry, Deanna knew, without voicing the thought. "Data . . . it's time. We have the VISORs, we have the containment device . . . and we also have the lure."

The android turned to regard her with his golden eyes, but there was no curiosity in his expression. He clearly had come to the same conclusion Deanna had, but was leaving it to her to make the decision.

"The lure?" Dannelke asked, long arms folded atop long knees, her pale hair falling forward out of its braid to frame an equally pale face.

Deanna paused, choosing her words carefully. "Right now, those infected are in a precarious state; the entities had adapted most successfully to Vulcan hosts, but the human hosts are not able to contain the entities' desperate hunger for very long. And now that they've lost their opportunity to infect the Vulcans, they are even more desperate; their controls are breaking down.

"Now, when they are especially vulnerable, we can lure them to us . . ." She paused and drew in a steadying breath. "By my opening my empathic sense and actually broadcasting to them to come to me. To feed."

Beside her, Kyla Dannelke shuddered and closed her eyes.

"I will not permit it!" Worf exclaimed. Deanna let the heat of his anger bathe her, protect her for a few seconds' blessed relief before the onslaught. Worf turned toward the android. "Commander, do not tell me that you will allow her to do such a thing!"

Data blinked as if he, too, were buffeted by the powerful Klingon emotions. "This is not something I can order her to do—or not to do. This is a very personal decision only she can make. And I suspect she has already done so."

Deanna glanced up at him gratefully; the android was becoming more insightful into the human condition every year.

She'd resisted the idea herself when Skel's mother had first proposed it. It had taken time for her to accept the ramifications—especially if their apparatus should fail. But as she thought of T'Reth, of the horrors that had been visited upon that courageous Vulcan woman and the strength with which she'd faced them, Deanna knew she could do no less. Realizing that Data's statement had implicitly put her in charge of this current tactical situation, she fingered her VISOR and the containment box it was attached to.

"The frequency modulation Data and Kyla programmed into the VISORs will enhance this lure. You will all be here to help control the hosts," Deanna went on, "and assist me in handling the crew so that they don't go berserk, or try to crush us. Since you will each be wearing VISORs, it won't be necessary for me to collect the entities from each crew member. Every person with whom you can intervene will spare me."

Data nodded. "Since we are in the cargohold, we can utilize the temporary force shields that hold the cargo in place when the ship is destabilized. If the crowd becomes too large or unruly, these small forcefields can restrain them. Twenty or thirty crew members can be contained by each forcefield, until we are capable of handling everyone."

"Like so many barrels of ale," Kyla remarked.

Deanna managed an uncertain smile.

"The forcefield units are small," Alexander piped up. "I can handle them while Father and Data manipulate the group."

"A good idea," Deanna agreed. "It will be critical that we all work as a team, and—" Her voice almost caught, but she stopped and collected herself in time. "And try to contain our fears. Remember, the most important thing is to keep your VISORs on and functioning. Are we ready?"

Troi nodded her readiness to the others, and silently they donned their VISORs.

The others took up positions on either side of her, except for Alexander, who hung behind them lest he be overwhelmed by the crushing tide of adults. The others formed a short funnel, with Worf in front of her, to blunt the numbers of victims who would—

Who would touch me, feed from me, like a thousand strangers fondling me over and over. She shook off the thought and closed her eyes, then opened her mind and emotions to the swirling, maddening evil that engulfed the ship.

The force of the desire nearly knocked her off her feet. She staggered, reeling.

On either side of her, Kyla and Data each grabbed an arm and supported her; she could not have resisted their aid had she wanted to. The lust, the hunger, the insatiable need pressed against her, smothered her, filling her mind, her body, her soul with dread and disgust.

"Breathe deep, Deanna!" Kyla's voice came to her faintly through the horror, as if from a great distance. "Deep, steady, breaths . . . you can do this . . ."

No! Behind the VISOR, tears of panic filled her eyes, spilled down her cheeks. *No, I can't . . .*

Amid the maelstrom of depraved desire came a soft still voice—a voice infinitely strong, infinitely soothing, infinitely serene. *I am here, Deanna.*

"T'Reth . . ."

Deanna reached for that calm and pulled it to her.

I am here, the voice assured her. *I will not leave you. You can withstand their force. Take strength from me, from my Vulcan discipline. Touch my mind . . .*

The bay doors slid open. In the dimness, a thin figure dressed in medical blue staggered toward them. In its desperation, it stumbled, falling to one knee; behind its frame of red hair streamed an eerie violet halo.

"Beverly." Deanna gasped. Crusher's eyes were wild feverish pools of darkness in a pale face slicked with blood and sweat. At the sight of Troi, she released a gasp of pure craving.

"Hungry," she whispered, her eyes growing impossibly huge. "So hungry . . ." She reached for Deanna's face with a trembling hand.

Touch my mind, child.

Deanna drew a breath and reached out, mentally, for the soothing balm of T'Reth's Vulcan control, then opened her eyes to see Worf, blocking Crusher's advance.

"Let her come to me," Deanna whispered.

The Klingon drew back. The infected woman surged forward and consumed Deanna in a crushing embrace, pulling Troi's face toward hers.

"So hungry!" Crusher's uniform was damp with perspiration, her body trembling uncontrollably. For a terrifying millisecond, her eyes blazed in a brilliantly colorful nova.

Deanna pulled back, gasping at the loud crackle of power, at the electric blue sparks that attacked the VISOR like a swarm of maddened bees.

Be calm, little one. This will pass.

A soft hum; the sparks faded as abruptly as they had appeared. For a breathless moment, Crusher stood swaying, eyes closed, arms still enfolding Deanna.

The violet aura abruptly vanished, like a forcefield damped. Crusher's grip eased; she opened her eyes and drew back in confusion. "Deanna?" She glanced from Troi to the other three VISORed adults. "Good Lord, what's happening?"

It continued for what seemed to Troi to be hours; at one point, the cargohold became a Hieronymous Bosch vision of hell, with dozens of crew members held by invisible fields—all of them reaching, screaming in desperation for Deanna. But T'Reth remained steadfast throughout, helping Deanna maintain her tenuous control as they painstakingly freed each person. At last, no new crew members were entering the hold, and the forcefield corrals were gradually emptying.

But there were more, still more.

Picard, trapped in the brig. Deanna opened her mind, searched for him, then immediately forced herself to shut him out: He was wild, insane, screaming for her in his confinement.

And there was one other who had not come: Skel.

You will have to go to him, Skel's mother warned. *He has lived with them too long; their hold on him is strong.*

Deanna sensed a startling emotion in the Vulcan

voice. *You're* afraid, *aren't you? You fear he may not survive the cure.*

I cannot know the effect it will have on him. They have been with him since his childhood. He may not survive the cure—but his death will be a relief to him, even so.

But if he dies, Deanna realized, *your spirit*—and his—*will be loosed upon the winds.* That was something no Vulcan would want.

I accept whatever happens, T'Reth answered placidly. *But my son will, at last, be free.*

Chapter Twelve

JEAN-LUC PICARD HUDDLED shivering on the brig deck, allowing his entities to gorge themselves on his terror and rage. His eyes were wide, yet he saw not the bulkheads of the *Enterprise*'s cell, but the gray metal honeycomb interior of the Borg ship.

They won't use me—I won't let them use me . . .

Footsteps behind him, soft voices—he laughed at the sounds. Let them come for him—he would not permit them to use him. He would die here first, alone in his madness, and *they* would die with him, too.

He turned and peered—delirious, sweating—at the faces that gathered on the other side of the forcefield: the pale moon that was the android, the darker countenance of the Klingon, Will Riker's bearded face . . .

Yet they were different—the eyes were covered in metal. Picard released a laugh that escalated into a sob. The Borg—they had transformed his people, even as they had once transformed him into Locutus, into neither human nor machine, but a monstrous marriage of metal and flesh.

"No," he murmured, hugging himself. "No!"

Voices beyond the field.

"Take it easy, Captain. We'll have you out of there in a minute. Data?"

"I'm afraid I was quite thorough, Commander. These circuits are fused beyond repair."

"Then stand back—I'll blast them until the power is interrupted and the field collapses—"

"The conduits provide too much power, Mr. Worf. You would be fatally shocked. I am afraid that only I can release the captain—"

An abrupt sound of metal slamming against metal—Picard glanced up and saw a bright shower of sparks, heard a hum followed by an abrupt pop.

Riker's bearded face, the eyes hidden behind a metal band. Not the blinking red Borg sensor-scope, at least, but Picard cringed nevertheless. *"Captain, can you hear us? Do you know us?"*

With a roar, he flung himself upward at his first officer—and struck an immovable object with a gasp. He flailed, only to find his arms pinned.

"Captain—it is Commander Data. Please do not resist us; I do not wish to harm you."

He howled in pure frustration, a sudden unbearable surge of hunger causing him to seek their eyes, their eyes—but there were none to be found.

A soft voice: *"Let me get close to him . . .* And then, *Captain. Look at me. It's Deanna. Let me help you . . ."*

Her presence pulled at him like the moon at the tide; he stared up at her, seeking her dark luminous eyes, but they, too, were covered by metal. And yet—here was relief: emotional warmth, compassion—but, best of all, anguish at the sight of him. He reached for that pain, gazing deep into the metal facets of her VISOR.

His entities surged up and out, racing toward her, making his nerves sing. They were ravenous, and for a moment he feared for her, but there was nothing he could do. They flooded from him into her; his sorrow was incalculable as they drained out of him leaving him empty, hollow.

At the same instant, the metal band across her face shimmered with electric blue light. He blinked, dazzled . . .

Then he smiled at the realization that he was free, his enemy defeated. The momentary pleasure filled his hollowness and made him whole again.

The next moment he stared back in utter confusion at Counselor Troi, Number One, Mr. Worf, and Commander Data—each of them sporting VISORs and huddling around him on the floor—of the *brig?* Even more disturbing was that he was being held protectively by Data.

He pulled away from the android, reorganized his uniform, and attempted to stand—but his body felt as though he'd run a marathon and lost, then been beaten severely by the disappointed spectators. He staggered. Lieutenant Worf caught and supported him, and this time he did not resist.

"What—what's happened here?"

Troi removed her VISOR; the others followed suit. "What's the last thing you remember, sir?"

The memory of Riker's attack returned to him; instinctively, he recoiled from them.

"It's all right, Captain," Deanna assured him. "Commander Riker is cured, as are you. He infected you with the alien entities. You've been under their control."

Quickly, Data, Riker, and Troi briefed him on all that had happened while the *Enterprise* had been under seige.

"I should've listened to you," he told Troi, when she was finished. "I should've beamed those things out into space, and to hell with the Vulcans and their research."

"It wouldn't have mattered if you had, Captain," she said wryly. "Skel has been harboring the infection inside him since his childhood—something of which he was completely unaware." She paused, letting Picard digest the horrific fact. "I'm afraid you're needed on the bridge now, sir. We're having a small problem with some . . . visiting starships."

In the vast silence of Ten Forward, Skel sat at the bar, one hand clutching the smooth shining counter as he trembled, struggling to resist Troi's siren call. The other hand gripped a phaser, set to kill. His mind was a swirling battlefield where two forces collided: the entities—full of venomous rage and desire, who felt the lure of the counselor's emotions, yet would not yield—and his true Vulcan self, who felt no hunger, yet struggled desperately to push himself away from the counter, to stand, to turn and move toward deliverance.

Beneath it all, T'Reth's soft voice urged her son to be strong, to have hope.

But the entities were too strong, and so Skel sat, shivering, waiting, struggling to loose his grip on the weapon, to change its setting—and failing.

Soon. Troi would come to him soon.

And so he sat, trembling, waiting, until at last he heard the doors open behind him. He did not turn, did not move except to draw the hand that clutched the phaser close to his body, so that the others could not see it.

Behind him, the deep voice of the Klingon: "Counselor, let me stun him now!"

And the soft reply: "No, wait . . ."

Skel listened to the sound of their footsteps, waiting until the last instant to rise, wheel—

In less than a heartbeat, T'Reth shrilled in his skull. *Take care! He is armed—*

At the same instant, Troi screamed. "Look out! He's armed!"

Unwillingly, Skel squeezed the phaser's trigger.

Before him, the three Starfleet officers parted like a wave as the dazzling shaft of phaser beam streaked between them, then seared a black smoking scar into the far bulkhead. The dark-skinned Klingon had seized Counselor Troi and pulled her to one side; meanwhile, a golden blur hurtled toward Skel and seized his wrist with impossible speed and strength.

Before Skel could so much as blink or fire, he found himself staring into Commander Data's pale bland countenance and realized that the android had wrested the phaser from him.

The entities within Skel roared. He swung with his free arm at the android, then shuddered with shock as his fist met a firmness more unyielding than bone.

Data never reacted.

The rage and pain fed Skel's entities. With a manic surge of strength, the Vulcan lashed out again, but the android seized both his arms and held him fast. Skel hurled his body at the android, slamming them both off-balance to the deck.

Data rolled so that the Vulcan lay with his back pinned against the deck. "You can only hurt yourself, Skel. I shall not release you."

Even as the entities within him bellowed their fury, the Vulcan within him watched with relief as Counselor Troi approached. Her dark eyes were masked by a VISOR, similar to the one worn by La Forge; despite his outer turmoil, Skel realized the device's purpose. A small part of him welcomed it . . .

Yet without us you will die! You must resist her—do not look! You have lived with us too long.

He squeezed his eyes shut, delaying the inevitable. Beneath the overlay of panic, a cooler voice whispered, *Do not be afraid, Skel. At last, we are delivered. . . .*

Trembling, he opened his eyes, yielding to the sweet pull of Troi's vulnerable emotions, of her fear. As he stared into the VISOR's gleaming facets, it lit up dazzlingly, as though kissed by blue lightning.

The image left him blinded for an instant; he blinked, then released a long deep sigh at the interior lightness, the profound silence, the freedom in his mind.

He closed his eyes again, still sighing, still sinking into the bliss of his own untainted consciousness, pure and clear.

And yet his mind was still not entirely his own, but this time, the realization evoked no dismay. Quite the opposite: Now that his thoughts were free from domination, he could clearly sense the other who shared it—an entity calm, controlled, compassionate.

"Mother," he whispered with dawning understanding, and the silent reply came:

I am here, my son. I have always been here. . . .

For a brief, blessed instant, two Vulcans yielded to joy and felt no shame.

With Riker beside him, Picard stepped onto his bridge, where a viewscreen displayed the image of two Galaxy-class starships hovering in front of the much smaller Vulcan science vessel in a protective stance. The screen blinked, then Captain Tiyo Soga's dark, normally friendly face filled the screen, but for the moment, his expression and voice were reserved.

"Captain Picard."

"It's good to see you, Captain Soga," Picard said, unsmiling. The situation demanded facts rather than diplomacy or charm. Both the *Skal Torr*'s captain and the *Odyssey*'s captain were listening and watching the encounter. "Have you been briefed on our . . . situation?"

"Your Commander Data has barraged us with information, to be frank," Soga confirmed. "We have not only the historical information from Starfleet and Vulcan archives, but logs and a summary of events leading up to this moment, including detailed plans on the devices he claims captured the infectious entities. My staff are still reviewing the material; they confirm the likelihood that Commander Data is immune and probably telling the truth."

Picard wanted to relax but couldn't. "However, *you* are still feeling a great deal of concern."

"Yes," Soga admitted gravely. "Your ship is carrying a full complement of crew, and you're ferrying almost half of the Federation scientists slated to attend the TechnoFair. The possibility of spreading this infection at the fair—"

"Understood," Picard interrupted. "Tell me how we can prove to you that we have indeed eradicated the infection."

"Well, that's just it, Jean-Luc," Soga admitted, with a faintly sheepish expression. "My staff has yet to be able to come up with a sure-fire way to guarantee you have wiped out this threat. My Betazoid counselor assures me that you and your staff 'read' clean, but—"

"You still have your reservations," Picard finished. "Just as I would have mine."

"Captain," Ensign Bron interjected from her station. "All ships are being hailed by the Vulcan vessel."

"On screen."

Soga's image wavered and metamorphosed into that of the Vulcan captain's. Beside her stood another female wearing the traditional long robes of a healer.

"Federation captains," the woman said, addressing her audience, "I am the Healer T'Son. I have come from Vulcan to help my patient, the Master Scientist Skel. Skel and I are mentally linked. Since he has been the carrier of this terrible infection, and you believe you have freed him of it, I can confirm that through a mind meld."

"Excuse me, Healer," Picard said apologetically, "but you've melded with Skel in the past, and never detected the entities hiding within him. Why do you think you would now?"

"There are many levels of the mind meld, Captain. Mine did not extend to the deepest reaches of Skel's consciousness, where the entities apparently dwelled; I am prepared to do so now. Also, if I come aboard your vessel and am infected, we will know you have not completely contained the entities. But if my meld is successful, I believe I can guarantee the safety of all."

"I am willing to agree, Healer T'Son," Picard said. "Captain Soga?"

"My counselor assures me this will be a trustworthy test," Soga replied, after a pause. "Good luck, Healer T'Son."

Captain Picard stood alongside Will Riker and watched the stately form of the Vulcan matriarch coalesce on the transporter pad. When she was fully integrated, Picard stepped forward, consciously reminding himself not to offer his hand. "Healer T'Son. I am Captain Picard, and this is my first officer, Commander Riker."

"Captain." With her flowing robes and plaited hair, T'Son seemed a vision from Vulcan's past; in one arm, she cradled a dimly glowing globe. "Commander." She nodded at each man in turn as she stepped from the platform.

Picard had never seen such an object before, but he surmised what it was that T'Son held so gently: a *vrekatra,* a receptacle designed to house a Vulcan's intelligent essence, a Vulcan's soul. "If you will follow me, Healer . . ."

Picard led the way to Skel's guest quarters.

"Captain," T'Son said, as they walked, "I have been in contact with the other healers who work with childhood victims of the plague. They are aware of Skel's unusual 'carrier' state, and have examined their patients. None can be found to harbor any entities at all. We will take the plans for the detection device your Mr. Data transmitted to us, and will construct one in order to verify our conclusions. But our current consensus is that Skel was the only child so infected."

"Well, that is partially a relief, and partially a tragedy," Picard remarked. She gazed at him silently.

"Healer," Picard said, "I plan to inform your captain that I will be destroying the entities—all of them. I will not permit them to leave this ship." He paused, knowing he was violating several protocols and could be disciplined for his action. Beside him, Riker struggled to suppress a smile.

T'Son's expression remained bland; if the notion disturbed her, she showed no sign. "I did not know they could be destroyed, Captain. How will you accomplish this?"

"Skel's research has determined that the entities only function as an infectious organism when they are bonded into groups—that is how they infect, feed, and procreate. Mr. Data has formulated a transporter dispersal pattern that will disrupt the frequency that bonds the entities together, so they will be forced into individual units. Data hypothesizes that this individual, harmless state may be their original, natural condition, and that the people who fashioned them into a weapon of war artificially bonded them to do so."

T'Son considered this in silence; when she did not reply, Picard asked pointedly, "Do you anticipate that your government will protest this decision?"

T'Son permitted herself a small sigh. "It is entirely possible that the entities have an innate intelligence. Victims of the plague spoke of their infection as if another, conscious being was inside them."

"Our counselor, too, sensed that," Picard admitted. "But she felt that any intelligence there was a completely malevolent one, totally incompatible with any other life-forms it would encounter."

"Yet Mr. Data's solution would merely return them to their natural condition as harmless individual entities," T'Son said. "It would seem to me that you are simply restoring the natural order, Captain. And the victims have suffered quite enough. I will support your decision before the Vulcan Council."

"Thank you, Healer." He bowed.

They stopped before the doors to Skel's guest quarters, and Picard watched the woman collect her sedate, emotionless demeanor about her like a robe.

"And now it is time for Skel and T'Reth," she said softly, and moved toward the doors.

Deanna Troi and the entire senior staff—Geordi, Beverly, Will, Worf, Data, and Jean-Luc Picard—stood in the transporter room shoulder-to-shoulder. Alexander was there as well, as was a healthy George Tarmud and a smiling Kyla Dannelke. There was barely room to breathe, but it seemed to Troi that they were all breathing in unison anyway.

On the transporter pad sat the quarantine unit with the two alien artifacts, and all of Data's containment devices that had trapped every entity infecting the crew.

Skel had opted not to be present; at that moment, Deanna knew, his consciousness was being separated from that of his mother, T'Reth—a woman whose concern for her child had become so desperate that, with her dying breath, she had ejected her *katra* into Skel's mind. But because of the entities' influence, Skel had not realized for all these years that his mother truly was with him, offering her assistance.

It was an unheard-of event, a Vulcan being able to transfer her consciousness without the medium of direct physical contact; Deanna had no doubt that the Vulcan metaphysicians were puzzling over the fact. To Troi, it was resoundingly simple: logic might fail when faced with the impossible, but love would not.

The emotional overload in the room was overwhelming, but Troi basked in it. Never had she felt this much power from the people around her, this much anticipation, this much resolve. It was a heady reaction and it made her feel a little woozy.

"Are we ready, Mr. Data?" Picard asked.

"Yes, sir," the android responded from behind the transporter console. "Dispersal pattern is laid in. The computer estimates that the probability is twenty-five billion, seventeen million, two hundred and fifty-eight thousand to one that any single entity will ever intersect with an inhabited planet, and that the probability of that individual entity being able to infect a living creature on that planet is—"

Everyone in the room turned to stare at him impatiently.

"Very, very small," he concluded. "Ready to transport on your command, sir."

"I think that honor belongs to Counselor Troi." Picard turned to her, smiling. "Counselor?"

With pleased surprise, she moved to the console beside Data and placed her hand on the lever he indicated. "Energize!"

A familiar whine filled the room. The objects on the transporter pad shimmered for a few moments, but the dispersal beam had been calibrated to transport only the entities and leave the equipment behind. As the whine subsided, the small shell-shaped artifacts fell open—dark, lifeless.

The final tendrils of their possession were cut adrift; Deanna laughed aloud at the sensation of utter freedom. "They're gone! We're free. . . ."

Epilogue

GUINAN WALKED LEISURELY through the multitudinous displays of the enormous TechnoFair, scanning the roster in her hand for Data and Geordi's booth. She was both surprised and amused to learn they had a display; when she'd left for her convention, Picard had insisted they wouldn't have time even to disembark here, what with the *Enterprise*'s impossible schedule of ferrying scientists here and there. Luckily, he'd gotten some other ships to assist with the transport, so that his crew could enjoy the fair.

And an amazing thing it was. In all her years, Guinan didn't think she'd seen so many different races or species in one place, all of them sharing their knowledge to promote science and its peaceful use.

She grinned suddenly at the familiar face in the distance, at a small booth nestled between two larger displays. She scurried over, her long mauve robes rustling, her enormous hat carrying her along like a sail through the parting crowd.

"Guinan!" Deanna cried happily. The empath stood with Will Riker to one side of Data and Geordi's little booth, in front of another booth featuring an android display. "How good to see you! You look so rested!"

The darker woman patted her friend on the arm. "I had a wonderful time! I just can't wait to tell you! I mean, I feel a little guilty leaving the rest of you to the drudgery of all that moving around, all that transporting, all those grim-faced scientists going on and on about their work." She peered at La Forge and Data suspiciously. "So, what condition is Ten Forward in?"

"Exactly as you left it," La Forge promised her, with an oddly secretive little grin. "You don't think Data and I were ready to face the wrath of Guinan, do you?"

"Not if you're smart! So what is this you guys have here? I didn't know you had plans for a display."

La Forge shot Data a bemused look. "It was sort of a last-minute thing."

"Yes," Data agreed. "Very last-minute. By using Geordi's VISOR, we have perfected a frequency-modulation device which will—"

"Sounds fascinating," Guinan agreed half-heartedly, knowing if she didn't cut him off the android would quote her chapter and verse of a scientific discovery she had no interest in. "Nice booth. Good color scheme."

Glancing around, she noticed the booth next to Data and Geordi's had a display featuring an enormous hologram of a floating Klingon eye, which was currently glaring down at her. Alexander, Worf's son, stood behind the display, manipulating the eyeball and clearly having a wonderful time doing it. Worf was standing close to a tall blond woman—very close.

Guinan's smile widened; this was looking more interesting by the moment.

She walked up to Alexander. "I didn't know *you* were planning a display at the TechnoFair either, young man. And you usually tell me *everything.*"

The boy smiled delightedly. "It's not *my* display, Guinan. It's Kyla's. She just let me set up the eye."

Worf, in a surprisingly gentlemanly manner, introduced Guinan to the scientist Kyla Dannelke. Their body language was *most* interesting. Guinan thought of all the evenings Worf sat in Ten Forward alone, insisting that human women were "too delicate" for him. There wasn't much about Kyla Dannelke that seemed delicate to her.

"So, have you two known each other long?" Guinan asked conversationally.

"Oh, it feels like *forever,"* Kyla replied drolly. Worf looked surprisingly embarrassed and everyone else broke into much more laughter than the situation seemed to call for. What had been going on while she was away?

"I want to hear *everything* that happened during the day devoted to the 'Use of Chocolate as an Entertainment Consumptive,'" Troi declared. "Start talking!"

Guinan grinned. "The recipes! You just won't believe them. For example: Rich Andusian chocolate bars, melted into Saurian brandy, with a little Terran vanilla, topped with whipped cream—"

Just then Picard strolled into view. He seemed tired, Guinan thought, but otherwise his usual self. The transport job must've been much more than he'd anticipated. And she'd heard about Ensign Ito's tragic death. No wonder he looked weary. If she couldn't lure him into Ten Forward, she'd beard the lion in his den. She couldn't wait to try some of her new concoctions on him! She didn't know anyone else who needed to relax more.

Picard was flanked by a tallish human male with a

pleasant face and a pronounced widow's peak. Picard said something, and the man gave a warm hearty laugh and replied with a pronounced New England accent. Beverly Crusher walked beside this man, and she, too, laughed.

Even the serene Vulcan male walking on Picard's right seemed more placid than the average Vulcan. Yet there was a sadness about him.

"Guinan!" Picard said as he spotted her. "It's good to see you. I certainly hope your . . . religious retreat fulfilled your spiritual needs and helped you find the peace of mind you were looking for. We'll all certainly enjoy the advantages of your counsel."

Religious retreat? What was he talking about? Oh, yes! She'd completely forgotten the "official justification" for her trip. She had been afraid he wouldn't have let her go during the hectic transporting assignment if he thought she was just going to have fun. She blushed darkly as everyone but Data swallowed their smiles.

The android only looked confused. "Why would they discuss the consumption of chocolate at a religious retreat?" he asked La Forge, who only jabbed him into silence.

"Yes, it was wonderful," Guinan assured the captain with only a little guilt. "Very . . . enriching." *Enriching* wasn't the word. She knew she'd put on at least five pounds.

He introduced her to the Vulcan scientist, Skel, and the android-builder, George Tarmud. *Another* android-maker! Guinan could see if she didn't get out of here soon she'd be trapped into science-speak for hours.

Snagging Deanna's arm, she said, "If you'll excuse us, I promised Deanna I'd show her the recorded scenes from the seminars on 'Religious Counseling Today.'"

Troi's eyes widened in horror as Guinan wrested

her away from a chuckling Will Riker and pulled her quickly out of earshot.

"So, what's with Worf and that woman?" Guinan hissed at her friend as they left the others. "I want details! And I thought it would be boring to have all those scientists on board."

"Oh," Deanna said mildly, "I wouldn't call it boring, exactly . . ."

As Guinan left them, Tarmud and Crusher remained at his booth, talking, while the rest of the group continued to interact with one another. Picard took the opportunity to follow Skel to his display on forcefield technology, which was set apart from the others. He'd had no chance to address Skel in private.

Now that they were, in effect, alone, Picard wasn't even sure what he wanted to say to the Vulcan. *I'm sorry about what happened to you. It was criminal, and should've never been inflicted on anyone, least of all a child.*

Finally, as he stood beside the Vulcan—both of them gazing silently up at the display—he murmured, "Skel, I am sorry about your mother. She touched my mind, spoke to me in my own mother's guise; it made me feel I knew her. She was an amazing woman. I wanted to tell you—I grieve with thee."

Skel turned to him, his expression relaxed, his air that of one who had resolved many problems. "It is not logical to grieve for my mother, Captain."

Picard felt awkward. "Perhaps not, but we humans—"

Skel held up his hand. "My mother's *katra* was not loosed upon the winds, as I had so long thought. Believing that, I had grieved for her all of my life. Now I know her *katra* reposes in the Hall of Ancient Thought. I can consult with her whenever I feel the need, and she can communicate with the *katra* of my father, and bring him peace. My mother is aware that her years of struggle were successful. In many ways, she was responsible for saving all of our people from being revisited by this dread infestation—indeed, all of the Federation. Even in death, she succeeded. So there is truly no reason to grieve, Captain."

Picard smiled slightly. "No, I suppose there isn't. Especially when I remember that the entities have been completely annihilated, that there is no possibility they can ever harm anyone again."

The faintest hint of shadow crossed the Vulcan's face and was gone. "Is that what you think, Captain? I thought you were aware—"

"Aware of what?" Picard demanded, a sudden knot of fear coiling in his stomach.

"The two artifacts in my possession," the Vulcan replied. "They were but a sample, recovered by a Vulcan archaeological expedition from an uninhabited planet in the Hydrilla sector. Thousands of artifacts remain there still. . . ."

ACKNOWLEDGMENTS

Somewhere there is a book that's been written by an author completely on her own, without her ever asking anyone a single question, or looking up an obscure reference, or quoting from an unknown source. Whatever that book is, and whoever its author, it ain't this one. No, this one had plenty of help.

Thanks go first and foremost to my co-author, J. M. Dillard, who has now heard every excuse under the sun for why the writing might not be going well. ("Well, the crane chicks are hatching. . . ." "Well, I'm doing lots of research. . . ." And the best one of all—"Well, I broke my ankle. . . .")

Invaluable techie advice was obtained from the ever helpful Michael Capobianco, and those renowned experts in graviton fluxes and warp drive complications, Chris Bartus and Brent Bowles of Treknobabble, Inc. (And they're not out of the Academy yet!)

Nothing written in this house has ever left the premises without suggestions, proofreading, and untold help from the one constant in my life, Anne Moroz.

And very special thanks must go to my longtime friend and writing partner, Ann Crispin, without whom this book would never have been finished. You're always there when I need you, Ann. What better definition of friendship is there?

Kathleen O'Malley

My thanks as well to all the helpful souls Kathy just mentioned—as well as to the Divine Ms. O'Malley, a true talent and steadfast friend. She came to my rescue during a very difficult year. Love you, Kath.

Jeanne M. Dillard